Danny King was born in ? up in a one-horse town (the horse drove an XR3i and ~~thought~~ policies on immigration weren't tough enough). He (Danny that is, not the horse) has worked as a hod carrier, a shelf stacker and a postman before being inspired to move into journalism and expose injustice and corruption wherever it lay in a never-ending fight for truth. He now works as the editor of top-shelf bongo mag *Mayfair* (still excellent value at £2.65). He moved to London in 1992 and is currently working on the third in The Crime Diaries series, *The Hitman Diaries*; the first, *The Burglar Diaries*, was published by Serpent's Tail in 2001.

Praise for *The Burglar Diaries*

'An absolutely hilarious, laugh out loud book by someone who has been there' Bruce Reynolds, mastermind of the Great Train Robbery

'Occasionally hilarious, if morally dubious, *The Burglar Diaries* is well worth buying – and definitely worth half-inching' *GQ*

'This is the sweet-as-a-nut, hilariously un-PC account of the jobs [Bex] has known and loved – the line-ups, the lock-ups and the cock-ups. If ever there was an antidote to *Bridget Jones's Diary* this is it. *The Burglar Diaries* is the first in a series. Long may it run' *Mirror*

'The perfect escapist read' *Buzz*

Also by Danny King and published by Serpent's Tail

The Burglar Diaries

The Bank Robber Diaries

Danny King

SERPENT'S TAIL

Library of Congress Catalog Card Number: 2001092088

A complete catalogue record for this book can be
obtained from the British Library on request

The right of Danny King to be identified as the
author of this work has been asserted by him
in accordance with the Copyright, Designs and Patents
Act 1988

First published in 2002
by Serpent's Tail,
4 Blackstock Mews, London N4 2BT

website: www.serpentstail.com

Phototypeset by Intype London Ltd
Printed in Great Britain by Mackays of Chatham plc

10 9 8 7 6 5 4 3 2

Acknowledgements

First off, I'd like to thank John Williams for championing my books and helping me get started. I can't speak highly enough of him. In fact I think I'd even go so far as to say that if he lost a bit of weight, grew some hair, was a few years younger, became a woman and had a few quid in the bank I'd be half-tempted to give him one (if I was really pissed). I'd also like to thank everyone at Serpent's Tail for putting me on the shelves — Peter, Jenny, Jackie, Ruth, Katie and that bloke whose name I can never remember; to my agents Kerith Biggs and Carrie Neilson for taking care of business and laughing at all my jokes; to Clive Andrews for working on an even sadder mag than me when we both got started in journalism (he worked on *Park Homes and Holiday Caravans*, ha ha ha – not telling you what I worked on); to Andrew Emery and Nat 'Mat' Saunders for ridding my manuscript of most of its exclamation marks!!! To Brian McCann for buying me a pint in exchange for another mention in the acknowledgements; to Paul McCann for pointing out that, unlike his brother, he actually used to read my stuff before I was published (and for buying me some peanuts); to Richard in The Lyric for running a pub next door to where I work; to Grandpa in Clapham North for his contributions and finally to Ollie Scull's dad, David, for pointing out that the 'cunt count' was a bit high in *The Burglar Diaries*. I thank you all.

For Robin
Big Man, little bruv ...

1. Dealing with a corpse

'Fill up the bag!' Gavin shouted at the pretty young teller. The teller stared at Gavin for a moment, fear scrambling her mind, and was finally only able to move when Gavin added, 'with money.'

She quickly started stuffing the contents of her cash desk into the canvas satchel Gavin had thrown at her and went at it with such blind efficiency that she had to be shouted at to stop when she started sticking in the coppers and coins. 'Just the notes please love,' Gavin told her and then had to do all he could to stop her from rummaging around in the bag to fish out the ones she had already put in. 'Look, just leave them, leave them there and just pass the bag on to her sitting next to you.'

The teller had a look at her co-worker and then back at Gavin.

'YES, HER!' he shouted.

Vince had already had enough of this and yelled across the room at her.

'Are you deliberately trying to fuck us about or what? Give her the bag and hurry up or we'll start fucking shooting!'

An old lady somewhere behind Vince finally lost

control of all her senses and let out a cry of hysteria which, for some unknown reason, I found quite unbelievably funny, making me crack up. Nerves I guess.

'Hurry up,' I tried to shout along with the others, but the whole sentence came out as some sort of strangled laugh. Gavin, Vince, the teller, her co-worker and all the customers stopped what they were doing just for a moment and stared at me. Everyone that is except the old lady who, at that moment, lost it big time, and went into one, wailing and wriggling about on the floor like a demented banshee.

'Are you alright?' Gavin asked me.

'Fine,' I blurted out, but I wasn't fine. My sides ached so hard where I was trying to hold myself together, I could barely hold my gun.

'Get a fucking grip man and cover those people. And you, hurry up with that bag, we haven't got all day you know.'

I tried not to look at her but it was impossible. At that moment, she was the funniest thing I'd ever seen in my entire life and I just couldn't tear my eyes away from her. The only thing that stopped me from staring at her unblinkingly were the rivers of tears that ran down my face and blurred my vision. I wiped my eyes with the back of my hand and tried to get a handle on things but it was no use, a quick glimpse of the old dear rolling around on the floor with her big old bloomers on show for the world to see was enough to effectively disable me.

'CB!' Gavin shouted at me and gave me the daggers. I took a deep breath and tried to count to ten, but couldn't get past three without images of elderly women making fools of themselves on cold hard tiles.

Looking back on it now, I have no idea what I was

laughing at and indeed, fail to see anything even vaguely funny about the whole situation. But then, that's so often the case with these uncontrollable fits of laughter, they're not caused by anything particularly funny (good job too I guess, otherwise everyone in the bank would've been falling about the place and we would never have gotten out of there) but they are horrendous because once you start, you just can't stop. Actors, I think, call it corpsing. They do it all the time and most Saturday evening television is taken up with clips of them falling about, calling each other darling and patting themselves on the back for fucking up the scene for everybody.

Gavin shouted something else at me but I couldn't make out what it was he said. I was in agony. Despite my outward appearance I wasn't enjoying myself at all. I just couldn't control myself. And the sight of me laughing like some deranged madman must've driven this old lady out of her mind, because she suddenly went into total meltdown, pointing at me, covering her eyes, trying to squeeze behind a huge plastic pot plant. All this in turn did me absolutely no favours whatsoever and I responded in kind with hysterics of my own until I was eventually rewarded with a growing feeling of warmth running down my leg.

'Oh god no!' I spluttered and tried to slam on the brakes but every ounce of strength around my midriff area had already been spent trying to keep my sides from spasming out of control. Sensing my complete helplessness, my body turned the taps on full and within seconds a huge dark patch was spreading across my cords. In this instant I managed to regain some control over my limbs and tried to wrestle open my zip. This proved more difficult than you would imagine as I was holding a lumpy old revolver in one hand and wearing thick leather driving gloves, which refused to purchase any sort of grip on the zipper.

The patch had now spread as far as my knee, and was making steady progress towards my trainers, when I finally freed myself up, pulled the old fella clear of my slacks and pointed it out of harm's way. I couldn't help but splash several assorted customers and bank personnel on the floor around me in the process, and I have to say they didn't look too happy about it, particularly the natty little blonde I'd been getting the eye off up until that moment.

'Urgh, you bloody animal,' she shouted at me. 'You absolute pig.' I should've turned back round and let her have the lot for her trouble but at that moment I was too preoccupied with an overwhelming sense of relief at regaining a little of my composure; although some might argue that standing in the middle of Barclays, laughing like a hyena and pissing over people at gunpoint, is hardly what you would call composed. A sharp looking lad in a pin-stripe suit slowly started to edge back from the pool of urine which was flowing in his direction. Several others did likewise until Vince shouted from across the room for everyone to stay still.

It was then that it caught his eye why they were all on the move.

'What the fuck are you doing now?' he shouted at me in disgust. See, all this happened in just a few short seconds. The old lady going haywire, me corpsing and then the floodgates opening. All this took place in little more than ten or twenty seconds. The entire job only lasted about three or four minutes as a whole, but when we were doing it – and indeed, when I look back on it – time slowed down to a crawl. I don't know why.

Maybe because in those few short moments, you are more alert and aware of everything around you than at any other time during your life. I have so many vivid recollections, so many details, but when I try to play them back in my head it can take over twenty minutes to get through them all.

Anyway, the point is that this all happened in such a short space of time and Gavin and Vince were so preoccupied with their own tasks that they hadn't noticed me until then. And boy, did they notice me.

'What the fuck are you doing?' Vince exclaimed. 'I don't believe you.'

Gavin spun round and stared at me as I shook off the last few drops. 'What the... what... what are you doing?'

'I'm sorry, I couldn't help it,' I replied.

'You couldn't help it! You... I... You dirty little bastard. Put your dick away and stop fucking about. Do what you're supposed to do and cover those people.'

I was, I was covering them in piss.

'We're going to have a long talk about this later.'

'But Gav...' I started to say.

'LATER!' he shouted back at me.

This was like a wake-up call for me. A bucket of cold water in the face. A sober pill. Gavin was the scariest man on earth to be on the wrong side of. See, besides crew leader, hard man and professional criminal, he was also my older brother. And there I was, stupid little moron, who didn't even shave properly yet, screwing everything up and acting the spastic on my big chance to prove to him that I was worthy of joining his crew. Gavin scowled at me from beneath his Balaclava. It was a scowl I knew all too well. A cross between deep disappointment and disapproval, with perhaps just a hint of mad violence. I knew what was coming. I've had these 'talks' with Gavin before and he's not a man to waste words. I wondered, just momentarily, whether I should shoot him while I still had the gun. Or better yet, just shoot myself and save the NHS some bother. Or even better yet, shoot the old lady for making me wet myself, after all, it was her fault in the first place. In the event, I didn't do any of these things, not least of all because Gavin had made sure before the job that he'd given me an empty gun. I suppose he didn't fancy getting shot in the spleen before we were even out of the getaway car, as I tested the trigger to see how taut it was. And by the way things had gone, you had to admit it was a good call.

I didn't know this at the time though, and I only found out when I accidentally squeezed the trigger whilst scratching my leg with the gun barrel. Gavin must've heard the click over everything else that was going off because he shot a glance over to me (probably to see which way the gun was pointing) and made a mental note to have another 'talk' with me about weapon safety. Besides Gavin, I think the guy in the sharp suit must've noticed as well, because his attitude towards us, well me, became noticeably more surly. Gone was the fearful, cowering wretch of two minutes ago, who would lie in a puddle of my piss and think himself lucky. Here now was a man who had hate in his face and was not afraid to show it. Here now was a man who had been humbled and humiliated, subjugated and splashed, all for fear of being shot, only to discover that there were no bullets to be shot with. Here now was a man who wanted to kill me. Not that he did anything though; after all, even without bullets, a gun is a heavy old lump to get hit round the back of the head with.

And there were three of us. So he continued to lay there, scowling at me along with everyone else doing nothing. Well, almost nothing. I did see him out of the corner of my eye sticking two fingers up behind my back as we left, an act of bravery he probably still tells his friends about today.

As we left the bank and jumped into the waiting Cortina outside, I was suddenly full of fear and trepidation myself. I knew what my cut of the robbery was going to be, and frankly, I didn't fancy it. Gavin threw me into the back seat and jumped in after me. Sid floored the accelerator and away we sped. Gavin must've known what I was going through. It was probably the momentary pause as I stood on the pavement outside the bank wondering if I should just try and leg it, get a bus and get back to our mum's house before he had a chance to beat me up.

No chance.

That afternoon, as Sid and Vince divided up the money (three ways) Gavin gave me a thorough grounding in the rules of robbery. He repeated them several times to be sure I wouldn't forget them, along with, 'not laughing now are you, hey?' and, 'come on then, give us a laugh you little bastard' etc. Vince wanted to come over and help him out as well but Gavin wouldn't let him near me. I was his baby brother and no-one got to touch me but him.

Well, what are brothers for!

It was a lesson that left a permanent mark on me.

Literally.

That was my first robbery. I was only seventeen. And at the time I thought it would be my last. Gavin promised me that he would never do another job with me ever again.

Ever.

It only took me five years and a lot of pleading to get him to change his mind.

And when I got it, I was determined nothing was going to fuck it up for me.

2. Memories of Melvin

I checked the gun before I got out of the car to see that it was loaded and was more than a little surprised to find that it was. Gavin had obviously forgotten about my lapse in concentration last time out and entrusted me with a clip of live ammunition (assuming that it was live of course). This boosted my confidence no end and made me feel like a part of the crew for real. I was determined to repay that trust by not shooting myself or any other part of the gang by accident for the next ten minutes. I was older, wiser and dryer and I had the second chance I'd thought I'd never get.

Nothing, and I mean nothing, was going to get in my way.

'Ready?' Gavin asked staring hard into my eyes.

'Yeah. Ready,' I replied with a steely look of my own.

'Okay Sid, this is it,' Gavin told him as we pulled up outside the building society. 'Remember everyone, three and a half minutes max, then out. Okay?' We all said okay, pulled our masks down over our faces, climbed out of the car and went for the door. A fraction of a second before we entered Vince nudged me in the back and said:

'Oi, piss boy, squeeze one drop and you'll have me to deal with.'

What a reputation to get stuck with!

And that's what has happened. Even now, after twenty years of professional thievery and probably more than a hundred jobs, I still sometimes catch the lads checking my trouser legs out of the corners of their eyes. I've long since given up trying to explain what happened and why and have accepted the fact that it will stick with me for the rest of my life. It'll probably even get a mention in my epitaph. I can see it now:

RIP Chris Benson
1962–20??
He pissed his pants in Barclays.

Not quite how I planned to be remembered, but I guess there's precious little I can do about it now. What was it that Oscar Wilde said?

'The only thing worse than being talked about is not being talked about.' This, of course, is a load of bollocks. I'm sure if the whole of polite London society went around cracking jokes about Oscar shitting himself all the time, he'd soon want everyone to shut up.

Vince didn't want me along. Neither did Sid for that matter, but Gavin had told them I was in and that was that. They both knew which side their bread was buttered and wouldn't argue with Gavin. They'd moan and whinge and say 'I told you so' in the police van on the way to court but neither would take on Gavin. Some things just weren't worth it. Gavin told them that they *needed* me, I liked that, they *needed me*. The bloke I was standing in for that day had the flu and couldn't make it (even bank robbers have to go off sick), so I was drafted in as a last minute replacement. All other possible substitutes were either in prison or on holiday or just couldn't be trusted.

'Everybody on the ground, this is a robbery!' Gavin shouted the moment he was inside. I was in next, darting off to my right to batter people to the ground, while Vince brought up the rear and guarded the entrance.

'Down, down,' I shouted at the thin scattering of customers and threw them to the floor (are they customers in a building society or are they members? Either way I had them all face down eating lino in a matter of seconds). It's interesting you know, but the fitter they are the quicker they drop. You'd think that the strong, young virile guys in suits would make more of a scene of it for the sake of bravado and that it would be the old, fat housewives who would be the ones who faint away like blushing violets, but it's not. In my extensive experience it's these old moaners that'll grumble and complain and take you to task over what a cowardly disgrace you are waving a gun at a lady and how 'if my Ron was here, he'd soon show you a thing or two', while the young suits shout at them from the safety of the deck, telling them to shut up and get down before they get everyone killed. It's old battleaxes like this that cause all the trouble for everyone and get poor old Ron killed. If they're not rolling about on the floor screaming blue-bloody-murder, they're lashing you with their tongues and standing proud in the face of aggression.

I hate them.

Although, I should say on this job I had no such trouble.

'Stay down,' I shouted and brought my foot down hard on the back of some young buck's neck. Vince was doing likewise behind me, kicking down and frightening any would-be heroes.

Gavin threw the bag to the nearest girl and told her to fill it up and quick about it. Good as gold, she emptied her till into the bag and passed it on to her left.

'Hurry it along,' Gavin shouted a bit unnecessarily, as it seemed to me that they were doing alright, but Gavin was the boss and an old hand at that.

I was hardly about to try and teach my grandmother to rob banks.

I guess what Gavin was doing could be parallel to cowboys driving cattle across the plains in the old West. From Montana to Mexico these toothless simpletons would shout 'yee-hah', 'giddy-up' and 'woh-woh-woh' and suchlike, at an enormous amount of cows that, frankly, showed not the slightest sign of slowing down. They'd do it though to keep the herd moving – and probably because they were bored.

'In the bag, hurry,' Gavin was shouting. 'Move it.'

'Two minutes,' Vince shouted from behind us somewhere. 'Come on, let's move.'

Someone to my right looked up for a fraction of a second and was rewarded with a kick in the ribs. 'Stay down you fucker!' I shouted at him.

'Pass the bag along, give it to him, come on.'

The last woman behind the counter handed the bag to Melvin and Gavin ordered him to empty his till into it. I don't know if Melvin was his name. I doubt it. But he looked like a Melvin and it's the name I've since given him. To me, he'll always be Melvin.

Melvin, at first, complied like all the rest, and filled the bag with the contents of his till as Vince shouted that there was one minute remaining to Gavin and me.

'Okay, okay, okay, that's it,' Gavin shouted as Melvin stuffed in the last of the cash. 'Throw us back the bag.'

Throw was the operative word, for this building society, like a lot of building societies and banks in those days, had a bullet-proof screen that stretched up from the counter, but fell just short of the ceiling. I never saw the point of this myself. Perhaps the designers of these types of screens thought that bank robbers were fundamentally thick or lazy and could either not see the chink in the bank's armour, or be bothered to exploit it. 'I'm not standing on the counter,' I'm sure they thought we would all say. 'Fuck that.' They might as well have knitted everyone a bullet-proof jacket while they were at it.

'Throw it back,' Gavin shouted. Melvin hesitated for a moment, took a deep breath and then said:

'No.'

'No! What d'you mean no? Throw the fucking bag over NOW,' Gavin screamed scaring the shit out of everyone. Everyone that is except Melvin.

'No,' he said again and just stood there shaking like a leaf, clutching the bag to his chest.

This has happened a few times to me in my long and illustrious career and it has never failed to amaze me. Why would you want to do that? Why would you risk your life standing up to a gang of armed and crazy gunmen just to protect money that doesn't belong to you? I don't get it, I really don't. In fact, not just money that doesn't belong to you, but money that belongs to your boss (what a fucking arse-kisser). A boss who pays you about £150 a week and lays you off the second someone invents a machine that can do your job for them. This money Melvin was risking all for, it was not only an insignificant fraction of what the building society probably earned in a day, but it was also insured and would've been recouped, to the penny, without so much as a zero slipping out of place.

What was he hoping to get out of it, employee of the month? Slap on the back and a hearty handshake? White-hot 12-gauge discharge in the face? Like I say though, Melvin was not the only wannabe hero I've met, but he was my first and the one I remember the most fondly. If it was me, and I had been in Melvin's shoes, I'd have handed it over and not given a monkey's. In fact, if it had been me, I'd probably've pocketed a few hundred before the bag even got to me and crossed my fingers that my building society could get robbed every week.

If it had been me in reality though, I wouldn't have even been there. I would've long since marched my co-workers into the safe at gunpoint and run off to Acapulco with its contents. And unlike Florida Phil, a Securicor guard who did much the same a few years ago, I wouldn't have left my workmates' wages behind. In fact, I would have probably even taken their handbags and wallets while they were all in there gasping for air.

'Give me the fucking bag!' Gavin screamed at him and pointed the gun straight at Melvin's head. 'NOW!!!'

'No,' Melvin managed to croak, tears welling up in his eyes.

'Give him the bag,' Vince shouted in support.

'Give him the bag,' I joined in.

'Give him the fucking bag,' Melvin's manager ordered him.

'No,' was his answer to each of us. 'Now get out,' he told us all.

'Thirty seconds,' Vince shouted.

Gavin shot a glance in my direction. I looked at him and said: 'What?'

'Get over there and get that fucking bag off of him.'

'What? Over there? Me?'

'Do it now,' he yelled.

I had to do it, this was my second chance. My last chance. I'd fucked up so comprehensively on the last job that I had to be James Bond this time out just to be taken seriously by proper people. In that split second I knew that I had no choice, I had to get that bag.

Nothing could get in my way.

I'd jumped on to the counter and had swung the first of my legs over the security screen by the time Vince called twenty seconds. I hauled myself up and over and looked down at Melvin who, along with everyone else, was staring up at me blankly. That was one of the interesting things about Melvin, which made him stand out in my mind so much; he never moved a muscle. He just stood there, at first staring at Gavin, and then staring at me, facing up to us like a defiant first-former standing up to the school bully.

I dropped down the other side of the screen and pointed my gun at him. 'Throw over the bag,' I told him.

'No,' said Melvin, and then just for a moment, I saw his eyes flicker left towards a pretty young cashier, all make-up and tits. Suddenly I realised what he was up to. He wasn't trying to impress his bosses, or make a stand against crime, he was trying to impress the birds. And by the looks of him, he needed all the help he could get; ginger hair, freckles, no eyebrows to speak of, fly-away collars. Of course, pissing off men with guns and sniffling like an eight-year-old, he wasn't exactly doing a very good job of impressing anyone, least of all old big tits, who, all said and done, looked more taken with me.

See, that's the thing about women, they're attracted to bad news like me, Gavin or Vince hands down over the Melvins of this world. Nothing gets a woman's juices flowing faster than wrong'un on a Harley in a leather jacket. I'm not about to give you a lecture on women and what they like; I can only draw from my own experiences and in my opinion, despite everything women say, they like their men to be bastards. This is because women are fundamentally vicious, spiteful bastards themselves, and nothing gives them greater pleasure than conspiring with lovers to inflict misery on any poor unsuspecting sap they take a disliking to. Believe me, I've seen this. Bullies pull babes. I guess there's also an element of taming tigers about them. They figure that if they can enchant and infatuate some evil nutter, who everyone else in the world is frightened of, then they, as women, must truly be something special. Of course, it doesn't take long before their spell of love starts to lose its grip and their sweetheart psycho turns on them and gives them a taste of his true intent.

But then, that's also what happens when you try and tame a tiger.

Not that I've ever hit a woman myself you must understand. I've shot a few, but I've never hit one.

I grabbed at the bag but Melvin pulled away and held on to it for dear life shouting 'No! No! No!'

'Time,' cries Vince. 'Get the fucking bag.'

I tried to yank it away from him but still he held on. 'You're not having it,' he was saying, the tears spilling down his cheeks.

'Give him the bag,' everyone was shouting at him. 'Hand it over.'

'No, I won't, I won't, I won't,' he was ranting while I tried to tug the bag free of his vice-like grip. The whole bank was watching, Gavin and Vince were screaming at me to hurry up and I was shouting all sorts of abuse at him, but still he would not relinquish his grip. I looked around at Gavin and saw the anger in his eyes and couldn't tell whether it was being directed at Melvin or me. Me, I quickly concluded.

He was angry with me for not getting the bag. He was angry with me for not doing my job. He was angry with me for failing him again.

Melvin jerked the bag back out of my hand and clutched it to his chest. Some people, you quickly realise in life, are just arseholes. Plain and simple. There's no rhyme, there's no reason, they're just arseholes. Arseholes, for the sake of being arseholes. They were born arseholes and they'll die arseholes; and that's all there is to it. Melvin was an arsehole. But what was I going to do, shoot him?

Of course that's what I was going to do.

So I shot him.

I was a bank robber, I had a gun, he was in the way – I mean, what did he expect?

Now, I don't know if you've ever shot anyone before, but there's this delicious moment of horrible realisation on the part of the victim about half a second after the bullet sinks in. A sort of 'Oh my god, I've just been shot. That's a bad thing. I wish it hadn't happened.'

Melvin's face was a picture. It was a real Kodak moment. In fact, I wish I'd had a camera with me and taken a quick snap, but I guess that would've probably seemed a bit callous to everyone looking on.

Melvin stumbled back a step or two and then fell on his arse. A white glaze spread across his face as the shock set in and a large messy red stain appeared just above the knee where I'd let him have it. Several customers gasped, the cashier closest screamed and the blonde with the big tits almost swooned with desire for me.

When I pulled the bag from his, now feeble, clutches, I almost expected him to continue to put up a struggle, but Melvin had other things on his mind and barely noticed me take it from him. I slung it over the screen to Gavin and climbed quickly after it. No-one tried to stop me. No-one even looked at me. Everyone now knew not to fuck with me. Suddenly, I was the scariest and most dangerous man they'd ever met.

Suddenly, I had respect.

As we fled the building and jumped in the car, I almost felt like I didn't want to leave. It sounds strange I agree, but the adrenaline was surging through my veins and all I could think was that I wanted to go back. I wanted to frighten those people some more.

Gavin brought me back to earth when he snatched the gun from my hand and ripped my mask off.

'You fucking shot him!' he growled at me menacingly. And for some reason, all I could think to say was:

'I'm sorry Gavin, don't tell mum will you!'

Gavin, Vince and Sid laughed their heads off at that and after a while I realised that they weren't laughing at me, they were laughing with joy. Joy at getting away from the building society clean, at having a big bulging bag full of money in the car with them, and at seeing the newest member of their gang do the business and bust his cherry.

Oh yeah, I had respect alright. And not just from the plebs. I had the respect of my gang. And that mattered more to me than the money.

Thank you Melvin, you wonderful, beautiful arsehole.
Wherever you are, thank you.

3. The enemy on all sides

The cops were all around. Ultimatums were being shouted through bull-horns while tactical firearms officers took up position back and front. The hostages, sensing what was coming, started to panic and one or two of the more religiously inclined crossed themselves.

'This is your last chance,' the police chief shouted. 'Throw out your weapons and come out with your hands up.'

'Fuck you copper,' was the reply he got back.

BANG. The first of several tear gas canisters crashed through a window and rolled across the floor.

'Get down, get down,' someone shouted as the doors blew off their hinges and in burst the filth shooting in all directions.

Suddenly Glenn Close was telling Michael Douglas that she was pregnant, that gay decorator was ruining someone's house and West Ham had taken the lead at Blackburn.

'Oi,' I said, 'put the film back on, I was watching that.'

'I'm bored,' Debbie replied.

'I don't care, put the film back on.'

'I want to go out,' she simpered.

'Then go, I'm not stopping you. Just stick the film back on and close the door behind you.'

'Chris!' she started, but I'd had enough.

'Put the film back on. Now!'

Debbie lifted her arm reluctantly, hit the button and slumped back into a silent sulk. It wouldn't last long.

I mentioned before that I thought women were vicious, spiteful bastards, well this was my case material. Deborah Weller – Debbie for short – my wife-cum-partner-cum-personal tormentor, for the past nine years. We'd met at this club my brother had a part-share in back in the eighties. She used to dance in a cage flashing her flesh at all the low-lifes and I used to sit at the bar and watch her do it. Benny, the manager of the place, introduced me to her one night, after the place closed. Actually, that's not strictly correct. I should have said: Benny, the manager of the place, set me up with her when he heard I was interested in order to earn a few brownie points with Gavin. Not that Debbie needed much of a push in my direction. She knew what sort of place she worked in and what sort of customers got in there after dark. Once she found out the sort of serious customer I was, the rhino horn wasn't needed.

I told you, it's a danger thing with women.

And dangling on the arm of one of the local faces did as much for her ego as being with the most desirable woman in the room did for mine.

All this asides though I think we were as good as made for each other. See, I'm not really much of a talker and she finds herself hard pushed to think up anything to say, so once we established the boundaries of our relationship and realised that we didn't have to bore each other half to death with every single little unimportant bit of gossip just to fill in the silence with conversation we got on well. Good sex, nice living and a lot of shopping. For a few years we were almost happy.

Things went sour shortly after Gavin went down though. I'd never really been one for living up the high life; clubs, racetracks, restaurants and the like, I find them all a bit of a yawn. I only really used to go along because I liked to hang around with my brother. And once he was gone, they lost all their appeal for me. At the same time I refound my caution. Gavin was the last person in the world I thought would ever do a serious stretch and it made me realise that what with the lifestyle we were leading, we were all on borrowed time. It's one thing to make a name for yourself – but you have to remember, once you've got it people are always using it.

I decided to quit the Smoke, get out of the country and live the quiet life in the sun for a while. My brother had invested a few grand in a villa and a couple of bars in Greece (Corfu to be more precise), so Debbie and I packed our towels and headed for the Ionian for a few years.

Greece suited Debbie more than it suited me. She spent the better part of four years photosynthesising around various pools, beaches and boats while I spent most of the time walking around with my hands in my pockets kicking pebbles. Well, maybe not, but it seemed like that sometimes. The one thing I enjoyed was returning to Britain once every four months or so to pull a job. See, even though Gavin was away doing fifteen years, Vince, Sid and I stuck together for the sake of business and became a working crew in our own right. Vince appointed himself Number One, though in reality, we all had an equal say in what work we took on.

These trips back to Blighty, though, did little to allay

my homesickness – if anything they just made it worse – until after a little over four years I decided I could take the sun, sea and sand no more and moved back to Britain. It sounds a bit weird, I know, when it's put like this, especially if you work in some drab little office or factory somewhere and spend the whole year dreaming, planning and packing for your two weeks in the sun. But just try it for longer and see how insane you go.

I did.

See the fact is I'm a Northern European, I was born under the grey skies of Britain and know them as home. I feel uncomfortable if I have to go more than a few weeks without a complete blanket of cloud cover to blot out the sun.

Debbie didn't take it too well at all and practically had to be dragged on to the plane kicking and screaming. But her meal ticket was leaving, so short of getting a job in a bar out there she had no choice. She lost heart even further when I told her that we weren't returning to our old stamping grounds in London, but heading instead for the wilds of Kent. I didn't really fancy picking up with Vince, Benny and the rest of them all over again, so I bought a four bedroom detached on a new estate that three years ago was home to foxes and badgers, and set about establishing myself as a respectable member of the public.

This was all a facade of course, I would still be pulling jobs with Vince and Co to keep me in the style I had no right to be accustomed to, I just wouldn't be socialising with the scum afterwards.

Debbie moaned and objected every step of the way about not being able to see family and friends (who she hadn't bothered to stay in touch with the whole time we were in Greece) but she ultimately knew which side her bread was buttered. The notion of leaving me wasn't even given a moment's consideration. Mercenary little bitch knew a good gravy train when she was riding one.

As for myself, I can't really say whether I was glad about that or not. We'd been together so long it was just the way it was. Sometimes I couldn't remember why it was we ever got together in the first place, and other times I couldn't imagine life without her. I guess in that respect I was no different from most other blokes. If it wasn't her, it would only be someone else, so what does it matter?

'I'm bored,' she said again after five minutes of relative peace. 'Let's go out.'

'Debbie, shut up please.'

'We never go out any more, let's go out.' This wasn't strictly true. We never went out *together* any more. For years we'd had our own lives, she did what she wanted to do and I did what I wanted to do. In truth, all I ever really wanted to do was rob banks, beyond that I was never too bothered; read, watch television, eat well, have the money to buy nice things if I wanted, generally lead the quiet life. I didn't care. Debbie, on the other hand, what she liked to do largely involved discos, shops or bits of rough trade she thought I didn't know about.

You'd think I would've minded more wouldn't you? I think I should've minded more but I didn't really. I just didn't care. As long as she didn't give me some nasty disease, or take the piss too much, then she could do what she otherwise pleased.

'Chris?'

Most of the robbers had been captured, though a couple had managed to slip the net. I'd spent the last five minutes trying to work out what had happened to

Lenny before coming to the conclusion he must've been killed while we were on the other channel.

'Chris?'

Bruce and Ryan had made it to a patrol car behind a shield of a beautiful female hostage and roared off to signal the start of the obligatory car chase. Obligatory car chases always make me laugh. They're nothing like that in real life of course. In real life, none of the other drivers on the road get to be instructed on which way to go to get out of the way to keep the chase going for the maximum length of time. Most drivers are bastards. Simply driving down the pub or the shops or to work or whatever is frustrating enough. You try having a car chase in the middle of a city in broad daylight and see how far you get.

'Chris?'

Ryan leaned out of the passenger window and shot the tyres out of the first couple of police cars while Bruce drove at 80mph the wrong way up a one-way street in the middle of rush hour.

What a load of bollocks!

'Chris.'

'For crying out loud Debbie, give it a rest for Christsake.'

She leapt across the room, her eyes wild and full of hate, hissing and screaming like a mad mullah. Michael Douglas swung a punch which knocked her back on her heels for a moment, gay boy was stapling up lace and Blackburn had equalised against the run of play.

'Oi,' I bawled at her. 'Give me that fucking remote control here.'

'Chris, I am bored with watching telly. Can't we just go out for half an hour?'

'No,' I told her, determined for once not to let her

get her own way. 'Now throw it over. Come on, give it here.'

Debbie clutched the control to her chest and shook her head.

'Debbie, give me the fucking control,' I swore at her.

Debbie smiled ever so slightly. 'No, you'll have to come and get it.'

I stared at her for a moment as I tried to decide which course of action would annoy her the most.

'Fine. Keep it. I'll go upstairs and watch it in the bedroom,' I said getting to my feet. This did the trick and Debbie jumped up to explode but was halted in her tracks by the doorbell. I thought for a moment she was going to ask me who that was, like she usually does, but she didn't. Instead she lit up like a Christmas tree and bounded for the door. I'm not sure what she was more pleased about, the company for her or the intrusion for me. Both probably.

She opened the door and standing there were a rather dull-looking middle-aged couple wearing loose clothes and tight smiles. They had to be my neighbours. I'd been in the house only four weeks but had successfully managed to avoid meeting any of them until this moment. I guessed they'd finally got tired of waiting to bump into me by chance and so took the decision to take the bull by the horns, bite the bullet and bring over some cake.

Just what I needed.

'Alan Robinson,' said the slightly more male-looking of the two. 'And this is my wife Brenda. We live across but one and thought we'd pop over and say hello.'

'Oh, you shouldn't have bothered,' I almost replied, but instead just gave them our names.

Alan reached out and pushed his hand my way. I

responded in kind and instantly took a disliking to him. You can tell a lot from the way a man shakes hands and with Alan it was obvious to me it was a one-upmanship thing, as he did the old *grab-the-fingers-and-squeeze* grip before I had a chance to get my hand fully in the proper handshaking position. This has two effects; one, it hurts your fingers and exaggerates the strength of the shaker; and two, it allows you no purchase or grip to respond and so it makes it feel, to the other person, like you have a really weak handshake.

I hate people who do this. Vince was always doing this and it never failed to annoy me. It's pathetic. Totally pathetic. A juvenile, puerile method of asserting authority over someone that I personally left in the playground. Mr Robinson's card was well and truly marked within the first ten seconds. Don't get me wrong, I wasn't about to go and get my gun or nothing but it certainly placed him firmly in my black books from the start.

And he never managed to climb out of them.

'How are you settling in?' he asked.

'Fine,' I told him wiggling my fingers. 'Just fine.'

'Lots to do I should imagine, new house and all?'

'Quite a bit,' was all he got back from me. He smiled at me for a moment while I stared back.

'Where is it you're originally from?' he asked changing tack.

'London,' Debbie cut in. 'North London,' she told him, which was a lie, because we came from East London but I guess that just sounded a bit too jellied eels for her liking. 'Do you know London at all?' she asked him.

'No, not really, we're originally from Attleborough ourselves, which is just outside Nuneaton.' I shrugged my shoulders like it was meant to mean something to me. He spoke with that dreadful, dreary Midlands accent, but had worked hard to try and lose it. 'Very close to Coventry,' he told us both.

'I've been to Coventry,' Debbie piped in, ending that particular conversation.

'Oh before we forget, we brought you over some lemon cake, thought you might like a couple of slices.' I'd never heard of lemon cake before, but it sounded like it was probably cake made out of lemons. Didn't know, wouldn't find out, as it would go straight in the bin.

'Thank you, that's very sweet of you,' Debbie said, taking the cake from them. They stood there for an awkward moment or two waiting for the invitation which was never going to come, before deciding that if the cake didn't swing it for them, nothing would.

'Well, I can see you're both very busy so we'll . . .' he had started to say when Debbie, the scheming little bitch, jumped in with her latest sucker punch to my evening.

'Wait, we were just about to go to the pub for a quick drink, perhaps you'd like to join us.'

Suddenly, I found myself tripping over my jaw as I tried to untangle myself from this pressgang invitation. I launched into one about not wishing to impose on the pair of them – 'It is a Tuesday night after all Debbie' – but Alan and his wife (I'd forgotten her name already) thought it was a capital idea, and Debbie wasn't about to take no for an answer and had me walking down the road, coat in hand, before I could think of a better excuse.

Well what else could I do? Short of cutting all of their throats and flushing them bit by bit down the toilet, there was no way I could get out of it without creating a scene and becoming the hottest bit of gossip on the Beech Tree estate.

Bollocks!

We got to The Beech Tree pub and I spent about two seconds wondering whether the estate was named after the pub or the pub was renamed after the estate before deciding I didn't care either way, it looked like an awful place whichever way round it was.

I'm not much of a pub person really, I don't hate them but I'd just as soon have a couple of drinks in front of the television in my own home than surrounded by a bunch of strangers. If, however, I am going to go to a pub, I like a pub to be a pub and not, as The Beech Tree was, half pub, half rustic steak house; place mats, salt and pepper, noisy kids and the whole place smelling of chips. The Robinsons loved it. Alan strode up to the bar and greeted the barman by name just to prove to one and all that he was a regular – yeah, a regular arsehole.

'What's your poison?' Alan said, thrusting his hand into his pocket before realising he'd come out without his wallet. I saw this and frowned. Not only did I get to miss the end of my film and get forced down the pub with a couple of dullards, I also got to pay for the privilege.

All night.

I half-thought about pretending I'd come out without mine too, but Debbie had seen me pick it up and would happily grass on me in front of everyone rather than let me 'pop back for it'.

The ladies found room in the snug for us while I got the round in. Alan stayed with me at the bar, told me what a peach my Debbie was and introduced me to a couple of tankard drinkers from the Rotary Club, while I waited for my change. I nodded a quick hello and made for the table before they had a chance to engage me in mindless prattle about this year's tombola.

I handed Debbie her vodka and tonic, while Alan gave his wife her gin, sat down and saw that Debbie was all done and ready for another drink.

'Oh pardon me,' she giggled to Alan and co. 'I really needed that, I've had such a day you know. Be a darling would you,' she said handing me the glass back. I climbed back out of my chair and fetched her another from the bar. When I got back Alan droned on for the next hour about the residents' association, smokeless fuels and the guy at number 16, his taxi firm and the amount of cars he sometimes had parked outside his house, while Debbie got pie-eyed and looked about for mischief.

One thing I'll say about Alan was that he liked the sound of his own voice and by and large that was alright by me. It saved me having to field off questions, make up bullshit and tip-toe around subjects. Being a professional criminal you see, you have to be very careful what you tell people. And I don't just mean watch out that you don't mention robbing banks for a living. Any slip-up in your cover story, no matter how slight, can stir suspicion and lead to your ultimate downfall.

Especially with neighbours. Nosiest creatures in the universe.

Billy Archer, a blagger I knew from way back and a more cautious man you could never wish to meet, ended up doing a ten stretch because he forgot himself one time and told two different neighbours he did two different jobs. Seems innocuous enough, but it was enough to get one guy talking to another guy, who mentioned it to another guy, who told it to his neighbour, who discussed it with his brother, who checked it with his files and told it to his sergeant, who reported it to his DI, who recognised the photo . . . etc. You see how it works?

And the more elaborate the lie, the easier it is to trip up. Sometimes it can make talking about even the simplest things seem like such hard work, watching every word you're saying, double-checking every lie. Who can be bothered?

Not that this proved much of a problem with Alan. With the exception of a couple of inconsequential questions about nothing, he mostly did all the gassing and allowed me to sit back, drift off and daydream about pistol-whipping him. He was a bore. Sid's a bore, but Alan was a different species of bore. Sid's a bore because he only likes two things, fishing and *Star Trek*, and only takes part in conversations which in some way cover (or can be turned around to cover) these two topics. A typical chat with Sid would go something like this:

'My wife's just gone in to hospital for a hysterectomy.'

'In the future women won't have to stay in hospital with hysterectomies because they'll have instruments like Bones has in *Star Trek* which work in an instant. Of course tench don't have this problem because they lay eggs.'

Alan's an altogether different sort of bore. Unlike Sid, he's the sort of bore who thinks he knows everything about everything, or at least feels the need to have an opinion about everything. Usually a strong opinion. And usually one that makes about as much sense as my shoes. He probably lies in bed at night trying to decide how he feels about Antarctic exploration and suchlike.

' . . . because if there's one thing that gets my gander up, it's people who say that breeze block walls are just as good as thermalite walls, which is ridiculous. When was the last time . . .' he was saying.

I knew just what sort of bloke he was. A fat little four-eyes at school, no doubt, with an expensive geometry set and no friends. Junior clerk's job at fifteen, the key to the stationery cupboard at twenty-three and his own desk a mere twenty years later. Probably filled his evenings with stamps, model railways or the Battle of Naseby Amateur Re-enactment Society just to make up for his complete lack of success with girls. Then along came Brenda – that was her name – still on the shelf at thirty-three and so blind with desperation that she leapt upon the first proposal that was muttered within earshot of her. Preprogrammed for domesticity and ready to fertilise; just add semen to create instant housewife. Two children John and Jane – I knew this part was true because they kept cropping up in the conversation/ lecture for no relevant reason – a mortgage, life insurance and a set of garage-bought patio furniture and that's it; sit out the rest of their days stopping in shop doorways and blocking up the outside lane.

I don't know what it is with some people. Some people just seem to exist for the sake of existing. They do nothing, contribute nothing, experience nothing; they simply use up valuable food and air and create a new generation of sloths to follow in their own inimitable arse imprints.

We should have another war, a big one, us and the Russians, or the Germans, or the Americans, I don't care. Just somewhere where we can send all the wasters, plebs and Alans of this world to soak up the artillery for a bit, and then call a truce. There would be less traffic on the roads, less queues in the supermarkets and less dullards like Alan and Brenda to drag you down the pub on a Tuesday night.

This might sound cruel, I know, but that's just because I am.

' . . . because not everyone has their own set of drainage rods, but I felt very strongly as head of the residents' association that we should all club together and buy some. After all, it can sometimes take a whole morning for the council to get its act together and send a van out,' he was saying. I nodded in agreement and wondered what would happen to those same rods if Alan were to move to another area.

'Which brings me to a, not too dissimilar, matter which I knew I wanted to discuss with you Chris and er, Debbie,' he started. 'As well as the residents' association, I also act as chair to the Neighbourhood Watch scheme.' Debbie, half-cut, sniggered at this and was going to make some stupid comment about Alan being a chair but couldn't think of one quick enough and the moment was gone. 'And so, in this official capacity I formally extend an invitation to you, and your lovely wife, to join our merry band.'

I took a moment to consider this before accepting.

You might think this a little strange, possibly even bordering on the hypocritical, for a career criminal to be joining a Neighbourhood Watch scheme, but what was the alternative? Turn it down? Refuse? Become the neighbour with something to hide? With organisations like this, the only way to go unnoticed by them is to join up. Even if I only put in the rarest of appearances, I'd still be above suspicion because I'd be one of them – cliquey little bastards.

'Splendid, splendid. You'll like the other members,

they're a riot some of them. Meetings are Thursday nights, 7.30 at my place.'

'Oh dear, I'm afraid we can't make this Thursday, it's my brother's anniversary you see. Terribly sorry.' This was partly true, Gavin was celebrating five years inside on Thursday, but that aside, it was really just the first in my vast arsenal of excuses as to why I couldn't make more than twenty-five per cent of the meetings.

'Oh well, not to worry, I'll sign you up by proxy and we'll see you next week then.'

'Super,' I told him, then mimed a look at my watch. 'I hate to be rude but it is a work night and I have to be up early in the morning, so if you'll excuse us.'

'Oh come on Chris,' Debbie whined. 'It's only half-ten, let's have another drink.'

'No really Debbie, I think it's time we were on our way. We can't keep Alan and Brenda up all night now can we?' I said pulling her up by the arm.

'Well I think Alan looks like he can stay *up* all night all on his own,' she sniggered smuttily. Brenda was so shocked she almost broke out into an expression. I hauled her to her feet, wished the Robinsons a good night and walked Debbie out of there before she could crack any more brilliant one-liners about our new neighbour's cock.

Alan might've acted the shrinking violet at the time, but once the initial embarrassment had faded, you could bet your life he'd be thinking of Debbie next time he was carrying out his husbandly duty to Brenda.

As we walked back to our suburban seclusion, Debbie was full of high jinks and mischief.

'Of course, you know what goes on in little respect-able estates like this,' she was saying. 'It's all bondage and orgies and wife-swapping behind closed doors. I bet Alan and Brenda are on that committee too hey. What d'you think, maybe we should give it a go too?'

'Wife-swapping hey?' I mused. 'Wonder what I'd get for you. Bit of peace and quiet if I'm lucky.'

4. Looking out for Gavin

That Thursday I made the trip back to London to see Heather and the kids. Heather was a strong woman, one of the strongest I'd ever known. She'd taken Gavin's imprisonment pretty badly at first, but quickly bounced back and had coped like a trouper since – well, what else was there to do? I popped down to see her once every few weeks to make sure she was okay, had enough money and the kids weren't running about in rags.

I liked Heather. I always had. She was the complete opposite of Debbie and then some. Practical, dependable, loyal and smart, she took from me only what she had to and hated herself for having to do so. She shouldn't have needed to in the first place really, but over the years Gavin had burnt almost as much as he'd earned, and what little he did have stashed away for a rainy day had been either seized by the police or plundered by former acquaintances.

Ryan Blackmore was one of these acquaintances. A trigger man from south of the river we'd had the poor judgement to hook up with for one or two jobs. Blackmore had never forgiven Gavin for cutting him out of the big score he thought he was owed. It goes without saying that this was crap. Blackmore was a troublemaker, an unprofessional arsehole who stirred it up wherever he went. Gavin, Sid, me and even Vince got bored of him quick enough and gave him the boot (and he's lucky that's all he got) just two weeks before almost £450,000 came our way.

Blackmore swore he'd been ripped off and when Gavin was picked up for the Fulham job, he saw his opportunity to repay him in kind. Blackmore and an accomplice broke into Gavin's house one afternoon and waited for Heather and the kids to return. When they did, he pistol-whipped the boys and told Heather that he'd kill them all if she didn't withdraw the contents of Gavin's security box.

We didn't even bother wasting a bullet on him when we finally caught up with the bastard. We just chucked him in the hole, trussed up like a chicken, and filled it in. Unfortunately though, we never got the money back. Blackmore's accomplice – a man he simply knew as Ken – had long since split with the lot, leaving Blackmore penniless and pissing himself with terror as the first shovels of dirt landed on him.

From that day on, Heather has kept a loaded pistol in their security box. Just let someone else try it again!

Blackmore was only the most overt of Gavin's plunderers, but there were plenty of them. As soon as my brother was off the scene and unable to protect his assets they were stripped. Business partnerships liquidated, capital relocated; Gavin liked to keep his fingers in lots of pies, but slowly, one by one, they were all chopped off, until eventually all he was left with was the house in Epsom, his property in Greece and a whole lot of hate. Heather was forced to sell their place in Epsom and downsize to Bromley to make ends meet but kept the place in Greece after I bought it off her in all but name. The way I saw it, we all needed a place to run away to sometimes and it was worth pretty much fuck all anyway, so why let it go?

There was precious little else Gavin, Heather or me could do about his other lost investments as most of them were undeclared and therefore didn't exist. And I wasn't about to go charging about getting my head blown off by some of the shady fuckers he'd been fool enough to give large chunks of bounty to on the security of a handshake. These were proper people, protected people, and I was just a blagger.

All I could do was see that Heather and the kids were alright and wanted for nothing. It was all I could do, and all I was expected to do. Gavin would take care of all other business when he got out.

I pulled up on to the driveway and gave Bobby and Barry a wave as they pounded the upstairs window furiously to get my attention.

'Uncle Chris is here,' I heard them shouting. 'Mum, Uncle Chris is here!' Heather opened the door and gave me a smile before I had a chance to ring the bell.

'Hiya Chris,' she said in that understated, almost sombre tone of hers. 'Much traffic?'

'No, I left early so I was okay.' I followed her into the house but didn't get more than two steps inside when my legs were suddenly weighed down with a couple of nephews.

'Leg bus,' they were shouting as they clamped themselves round a pin each and hung on for the laboured journey into the kitchen. This was their favourite greeting, a ritual they'd started when they were only toddlers but five years and an extra three stone of puppy fat each and it was no longer cute. Once in the kitchen

I threw the presents I'd brought for them into the corner and they disengaged themselves and hurried after them.

'Coffee?' asked Heather.

'Please.'

We sat and chatted for as long as we could before Bobby and Barry got bored with listening to grown-up talk and crowded out the conversation with pointless observations about Mr Blobby. Don't get me wrong, I like my nephews, I just get bored of them very quickly. They're nice enough I guess, no worse than any other kids, I'm just not really very paternal that's all. Debbie and I talked about having children a few years ago, to give ourselves something to do, but quickly decided against it; Gavin's kids provided me with all the exposure to children I needed and as for Debbie, well, she's hasn't really grown up herself yet. We concluded that looking after children would be a great deal of hard work and ultimately unrewarding.

Bobby and Barry carried on jabbering all through dinner and beyond before Heather decreed that it was bedtime and no arguments (of which there were plenty). We carried the kids up to bed, brushed their teeth, put them in their pyjamas, tucked them in, read them a story, kissed them goodnight and told them to 'get back upstairs' when they came wandering down again after five minutes, before silence finally descended.

Heather poured us both a drink and we settled in the living room.

'Sorry about that,' she said. 'They get a bit excited when you come round and like showing off.'

'That's alright, that's what kids are like I guess.' – Little fuckers!

'How are you settling into your new house?'

'Fine, fine,' I said and told her about my visit from

Alan and Brenda. 'I've got a horrible feeling they're not going to leave us alone.'

'And that's so bad is it?' she asked.

'Yes, it is. You haven't met them.'

'No, maybe not, but I've met you,' she said, her voice full of disdain.

'What's that supposed to mean?'

'It means Chris, that you're the one with the problem, not them. I think it's nice that they came round and introduced themselves to you, took you for a drink, welcomed you to the area. God knows there's precious little of that neighbourly spirit left in people these days, especially around these parts. Decency and courtesy in people isn't something to pour scorn on, it's something to be commended.'

'But Heather, you don't know . . .'

'I do know Chris, I know. I've lived in this god-awful crappy town for more than five years now and never get anything more than a grudging acknowledgement from any of the neighbours I pass on the street. I envy you, I do. I'd like to live in a place where a little bit of company isn't three bus rides away or I don't have to worry about my children playing out in the front garden.'

'I'd hardly call Alan and Brenda stimulating company.'

'Well, I'd hardly call you stimulating company either. You sit around in a world of your own, with hardly a word to say to anyone, let alone any good ones, sneering at anyone mug enough to actually go to work for a living and dreaming up your next fucking job. You're pathetic Chris. Personally, it's your neighbours I feel sorry for, not you.'

I took a sip of my drink and tried to explain to her

again how boring and dull Alan and Brenda had been, but she wasn't having it.

'Just because they don't rob banks Chris, it doesn't make them bad people. They're normal that's all, they're simply normal everyday people, the country is full of them. Give them a chance, be nice to them and you might even find you end up liking them.'

This was vintage Heather, ever the altruist, always ready to see the best in people and always on guard to take a stand against my all-encompassing cynicism. She'd shower the objects of my contempt with the benefit of the doubt and shoot down my arguments in flames until finally I threw in the towel and, just for a bit of peace and quiet, agreed with her point of view. It was her most annoying feature.

I don't know though, maybe she had a point. Maybe I did need to lighten up a bit. Maybe. But cynicism, suspicion and mistrust had kept me alive and free longer than most, so I wasn't about to change.

'You know you're so like Gavin in so many ways, except in this. Gavin – as hard as you might like to think of him – he always had time for others, no matter who they were. He could see that there was more to life than robbery, and he only did it for the money.' She leaned over and topped up my glass and then her own. 'I sometimes wonder Chris, why do you do it?'

'Money,' I told her.

'Really?' she said. 'Is that really all?'

'Yeah,' I replied. 'Why else?'

'I don't know, maybe you just can't think of anything else to do. Maybe you're still out to impress Gavin. Or maybe you just like being a bank robber. Whatever the reason, it's stopping you from leading a normal life, and gives you a problem with everyone you meet.'

'That's nonsense,' I told her. 'It wouldn't of mattered if I was a £5-an-hour clerk in a large insurance firm, I would've still thought that my neighbours were a couple of dullards.'

'Perhaps, but I bet you'd have a damn sight more people to tell it to than just me. You don't have any friends Chris, and you don't have a life.'

'I have got a life. I've got more of a life than most. How many people can claim to have done the things I've done? Seen the things I've seen?'

'Not many I should imagine,' Heather conceded. 'But then, who'd really want to?'

'Plenty,' I told her.

'I doubt it,' she replied. 'I'm sure it's everybody's favourite fantasy, but that's all it is really – a fantasy; like murdering your boss or screwing a whore, not many would really be prepared to actually do it, but that's not the point I was making. No ... actually, you demonstrated precisely the point I was making.'

'Which was?'

'Which was you, and your inability to see beyond the barrel of a gun. Let me ask you this then, what have Alan and Brenda got that you haven't? Happy marriage, kids, friends in the community, cheery outlook?'

'I'm green with envy,' I smirked.

'And so you should be, Chris. It's a cliché I know, but which of you is the richer? Alan or you?'

What a load of bollocks! I've had this little pearl of wisdom levelled at me on countless occasions and I still don't get it. How can a fat, pointless bore with a miserable wife, two ugly children, a colossal mortgage and a tedious pen-pushing job possibly be richer than me? Even if we're not talking money here, even if we're just talking say ... say women for example. I've probably had ten times as many – all ten times better-looking and ten times more animated in bed – than Alan.

As for careers, well, bank robbery might not be some people's idea of a contribution but it still beats the hell out of whatever it is Heather's all-time hero spends all day doing; filling in stationery orders or photocopying his arse.

'Nothing to say for yourself?' Heather asked me.

I didn't. Much as I believed in the legitimacy of my convictions, there was no point in arguing them with Heather when she was in this mood; it would have just gone on all night and I couldn't be bothered. Best all round just to nod and agree with her like a good little boy should. That's the problem with women when they've had a few children, they get so used to arguing the toss with back-chatting little know-it-alls that they lose the ability to recognise a valid point when one is made.

If I'd been a few years younger, she could've just got away with 'because I said so', and sent me to my room with a thick ear.

'Chris, I don't mean to nag, really I don't, I just . . . I just get worried about you that's all. I don't want to see you end up in the same place as Gavin . . . or worse. Sometimes, I just think that, if you gave life a chance, maybe you'd start taking a few less risks.' I took a deep breath, to give myself the appearance of understanding, before answering.

'I know Heather, I know, but really, you shouldn't worry about me, worry about yourself if you have to worry about something, I can take care of myself.'

'That's just it, I am worrying about myself. This'll sound selfish I know, but you're about my only regular contact outside of PTA meetings, doctor's appointments and the supermarket. You've been like a lifeline for me since Gavin went away, and I don't know what I'd do if anything happened to you too.'

'I'm sure you'd cope,' I told her, all chipper.

'Cope! Cope! That's all I've done these past five years. You know, sometimes coping isn't enough.'

For a moment I thought she was going to break down and blub but she didn't, she just sat there and stared off into oblivion at the life she thought she deserved. I'd never seen her like this before. She was always so strong, always so resilient. I hadn't seen this coming at all. I thought we were having an argument about what a social inadequate I was, then suddenly it all turned into a . . . a . . . well a cry for help I suppose you could call it. I thought about offering up a few words of support or comfort but dared not in case the topic of conversation switched back to what an arsehole I was before I finished talking.

You just never know where you are with women.

'I just, I . . . things have been so difficult for me you just can't imagine,' Heather said.

'I can,' I told her. 'I know what you're going through.'

'No you don't, you can't possibly. While you're out there acting like a bloody child, it's women like me who are left to pick up the pieces.'

Told you.

'Gavin's been locked up now for five years and everyone says "poor old Gavin, isn't it a shame, five years inside away from his wife, how does he bear it?" How does he bear it? What about me? How do I bear it? I'm serving the same sentence; fifteen years deprived of my husband and I haven't done anything bloody wrong! It's not fair, it's not bloody fair,' she said and started to sob. I reached across a hand and touched her elbow.

'Come on Heather, come on, chin up,' I said before realising what a pointless empty gesture that really was.

'Chin up! Chin up! I want my husband back here with me. I'm lonely, and it's been so hard for me and it just gets harder and harder.'

'Why don't you and the kids go to Greece for a few months? I'll give you the air fare and all the spending money you'll need.'

'Because I don't want to go to Greece. I want my husband in my bed.' She dropped her head into her hands. 'I want a *man* in my bed and I can't have my husband, but you're the nearest thing. Chris, please don't be angry with me, and don't judge me, just fuck me.'

Well, how does the expression go? You could've knocked me down with a feather. I didn't know what to say. I'd never thought of Heather in that way before, she was always Gavin's girl. My whole life I'd known her as Gavin's girl and therefore completely inaccessible, off-limits and almost sacred like. When Gavin went away I made a promise to myself to look out for him and make sure Heather was taken care of. I would've killed any man I'd found out had been with her behind Gavin's back and known right was on my side for doing so. But this . . . this . . .

'Please Chris, do this thing for me. I need it more than your money.'

She moved forward towards me and started to unbutton her blouse. I put my glass down and kicked off my shoes.

I know it seems like a shitty thing to do, what with her being my brother's wife and all, but I really had no choice. If she really needed it that badly, well then, better me than someone else.

5. Fifteen years of bad luck

You know, sometimes the difference between death or glory can be traced back to a single decision, a solitary coincidence or just a couple of seconds. How lucky do we call the man who misses his connecting flight because he forgot to put his watch forward after landing in a new time zone, only to hear with horror how the plane fell out of the sky not twenty miles from the airport? How unlucky do we call the passenger in seat 37B with her stand-by ticket and her last-minute call?

Life's like that though. Perhaps not as disastrous or as obvious as that for the most of us, but with five billion people in the world, leading five billion different lives, it's no wonder nearly all of us, at some point, feel like we're merely five billion stooges to some sick intergalactic joker.

My brother's arrest was like that.

'It was just one of those things.' That's what people said, as if it was some sort of comfort. 'It was just one of those things.' And they were right, it was. I'm sure Gavin was 'tutting' his fucking head off as he was driven off to the Scrubs for his fifteen-year stopover.

You know, sometimes, it doesn't matter how careful you are or how professionally you conduct yourself, if the stars aren't in your corner, then they're usually against you.

'Don't be a hero!' Vince shouted and whacked the most unhero-like manager I've ever seen across the face with the butt of his gun. 'Don't fucking try it.' All he'd said was, 'Please take the money, just don't hurt anyone' and he got a smack in the mouth for his trouble. But then, he was always on dangerous ground saying anything to Vince. See, Vince had such a big chip on his shoulder that he took everything you said to him as either a command or a goad; so to him 'please don't hurt me' came across as 'don't you even think about hurting me' or 'what are you going to do? You're just a big poof.'

I couldn't say anything really, it wasn't my place to do so. Everyone has their own way of robbing a bank, just as everyone has their own way of combing their hair or peeling a banana, and that was Vince's. Come to think of it though, Vince peeled a banana that way as well.

'You there,' Vince then screamed at some young lad fixated at the sight of his boss crawling through his broken teeth with one hand whilst trying to hold his nose on with the other (couldn't tell what he was thinking – 'ha ha' by the look of it). 'Who told you to stop filling that bag, fill that fucking bag or you'll get one in the mush too.'

The cashier finished filling the bag just as Gavin came out of the back with the assistant manager and another bag of notes. Gavin always used to tell me to take the assistant manager to the safe rather than the manager. His theory was that the assistant manager was less likely to know about secret alarms, trip codes and delaying tactics because it's usually the manager that got sent on these courses by their banks. He also used to reckon that the assistant managers were less likely to mess you about because they held a lower position, thus had less loyalty to the bank and were therefore less likely to put the lives of themselves and their co-workers at risk for the sake of a few quid. Personally, I disagree with all of this. Assistant managers, I reckon, are more likely to try and be heroes, because they're usually younger, less experienced, and eager to get noticed by the regional branch managers to try and swing promotion. They're also less answerable for the safety of the bank employees and more likely to be Bruce Willis fans than their bosses – just look at the cars half of them drive. Vince reckons we're both wrong and a sharp whack in the gob with a shotgun butt and there's very little light between them.

You know, sometimes you have to bow to greater reasoning.

'Did you get the cards?' Gavin asked Vince.

'In the bag,' he replied.

'And the book?'

'What book?'

'The fucking book!'

Prefixing the word 'book' with the word 'fucking' still didn't strike a chord with Vince, so he asked again:

'What fucking book?'

'Jesus Christ how many fucking times have I got to tell you this? We went over this only last night.' Gavin looked around and noticed that the lad filling up the bag from the tills had finished what he was doing and was now stood quietly staring at the pair of them with a mixture of fascination and servitude. 'Tell him,' Gavin ordered the lad. 'Tell him the book I mean.'

'He means the credit card book,' the lad duly obliged, snapping to attention like a toy soldier.

The credit card book. This, Gavin had explained to us the night before, had to be taken if we were going to nick the credit cards waiting for collection by the card holders. It gave a list of all the cards held at the bank, all those already collected and all those awaiting collection. Taking the book would lob a sparrow in the works (as Sid used to say) and buy us an hour or two while the bank traced and cancelled all the stolen cards; this was all the time that was needed by associates of ours to run them up to their limits – efficient and impressive, yet still nothing compared to the damage Debbie could do in an afternoon.

'Yes, the credit card book you doughnut, what d'you think I meant, *The Guinness Book of* fucking *Records*?' Gavin grabbed the book as the lad handed it to him. 'Christ almighty, he's more of a pro than you, you useless bastard,' he said bawling out Vince. 'I should have him on the next job and leave you to fucking whistle.'

Vince was just about to retort with one of his hilarious 'fuck you' or 'come on then' one-liners when the lad himself piped in and pleaded with Gavin to: 'Take me with you.'

For a moment no-one said anything, we all just stared at the bloke and tried to take in what he'd asked. And we weren't the only ones – me, Gavin and Vince – suddenly everyone was staring at him; his workmates, the bank customers, his boss – his boss most notably of all in fact.

Again he asked: 'Please take me with you, I can be useful to you.' I couldn't see how, we all made our own tea.

He was only a young lad – and if I remember rightly, quite unbelievably thick-looking in a kind of 'always-saying-the-wrong-thing-at-the-wrong-time' sort of way – and as young lads tend to be, he looked way out of his depth and hopelessly confused by life and all that surrounded him. He probably held some silly, romantic, wild west view of bank robbery, like we were The Hole in the Wall Gang or something, and hoped to ride out of town with us to a new and better life – or at least one in which he got laid occasionally. In many ways he reminded me of me when I was his age, although I pray that if I live to be 150 years old, I never make as colossal a cunt of myself as he did that day.

'Sorry Clive,' Gavin finally said reading the name on his trainee badge. 'Maybe another time.'

'Alright, come on let's go,' I shouted, shattering what was a truly touching scene. 'That's three minutes, come on let's move.' I glanced back as we left and chuckled with delight as Clive turned to examine the scowl on his boss's face.

Not exactly done your career prospects any favours have you mate, I thought to myself as we all jumped into the waiting Astra and sped off up the high street.

We laughed like drains about it as we counted out the cash back at the garage, but Gavin wouldn't hear a word against the prat. 'He was one of our own he was, young Clive, a proper little robber, with cheek, guile and nerve, and we should respect and admire him for the chance he took today.'

'He was a fucking idiot,' Vince said. 'What a cunt! Can you believe that, what a cunt!'

'Well I'll raise a glass to him tonight,' Gavin told us. 'I thought he was a top man.'

'So will I,' Sid agreed. 'A fucking idiot sure, but a top fucking idiot.'

'Oh come on . . .' I started to say, but Gavin cut me short.

'You've got no ground to comment, if you remember what you were like when you was a nipper. You couldn't wait to team up with us, get on the crew full-time and live the life, but we didn't all laugh at you did we.'

I thought about this for a moment. 'Yes you did, all the time.'

'No we didn't, well not all the time anyway. But the point is you turned out alright, you're a good little robber these days,' he said, a bit too patronising for my liking. 'So don't be too quick to jump on the bandwagon and take the piss out of poor little Clive. I hope he makes it, I hope he gives it a go and makes a success of it. I wish him all the best of luck for the future and I'd be happy to do a job with him in the future.'

This was bollocks. Gavin's one of the most fastidious people in the world about who he'll work with, he was clearly saying all of this just to get his point across, which, to be fair, he did. He was right about one thing, and I've admitted as much myself already, on the surface I don't suppose there was much between the young me and Clive. I guess the only real difference was that I had the good fortune to have an older brother working in the business I wanted to work in.

Maybe though, it was because I had Gavin as a brother that I chose robbery as a career. In this respect I guess, Clive's one up on me. What would I have done if it hadn't of been for Gavin? Would I still be a robber today? Maybe I might even be working in a bank, praying for The Hole in the Wall Gang to burst in and take me away with them.

It doesn't bear thinking about.

I found a new respect for Clive after that and also wished him well in whatever career he chose. For one thing was certain, he was going to need a new one.

Gavin finished dividing up the cash and we all pocketed just under £14,000 each. An extra few grand would be realised on the credit cards and Gavin stashed them back into one of the bags, along with his share of the money and the four guns.

'Phone O'Riley, tell him I'll be at his place with the plastic some time after three.'

Gordon O'Riley, con-man, crack-dealer, low-life extraordinaire. He was the associate we off-loaded our plastic on to. Plastic was good for him, plastic was very useful indeed. He had so many petty thieves, crack-heads and scumbags on his books, changing plastic into paper was a doddle for him.

Need a fix?

No money?

No problem. Take this card, go down to Dixons and get me a video camera, we'll swap it for some rocks.

By late afternoon, most of the main shopping centres and high street big names would, after one simple swipe, be instantly aware of the plastic's status – but that was okay, back then there were still plenty of places technology had yet to reach; hundreds, thousands even, of independent retailers who still relied on paper, pen, card presses and simple honesty. O'Riley knew them all and harvested in the cash with consummate expertise.

'Want a cup of tea before you go?' Sid asked.

'Er, no, better make a move, you know what the Friday traffic down to London and back's like,' Gavin replied. 'Right, okay then chaps, I'll see you all later, 7 o'clock at Benny's okay? See ya.'

'Mmm, yeah, see ya,' I murmured, looking up from my share of the cash just long enough to catch my last glimpse of Gavin this side of prison bars.

Gavin was already in cuffs when he came to in the ambulance. He tried to sit up but the pain in his back was crippling. He tried to turn his head but the brace around his neck prevented even that. A face appeared in front of him and told him that he'd been in an accident and was on his way to hospital.

And somewhere, off to the left and out of view, another voice spoke.

'And you're also under arrest,' Gavin heard and then slipped back into unconsciousness.

I mentioned, I think, how sometimes you can usually trace monumental catastrophes in your life back to a single, solitary, decision – or indeed, a whole combination of insignificant decisions, any one of which goes the other way and a whole different outcome unfolds – well Gavin's arrest, for me, was like that. I always wonder what would've happened if he'd stopped for Sid's cup of tea, or if he'd decided to take the A5183 instead of the B5378, or what if he'd left five minutes earlier or stopped for petrol ten minutes later or whatever. Any one of these decisions and Gavin would still be free today. Thinking about it is enough to drive you crazy.

But it doesn't really matter, none of these decisions are really to blame for Gavin's arrest, none of these decisions are the key catalyst behind his downfall, I mean how could they be? How could the difference between doing fifteen years and getting away really rest on the brim of a cup of tea? It couldn't and it didn't. It might've allowed Gavin to avoid his fate, but it wasn't that decision.

No, in fact, the decision that led to Gavin's arrest wasn't even Gavin's; it was William Paul Woodman's. It was his decision to knock back five pints at lunchtime. It was his decision to climb in behind the wheel of his company car. It was his decision to drive 60mph through a 40mph speed limit.

My brother didn't even see him coming. He pulled out of the station and next thing he knew he was in the ambulance. The accident knocked him out cold and left him at the mercy of the three emergency services, who turned up to deal with the mess.

'Is that a gun,' the fireman said to the ambulance man as he cut away the car roof.

'I think you're right,' said the ambulance man to the fireman. 'You'd better take a look at this,' the ambulance man shouted to the policeman, who, at that moment, was taking a sample of breath from the dead man.

He wasn't really dead. In fact William Paul Woodman, typically, came through the whole prang without a scratch. No, but he was as good as dead. That decision he took to have those extra couple of pints and drive like a fucking drunken maniac would be the one he would be able to trace his brutal and untimely death back to.

Me and Vince would see to that.

When he stood in the dock and received his eighteen-month ban and £750 fine, the magistrate remarked that it was only due to his remarkable good fortune that the man he had hit had been an even more reprehensible criminal than him, and that the bench had chosen to be lenient.

William Paul Woodman walked from court with a 'thank you your honour' and a tug of the forelock and even had the balls to try and sound heroic when he talked to reporters on the step outside; like he was some sort of crime-busting drink-driver or something, who went around mounting the pavement and smacking into bus queues of shoplifters – Super Swerve.

Gavin, on the other hand, received no such leniency. In fact he felt the full force of the law after repeatedly refusing to turn Queen's and hand up me, Vince and Sid. We were all questioned of course, as known associates, but Plod never had so much as a shred against us, so we all eventually walked.

You know, I can't believe that the police never gave Woodman protection. I guess they felt they didn't need to, I mean, he wasn't a prosecution witness or anything so I suppose they felt he wasn't at any risk. Actually no, the more cynical bones in me tell me it was probably because the Old Bill didn't need him; he wasn't testifying, they didn't need him to get a conviction on Gavin, so why bother wasting valuable resources protecting some old pisshead who might as easily have run a busload of kids or nuns off the road as a dangerous armed robber.

Me and Vince, we let it slide for three or four months after the trial anyway, just to be sure, before knocking on the bastard's door late one November evening.

Woodman opened the door in his carpet slippers and cardy and got a smack round the head with the barrel of my shotgun before his eyes had time to dilate. I could so easily have just pulled the trigger and legged it but I didn't want the drunken, flabby bastard to die before he knew he'd been killed.

Woodman landed heavily and immediately did what all people do when they have a gun pointed at them, he held his arms up in front of him to protect himself. This is a ridiculous thing to do, I know, but it's instinct, what can you do? I can't help wondering if somewhere, three million years down the evolutionary line say, a child will be born with bullet-proof arms.

Little gulps of air, that's all it is, little gulps of air.

'No, no, please God, no. Wait, wait, don't shoot, don't shoot.' It gave me great satisfaction to watch him squirm in terror those last final moments as I pointed the gun at his belly. 'No, god, no.'

'Die you fuck,' I screamed back.

'No, stop, don't!!!'

At this, I did stop and looked up to where this scream had come from. Standing at the end of the hall, just in front of the kitchen, was his wife and two little kids. It had been the eldest, a little girl aged about ten, who'd shouted at me to stop. Her mother was just screaming incoherently as she held the two tots back, while her little brother trembled with fear beside her.

'Don't hurt my daddy. Please, don't hurt my dad.'

'Shut up,' I shouted and raised the gun a little to warn them back, but still the little girl pleaded with me and struggled against her mother's grasp.

Suddenly I couldn't do it. I couldn't take his life. Not now, not in front of his kids. Whatever else he'd done to me, his kids had never shared any of the guilt. And I wasn't about to leave them with a nightmare that would haunt them for the rest of their lives.

I paused a moment longer to induce a few more seconds of trouser-wetting fear out of Woodman and was going to leave when he said something that suddenly changed my mind again.

'Please, don't shoot me, don't kill me,' he said. 'Please don't hurt me.'

This annoyed me because, here was an armed man, standing in his hallway, waving a shotgun about with his wife and kids not four yards away, and he was pleading for his *own* life? If ever I was in this situation, I hope to Christ I'd at least have the guts to plead for my kids' safety before my own. When Vince whacked that manager around the nut on that last job we all did together, and all he said was 'please don't hurt anyone', I at least had an iota of respect for him – the manager that is, not Vince.

But for William Paul Woodman, I couldn't believe it was possible for him to slip any further down in my estimation but he did. For all I heard, he might as well have said: 'Please, don't hurt me, kill the kids, but don't hurt me.'

Quick as a flash, I brought the shotgun barrel down again and pulled the two triggers before anyone else could come up with a decent reason why I shouldn't plug their dad. The only concession I made to my conscience and their terror was that it was his right and left kneecaps I pointed the gun at rather than his belly.

Woodman yelped like a big baby and then passed out almost immediately, as did his wife. This left just me and the kids, silent and staring at each other for one of the longest seconds of my life.

'It's alright, it's only his legs,' I told his daughter. 'He'll live. Go and phone 999, ask for an ambulance. And tell your dad when he wakes up, he was lucky. This was a warning. He had better never ever do it again. He'll know what I'm talking about.'

The little girl nodded and I turned and left.

Vince slammed the car into gear and we sped off down the road.

'Well?' he asked as I pulled the mask off. 'Did you kill him?'

'Kneecaps,' I replied.

'What? I thought we were going to kill him.'

'Don't worry about it, mission accomplished. One way or another, he'll never drink-drive again.'

6. Tons of guns

Of course, Gavin getting caught like that presented us with a very much more immediate problem than just a sense of sadness over the loss of a comrade – we'd lost all our fucking guns as well.

See, the guns that Gavin took off us after the job, and was found with after the accident, were the only four guns we owned. They were the crew guns, property of the crew, they didn't belong to any one of us as an individual, they were just our collective tools of the trade (as in, robberies: for the use of). I can't remember where Gavin got them in the first place, but I do know that he'd had them ages and that they were pretty hard to come by in the first place. I mean, this isn't America. You can't just wander in off the street, show the shop-keeper your driving licence and walk off with a bazooka. You want a gun in this country you have to have a licence; and to get a licence ... well, you've got less chance of getting a licence than you have of getting planning permission to pebble-dash Westminster Abbey. I said this to Vince and he ventured: 'Yeah, or arse-fuck the Queen live on telly on the National Lottery programme.' Personally, I thought my analogy was cleverer, but Vince always gets a bigger laugh with his, so I mention both here in the interests of fairness.

If you ever do manage to handshake your way round the licence review board, or whatever they're called, all you end up with these days is a piece of paper which gives you permission to own something marginally less powerful than a spud-a-matic.

This is all the fault of a few gun-toting maniacs who vented their frustrations at being labelled dangerous weirdos by workmates and neighbours by mercilessly hunting down their aforementioned workmates and neighbours with large automatic weapons, blowing them to bits and ruining it for the rest of us.

Up till a couple of years ago however, if you had a licence, you could still buy some half-decent artillery from respectable gunsmiths, specialist importers or through your local gun club. And if I was to sit down and look for a silver lining behind Gavin's arrest, I guess I'd say it was in the timing. See, Gavin was arrested and sent down before that evil nutter ran riot in Dunblane and the government introduced the .22 limitation on handguns. That meant that at least there were guns out there to be had.

The only problem now was getting our hands on them.

I flicked the cigarette butt out on to the pavement and started to roll the passenger side window up.

'Oi, what you doing?' Vince asked. 'Go and get that.'

I looked at him for a moment before offering him one out of my packet.

'I don't want a fag you stupid cunt, I want you to go and get that butt you just flicked away with your fingerprints all over it and not leave so much evidence all over the place for the Old Bill to find. Wanker!'

He was right of course, I felt really stupid. We were sitting not ten yards away from the gunsmith's we were about to rob and I was dropping clues like a coy young maiden at a cavalry ball. I might as well have gotten out of the car and written my name in the snow in piss. Not that that's what coy young maidens at cavalry balls do.

'Sorry Vince,' I said stepping out into the cold, picking up the offending butt and dropping it into the dashboard ashtray.

'And don't go spitting out any chewing gum either. Police find that and they can get your DNA off it from your spit.'

'Can they?' I wondered aloud.

'I don't know. Probably,' Vince said. 'Haven't you learnt anything in the last couple of years? Haven't you even grasped the fucking basics? Gavin ain't here to hold your fucking hand any more so you better start doing things right, or you'll be doing them alone. I ain't going down for you, and neither's Sid. Got it?' Sid would've probably agreed with Vince had he not taken to a little bivouac about fifty miles away to watch a glow-in-the-dark float bobbing about all night.

This was our first job together without Gavin and already tensions were strained. I know it was a stupid thing to do with the fag butt, but I didn't need the condescending lecture off Vince, I'd been robbing banks far too long for that. It was a genuine mistake, that was all, a momentary lapse in concentration, we all have those from time to time – even Vince. Only two jobs ago, Vince was ready to tear his ski mask off in the middle of the bank and had to be stopped at the last by

Gavin, just because he'd sneezed, but still, we didn't give him some long lecture after the job on the discipline expected from a professional did we?

No, we just laughed at him.

'I haven't got any chewing gum,' I told him. Vince growled in response.

Of course, I knew exactly the reason for his little paddy, and it had nothing to do with a shaken faith in my abilities as a crook; Vince wanted to be top dog now that Gavin was out of the frame. He was just testing his bark.

Well, it would be a cold day in the Scrubs before I bowed to that psycho's judgement.

Admittedly, this on the surface would've looked like Vince's job – he came up with the idea and found a shop ripe for the taking, but I'd provided the weapons; two ageing, but fully functioning World War II pistols I'd 'hired' off this little Czech fence I occasionally had cause to deal with (the same guy I'd got the shotgun off for Mr William Paul Woodman). We'd tested them out the previous night, firing one round from each gun, out in the woods, and they'd done what was asked of them, which was all we was after for one job. Just looking at the state of them though, I wouldn't like to get in a tight corner and have to rely on them. Probably as likely to blow your hand off as someone's head. Not only that though, I wanted to get shot of these antiques as soon as possible because you never know the history behind guns like these. Who knew what these guns had been used for in the past and by who? Knowing the bloke I got them off like I did, it could be anything and anyone. I didn't particularly want to get caught holding a weapon that'd been used in five different sloppy murders when all I'd done is borrow it for a quick robbery.

'What time have you got?' I asked Vince.

'Two minutes to three.'

I added a couple of minutes to my watch to catch up with Vince's.

'Okay, you ready?' I asked him.

'I was born ready,' Vince replied, nicking a line from a film. I struggled quickly to remember which film it was and pull him up on it, but before I could, he'd climbed from the car, crossed the road and entered the shop. I gave it about a minute, then clambered out from behind the passenger side and walked towards the shop.

Gunsmiths are prone to robberies from time to time; they have panic buttons and alarms everywhere so taking them out like banks doesn't work. You have to be more subtle, you have to take them by surprise, which was exactly the way we'd planned it.

Vince was standing by the counter going through his gun application licence with the manager, when I walked in and trudged past. The pistol hidden in my pocket felt like a lead brick and without my constant support, it would've stood out like a ... well, like a coy young maiden writing her name in the snow with her piss at a cavalry ball. I stopped by the Barbour jackets and began to browse. After several seconds, I heard the voice I'd been waiting for.

'Can I help you at all sir?' I quickly turned to face the manageress and shoved the gun in her belly.

'Yeah, freeze.'

That instant, with impeccable timing, Vince did the same with the manager's face.

'Don't move a fucking muscle, not a fucking muscle,' Vince told the manager in no uncertain terms as he clambered over the counter beside him. He looked around where the manager was standing and straightaway saw three alarm trips, one on the floor and two at hand level. Vince was satisfied that he hadn't managed to get to any in the split second we'd pulled the guns and indicated to me that it was a go.

I spun the manageress (the manager's wife I think she was and a bit of alright to boot) and frogmarched her into the back room, where I sat her down and tied her to a chair with thick plastic ties – you know, the kind with the teeth along the plastic tongue which you can pull tight.

'Please don't hurt me!' she started to plead until I told her to shut up.

'The video machine for the CC tape,' I asked her. 'Where is it?'

'In the cupboard, under the monitor. Over there,' she indicated with a nod of the head. I found it straightaway, hit the stop and eject buttons and pocketed the tape. We'd come in without masks on, you see, in order to spring the surprise, so taking the tape was probably not a bad idea if we wanted to retain a modicum of anonymity.

'The main lights to the shop, are those them on the wall here by the door?' She nodded, too frightened even to speak. 'Okay, keep your mouth shut and you won't get hurt,' I said and flicked all the switches off.

I walked back out into the now darkened shop, crossed the floor to the front door, bolted it and turned around the open/closed sign so that we wouldn't be disturbed. Vince, by this time, had the manager bound up, on his knees and sobbing like a little girl.

'Please don't . . .' he was saying as I joined them around the other side of the counter. 'Please, please don't kill me,' sniff etc, all the usual shit. You know, much as I hate these heroes we sometimes encounter, I probably get more annoyed by the blubbering wanting-to-hide-behind-my-mother's-legs weeping baby shit. Can't people, in a life-threatening situation, conduct themselves with a little bit of dignity these days? I mean, we are British aren't we!

Vince, I could see, was just as disgusted as I was.

'What's the fucking matter with you?' he said holding his pistol to the manager's temple.

'You're going to kill me, you're going to kill me,' the manager blurted out.

'No we're not,' Vince told him. 'We're going to *rob* you.'

'You're not, you're going to kill me, you're going to kill me. Oh Christ, dear sweet mother of Mary, please don't do it.'

'We ain't going to kill you,' I shouted at him, imploring the snivelling bastard to shut up.

'You are,' he said back.

'We're not.'

'You are.'

'We're fucking not,' Vince said. This slowed the manager's hysteria a little.

'You promise?' he asked.

'Yes,' I said.

'Honestly?'

'Honestly,' I reassured him, although to be honest if he carried this on much longer . . .

He stopped his snivelling for a full three seconds before lapsing into it once more. 'You wouldn't tell me if you was going to though.'

I found it hard to believe that someone who worked with guns all day should be so shit scared of them.

Surely he should've gotten used to them by now; well perhaps not at having them pointed at him while he was trussed up on the floor, but still. It's like a bee keeper being scared of bees, whoever heard of such a thing?

'Oh for fuck's sake,' Vince exclaimed. 'If you don't shut up we will fucking kill you, and you would've done it to yourself, you got it, now shut up.' The manager shut up a little, but not enough to be in the reckoning for any bravery awards. 'You know what we're here for?' Vince asked him.

The manager nodded.

'What?' asked Vince.

'Money and guns.' Correct, but not necessarily in that order.

Incidentally, there's a little tip for you here. If ever you're doing a job like this, always make the guy you're robbing tell you what you've come to rob him of. The reason for this is simple, if he's got half a million quid's worth of diamonds or heroin or cash hidden away about the place, he might mistakenly think that that's what you've come for and tell you about it. It hasn't paid off for me yet, but some day it might bear fruit.

'I want pistols, shotguns, ammunition, the combination to your safe and you to stop crying,' Vince ordered.

'Okay,' the manager croaked with effortless servitude.

'Right, let's move.' Vince and I were just about to frogmarch the manager into the back room when two voices, coming from the direction of the front door, stopped us in our tracks and caused us to drop to the ground for cover. Vince clamped his hand over the manager's mouth and stuck the gun in his ear just in case he got any ideas.

'Oh where is he?' said one of the voices.

'Roger! Roger!' called the other. Some forceful knocking followed to accompany a duet of: 'Open up Roger. Roger?'

I peered up carefully from behind the counter and could make out the two silhouettes pressing their faces against the glass trying to peer back into the gloom of the shop.

'ROGER?' shouted one of them through the letterbox. He sounded annoyed. Roger later told us that they were a couple of regular customers who'd left their shotguns with him for repair. Judging from their overalls I would've also said that they'd bunked off work for the afternoon, or knocked off early, to come and collect them.

'Roger you bastard, where are you?!'

'I bet he's down the pub again, the drunken old fucker,' one of them said, causing Roger to pull a wounded face. 'He's always doing it. Come on, he'll be down the King's Arms, let's go and drag him out.' And with that they left.

We gave it a couple more seconds to make sure they didn't come back before we got on with the job in hand. 'Come on,' said Vince, 'let's get cracking.'

We dragged Roger out the back and dumped him down on the arm of the chair next to his wife. Vince unlocked the gun cabinet with the key he'd taken off Roger while I went through the safe. We made a little over £2,000 in cash, which was in essence just a bonus. Vince even took ten seconds out to go through Roger's wallet and his wife's purse and scored another £50.

Now that's what you call thorough.

All very well and nice, but not the reason we'd come today. Here, we really hit the jackpot. .38s, .45s, .22s, shotguns, rifles and ammunition. We filled two great big holdalls with weapons of all descriptions in a little under two minutes and even had to leave some behind because the load proved just too heavy for us to carry (we were only making one trip from the shop to the car and had more than enough guns for our purposes so there was no point in being greedy just for the sake of it).

Vince was double-checking the load to make sure the bags didn't split halfway across the road and left it up to me to tie Roger up.

'Okay,' I said to him, 'sit down over here, I'm going to tie you up now.' I saw the absolute panic in his face and recognised it for the trouble it was. Just then, a thought occurred to me, something I'd heard one of the two guys at the door say.

'Listen,' I told him, 'you're going to be tied up for quite a while, so if you want to take a quick neck of something before I tie you down, you'd better do it now.' Roger responded instantly and rummaged a little quart bottle of Scotch out of the back of one of the drawers.

'So,' said the manageress as she watched him taking a huge swig from the bottle, 'that's where you've been hiding it!'

'Oh get off my back you cunt!' he hissed by way of reply.

I was going to take the bottle from Roger but saw, before I even held out a hand, that he'd already finished it. Now I saw why he was so worried about us killing him, he was saving that privilege for himself.

I tied him in place and stuck tape over him and his wife's mouth, but after seeing him chug that Scotch so quick, I worried about him chucking up and choking himself to death on his own spew. After a moment of consideration, I ripped the tape from his mouth and told him that if he tried to call out we'd hear him and come back. He was so petrified with fear I honestly believe he took me at my word that me and Vince were going to hang around outside waiting for him to open his gob. The manageress looked at me expecting me to do her the same courtesy but I left her gag in place. Well, I'm practically a married man myself and I wasn't about to leave poor Roger trapped and helpless at the mercy of that mouth.

I think Roger secretly appreciated it.

We crumped across the snow-covered road, loaded the bags into the boot and drove smoothly away. It had been a textbook success. Everything had gone to plan and then some. Gone were the feelings of anxiety and strain Vince and I had felt before the job. We'd done it together, and done it well. And although nothing was said, I felt a new, and mutual, respect grow between Vince and myself. We were able to work together, we did have a future.

We might not have particularly liked each other, but at a professional level, we'd be okay.

We got back to the garage and stored the stuff. Neither of us could wait to test the guns so we selected a pistol each. We grabbed some ammunition and drove out to the same patch of deserted woodland we'd tested our 'hired' guns at.

'Okay, I'll go first,' said Vince standing in front of the large oak tree we'd shot the previous night.

He raised his weapon and went to cock the hammer when he noticed that there wasn't one.

'Hey!' he pondered. 'Where's the fucking hammer?' I laughed at Vince then looked down at my gun and asked the same question.

'What's going on?'

Vince dropped to his knees and went through the bag.

'Useless. They're all useless,' he said.

'They can't be,' I replied. A number of the pistols did have hammers, these were the ones we'd taken from the display cabinet, but they didn't have firing pins.

'Oh well, let's try and shoot each other then shall we?'

'But why?' was all I could manage, almost mute with the enormous sense of disappointment.

'I don't know. He must've deactivated all of them. You know, to keep them safe unless they was nicked. What a cunt! I bet he's laughing his fucking head off at us right now,' said Vince shaking his head, the disbelief turning to rage. 'Incredible! Fucking incredible! YOU FUCKING BASTARD!' he screamed at no-one in particular. We'd been in such a rush to rob the place we hadn't even noticed, neither of us. The rifles and the automatics were just as disabled; slides and pins and springs and things missing so that they were all duff.

'Now wait, wait, think, where would all these bits be?' I said.

'Oh, I don't know, probably in his gun cabinet. I saw loads of spare parts and shit in there. He probably takes an order for a gun, then spends a little time putting it back together before handing it over.'

'Well come on then,' I told him.

'What?'

'Let's go and get them.'

'Are you fucking stupid or something? It's been over three hours, the pigs have probably found him by now.'

'That's just a chance we'll have to take.'

Vince pondered this a little longer then agreed.

'Yeah you're right,' he said, 'come on, let's get the cunt!'

7. Let's get the cunt!

We got to the shop and found that the police had turned the whole street into a disco with the amount of flashing blue lights they'd poured into it.

'I'll keep on driving then,' Vince said rather unnecessarily.

We cruised past at a leisurely pace with the rest of the rubberneckers and counted no less than three pandas, a meat wagon and two area cars parked up on the pavement outside the shop. Anyone would've thought there'd been a riot going on or a football match or something. Police procedure doesn't make any sense to me. Why tie up half the vehicles in town at the one place you can bet your nose the robbers aren't going to be? You can see why these young mothers, whose kids go missing, get frustrated with the Old Bill when all they seem to do is mill about the house en masse, asking the same questions over and over again, scratching their arses, and eating all the digestives.

It's almost like they were working on the classic Sherlock Holmes principle that the criminal always returns to the scene of the crime, which, as a rule, is usually bollocks. This day, however, was different; this day we did return, although thanks to Vince's almost genius-like grasp of the staggeringly obvious, we somehow managed to avoid their cunning trap.

'That was you, you know,' Vince said. 'Leaving Roger's fucking gag off. If you'd put it on like we agreed, he'd still be there now and we'd only have to stroll in to get the bits.'

'Slow down a little bit Vince. I didn't know we was ever going to have to go back and neither did you. Besides, he was tied up way back in the storeroom, he'd have to be some kind of pitch baritone to be heard all the way out on the street. It's more likely than not that those two blokes came back and found the door unlocked and we're both to blame for that.'

'You were last through the fucking door not me.'

'Oh this is pointless, what's done is done, arguing the toss over it isn't going to make any difference.'

'So you admit it was your fault?' Vince sniped.

'I never said that.'

'Well what the fuck are you saying, that it was mine?'

'I'm not saying it was anybody's fault, I'm saying it doesn't matter.'

'Well I'm saying it does and I'm saying it was yours, so that's one against you and none against me, so that makes it your fucking fault.'

'Whatever.'

It was pointless arguing with him, this was Vince country, and in Vince country it was always someone's fault. Vince country was a simple place to live, things were much more black and white than where I lived. Someone was to blame, that someone got hit. If someone couldn't be found to pin the blame on, then the search was widened, the facts blurred, someone was found and that someone was hit. There were two rules in Vince country: one, it was always someone's fault, and two, it was never Vince's.

'Fucking wanker,' Vince said by way of a warm-up.

'Listen, you want those hammers or not?'

'Oh yeah, and how we going to get them now dickhead?'

'Easy, all we have to do is pick up Roger when the Old Bill's finished with him, take him back to the shop and get him to open up the gun cupboard.'

'Oh yeah, like the parts are still going to be there! They'll have been taken away or moved somewhere by now.'

'What, why? It's a gun shop. It's still going to be in business tomorrow isn't it. It's still going to have some guns and some hammers there so we'll just have those away.'

'But what if . . .'

'What if nothing. The stuff's there, it's just a question of us going to get it. Besides, the fucking pigs'll never expect us to hit it again so soon after. We'd have to be idiots to do that and so that's what we'll do, and that's why it'll work.'

Vince thought about this long and hard.

'Did you just call me an idiot?'

'Oh for fuck's sake Vince, let's just go and do the job, we can have the punch-up afterwards.'

'You're on.'

And with that, he mirror, signal and manoeuvred us back towards the shop.

We parked up a little way past the shop and watched the flashing lights for about twenty minutes or so until they'd become imprinted on our eyes and we could still see them when we looked away into the dark.

They brought Roger's wife out first and sat her in the back of one of the pandas with only a chunky WPC for company. Then came Roger, with a blanket wrapped around his shoulders and some young flat-foot for support. Neither he, nor his wife, acknowledged the small huddle of neighbours that had formed just beyond the police cordon in the hope of seeing someone they knew brought out on a stretcher. Roger seemed to disappoint the lot of them and they soon dispersed once he'd climbed into the back of a second panda.

The two motors with Roger and the wife pulled off the forecourt and headed on up towards the high street. Vince and I, in our stolen Astra, moved out into the traffic, a dozen or so cars back, like crocodiles sliding into the Nile. We kept up easily and trailed them all the way to the local nick. There, we parked up across the road and waited.

Some two hours passed, until eventually the wife reappeared in the front office. She took a seat, lit a fag, crossed her legs and sat there for about half an hour before getting the hump. She climbed from her seat, had a go at the dopey-looking copper on the front desk and then sat down again. Five minutes later she was at it again, giving him the old 'we were the victims for God's sake' routine with a little bit thrown in from everybody's favourite 'what do I pay my taxes for?' just for good measure.

'What an old bag,' said Vince, awake at last after three prods in the ribs.

'They're keeping Roger in by the looks of it,' I told him. 'She wants a lift home and is tired of waiting around for the old man. Plod on the desk's telling her that they'll be through as soon as possible and she's telling him that ain't soon enough.'

'How do you know all this?' Vince asked.

'Obvious, isn't it? She isn't hanging around a police waiting room for her health is she.'

'Well where's Roger then, why's he taking so long?'

'They suspect him, don't they? Masterminds in CID probably think he's trying it on.' I looked at Vince for full effect. 'They're probably wondering why his wife was gagged and he wasn't. Can't figure out the favouritism motive.'

'Hello, what's she doing now?'

Roger's wife stormed out of the office and started straight for us. She walked across the car park and across the road and stopped not fifteen yards from us as we dived for cover under the dash. Vince reached for the keys to start up but didn't turn them. We continued to watch her for the next couple of minutes as she stood by the side of the road and shivered in the cold.

'Why don't we just grab her now?' asked Vince.

'No, let her go, it's Roger we want. He'll have the keys to the cupboard and besides, once they release him then at least we'll know that the Old Bill are through for the night. Get your head down, she's looking this way.'

Another couple of minutes and at a third attempt she got a cab to stop for her. Vince and I watched her pull away before we sat up and resumed our vigil.

They must've really given poor old Roger a good going over because it wasn't until almost ten o'clock that he was finally shown through to the front office by a man in a middle-of-the-range Marks and Sparks suit.

'Here we go,' Vince said eyeing the gunsmith like he was dinner. Roger paced around the office for a few minutes until his minicab turned up. He then vented some of his indignation at the copper on the desk and ran out of the office and into the cab before the copper could respond. With a quick 'go, quick, come on let's go' they pulled out of the station and off into the night. I can't know it for certain but I would bet my house Roger gave the entire station the two fingers salute as well, once he was safely out of sight.

Vince turned the keys and we started after him.

'Where is it he lives?' I asked Vince.

'103 Lightmeadow Drive. Know it, on the Clockhouse Estate?'

I shook my head.

'It's only just round the corner from his shop really, half a mile or so, not even that.'

'Good.' Vince, of course, knew where he lived because he'd spent a week casing Roger and the shop as part of general planning and preparation.

It was a good job too because it was only five minutes or so into the journey when we lost Roger after the idiot in the Mazda between us and the cab decided to brake rather than speed up when he saw the lights up ahead turn from green to orange.

'It's alright, no panic, we know where he's going. It just means we'll have to knock on the door to get him out rather than grab him when he gets out of the cab.'

Vince was right, no panic, although we were both well aware that if we were going to do him, it had to be that night. Roger – and the cops for that matter – would be off their guard. That night, everyone was safe because Roger had just been robbed already and everyone knows lightning doesn't strike twice in one day. The next day would've been too late. A lot can be achieved in a day. Shock can wear off, people can become more cautious, hammers can be moved, police surveillance can be organised. It was only really through good fortune and our own immature eagerness to try out the guns that we had found out that they didn't work. I doubted very much whether even the police expected us to go back for the missing parts, and if they did, they certainly wouldn't have expected us to be so unprofessional as to go back that same night. No, the ideal time to go back for them would've probably been after three or four weeks or so, let it all settle down and go back and get them when the heat had cooled.

That was why it was so important to get them that night.

We arrived at 103 Lightmeadow Drive about ten minutes later and missed the cab completely.

'Are we sure he's home yet?' Vince asked.

'Tell you what, we'll give it till half-past to make absolutely sure.'

At half-past I climbed out of the car and walked up the garden path. Vince peered through the curtain and nodded, so I rang the bell.

The latch turned, the door swung back and Roger's wife suddenly had a gun in her face again. Before she could say a word, the pair of us bundled her inside and slammed the door shut behind us. Vince ran through into the living room, then to the kitchen, through to the dining room and then upstairs.

'Roger, come out. Come out Roger, we've got your wife,' Vince called. 'Roger!!!'

After a while, Vince came back downstairs and looked at the wife.

'Well, where the fuck is he?' he asked her.

I took my hand from over her mouth so that she could answer.

'Roger? He's still at the police station.'

'No he's not, we saw him come out. Now stop playing fucking games. Where is he?'

'I swear I don't know, he's not here, honest.'

Vince looked at her for a few moments then rolled his eyes.

'Oh he ain't in the fucking pub again is he?'

Roger's wife suddenly looked as pissed off as we did.

'I'll bloody kill him,' she said.

'Not before I do,' said Vince, probably meaning it a bit more than she had.

' . . . bloody can't give it a rest for one day . . .' she was murmuring until I put my hand back over her mouth.

'Listen to me, have you got a set of keys for the shop and the gun cabinet?'

She nodded.

'You have? Brilliant. Where are they?'

We followed her through to the kitchen where she handed us a little set of keys which had been hidden away at the back of a drawer.

'Now please leave, you've got what you've come for,' she ordered us.

'Oh yeah,' Vince replied. 'Like we're just going to leave you up and about to bell the Old Bill as soon as we're out of the house.'

'I won't, I promise, I . . .'

'This way,' said Vince yanking her arm.

We tied her to the bed with blankets and towels and gagged her mouth with the little strip of electrical tape I'd brought with me. It's funny, it just goes to show how hardened you can get to something, even in the space of one day. She was nowhere near as scared as she was when we'd done the shop earlier in the day. In fact, if anything, she just seemed annoyed.

'Oh this is ridiculous,' she'd said as we were tying her up for the second time that day.

Was her own fault for owning a gunsmith's, silly cow.

'Where'll he be, the King's Arms?' Vince asked her. She nodded in reply, reminding me of Vince's nod five minutes earlier.

'I thought you said he was in here?' I said accusingly.

'When?'

'When I rang the door. I looked at you and you nodded.'

'So?'

'You was looking through the gap in the curtains and you nodded.'

'So?'

'I thought you was nodding to say you saw Roger and that he was in here.'

'Well I wasn't, I was nodding that I saw her.'

'Well how the hell am I meant to know that that was what you was nodding for?'

'Well how the fuck am I meant to know what you think I'm nodding about. You didn't ask me anything, you just looked at me. I thought you was looking at me to ask if I was ready.'

'Look, it doesn't matter alright, let's just go to the pub and get the bastard.'

'It ain't my fault,' said Vince. 'It's your fucking fault.'

'We'll talk about it later,' I tried to tell him.

'Oh yeah, well we'll also talk about this fucking nodding code of yours as well then because I ain't nodding again until we've got this fucking thing sorted out.'

'Okay, okay, alright, let's just go.'

'Hey, don't go telling me what to do or I'll nod you a good'un alright, right on the fucking nut.'

'Vince...' I tried to say but Vince was totally hyped up. 'Come on, let's just get the parts.'

'You ain't your brother...' he started but stopped the instant I shoved my gun in his eye.

'Not in front of the lady. You want to say something, save it for after the job. I'm not fucking around. Let's go.'

This was a gamble. Vince could've gone either way but as it happened he didn't have the chance. He was just about to make his move when the sound of the front door opening brought us both back to reality. We held our breath for a second, then the door shut, keys hit wood and footsteps started upstairs. Vince and I leapt out of sight either side of the doorway and readied ourselves. I looked across to Vince and guess what, yeah, you've got it, the moron nodded at me. I didn't even try to guess what he was nodding about, I just poised myself to welcome Roger home. Before I could though, Roger closed the bathroom door behind himself and slid the lock.

This was getting frustrating, the look on Vince's face said it all. I think it took all of his self-control not to kick in the door and start blasting there and then.

Five minutes, a short piss and a lot of teethbrushing later (presumably trying to hide the fact that he'd been to the pub) he finally emerged to a good, hard smack in the mouth from Vince. He tried to yelp out of fear but Vince was too quick for him. Before he was able to murmur even two syllables he found he had a gun in his mouth and a madman on the other end of it.

A few slavering, nasty threats later and he was the compliant rag doll we'd come to know and love from this afternoon again. What his missus ever saw in him I don't know; the fact that he owned a shop probably, that's usually the case. We picked him up, dragged him out to the car, threw him in the back and told him to shut up. Then we drove back to the shop to pick up what was rightfully his.

The police presence had disappeared from outside so we parked up and carried him inside, stopping only to switch off the alarm and chuck him forcefully against the steel gun cabinet.

'Hammers, now.'

Roger's hands were shaking so much it took him a full thirty seconds to unlock the cabinet. When he had, Vince pushed him aside and grabbed the box of hammers, slides, pins and assorted gun parts.

'These 'em?' Vince asked him.

Roger nodded weakly. Vince picked out one of the pistols we'd left behind from the cabinet, handed it to Roger, along with the box and ordered him to make it dangerous. Roger was so paralysed with fear he couldn't hardly talk until Vince stuck his pistol under Roger's chin and told him to stop fucking about. Amazingly, he recovered suitably enough to give us a quick one-step lesson on the dismantling and rebuilding of a firearm. Incredible to think that blind fear can be controlled and overruled by an even greater shit-inducing terror. Probably not too good for Roger though in the long term, but then, who cares? Vince grabbed all the manuals he could find and stuffed them in a bag.

We made him repeat this procedure three more times on several different makes before deciding we'd spent more than enough time in this shop to last a lifetime. Or, at least, twenty years. We had a load of guns, a box of spares, dozens of books and no day jobs. We'd eventually figure out how to repair the rest of the guns ourselves. Better steal his tools as well, I thought to myself.

'Please don't kill me,' he started to plead when he saw that we were done but Vince silenced him with a pistol-whip around the face that left him out for the count. Vince then levelled the gun to Roger's face and was just about to pull the trigger when I stopped him.

'Vince no, don't do it.'

'Why not? Give me one good reason why I shouldn't put a bullet in this little rat for wasting so much of our time?'

'Because if you do that, I won't be able to get the deposit back on the guns. It's £300 for God's sake.' After a second or two, Vince tucked his gun back into his belt and we hurried back to the car.

That was how much Roger was worth to Vince, less than £300.

Lucky Roger.

I took our 'borrowed' guns back for the deposit and realised what a risk I'd taken hiring them off Karel in the first place. He was small-time, strictly small-time. And mixing it with small-timers is a dangerous thing to do. Small-timers take more risks than proper villains; they're less careful, they're more stupid and they're more likely to talk.

Simply bothering to take the guns back I exposed myself to enormous risk. The moment he opened the door I found myself face-to-face with two dopey-looking low-lifes who gave me the old up and down and no doubt spent the next hour playing guessing games in the pub, with all and sundry, as to what my line of business was. I shouldn't have gone, I know that now,

I should've just chucked the guns in the river and let the tight old bastard keep his deposit, which he was a bit reluctant to hand over after he saw that Vince and I had used a cap each. He even tried to palm me off with some crappy old washing machine and video recorder the doughnut brothers had just brought round instead of the cash. In the event I took £100 less and gave him a stern warning not to ever mention me to anyone. I could've simply come on the heavy with him, but that would've been counter-productive and made it all the more easier for him to spill my name if he ever found himself in a corner.

That corner appeared about three months later.

8. Circumstantial suspicions

The inevitable happened, Karel's guns ended the life of some sub-Post Office cashier, the liberty of two desperate young junkies and the Czech genius himself. Karel, of course, tried to deny everything, as you would, but he was in it up to his eyeballs and there was no shortage of evidence. This was a dangerous time for me, Vince, the pair of losers in the hall and everyone else that could be linked with any of Karel's rackets. He could've offered the lot of us up on a plate for the cops to chew over, and probably would've had it not been for one monumental stroke of luck – he ended up on remand at the same nick as Gavin. He wasn't in the same cell, or even in the same wing or anything, but he was there and word could be got to him via the old lags' grapevine and that was the main thing.

Karel got the nod within a week of arriving: 'Keep your gob shut and life inside'll be easier. Open it, and it'll be short.' This did the trick very nicely. Much to the annoyance of CID, the old man kept silent and didn't offer up a single name for fear of reprisals (not even any of his little sneak thieves) and all would've been said, done and forgotten had the idiot not asked to be sectioned out of the general population. The authorities drilled him as to why he wanted to be sectioned, and I guess to his credit he kept even this to himself, but everyone suddenly realised that he'd been got to.

But by who, and for what reason? These were the things that CID couldn't work out. Karel was small-time surely, so who'd have the clout to silence him? And even then, why bother? A junk store fence wouldn't have any dealings with big players would he? What could he know that would merit such attention?

The cops and prison authorities went to work trying to find out and for a couple of months met with the same sort of success they'd had with Karel. But secrets never stay secret for very long, particularly when they're worth something to someone.

'Gavin Benson sir, he's the one that put the squeeze on the fence.'

'Gavin Benson?'

'He's a blagger sir. One year into a fifteen stretch.'

'I know the name, I remember the case, quite a scalp he was too. But why would Gavin Benson be interested in Karel Lecved?'

'I don't know sir.'

'You haven't got any idea?'

'No sir, all I know is that Benson got word to him almost as soon as he set foot in the nick.'

'Alright, leave it with me, I'll check it out.'

'Thank you sir. Er sir, about my transfer request...'

is how I imagine the conversation went.

It took a little while longer checking Karel's request against Gavin's visitors record for them to see that everything seemed to kick off just after my brother got a visit from his wife. Did the word come from outside?

'Get me a list of Gavin Benson's known associates, I think we may be on to something.'

'What were your movements, between 2 p.m. and 11 p.m. on February the 11th of this year?'

'I don't know, what were yours?'

'I'm asking the questions here Benson so unless you want to end up banged up with your brother you'd better start answering them.' At that, I had to smile. What did he have, papal powers of attrition or something? This wasn't confession. It struck me that in answering DS Evans' questions, I was guaranteed to get banged up with my brother.

'My client is attempting to answer your questions Sergeant, but I think his point is that it is rather difficult to answer this particular question, after some three months, off the top of his head. Indeed, if he were to, I would say that this would be cause for greater suspicion, wouldn't you Sergeant?'

'No I don't Mr Barratt, I think your client knows exactly what he was doing on that particular day and with whom.' Evans looked me in the eye. 'What was it Chris, out to impress big brother or something were you?' Again, I merely smiled.

'What are you smiling at Chris, you think this is funny do you? Think it's all a bit of a joke?'

'No,' I replied. 'I just like clowns.'

At this, Evans smiled too, though it wasn't the smile of a man amused, it was more the smile of a man discovering his hate for something, or someone I should say.

'You recognise this do you?' he said and slapped two large plastic bags containing Karel's guns on the desk. I studied them for a moment.

'Are they guns?'

'Don't be such a smartarse,' DC Roach (what an appropriate name) barked.

'They are the guns used to rob a gunsmith's just outside Oxford on February the 11th. Twice in fact.'

'Don't know them,' I told him.

'How do you know these are the guns Sergeant, the exact guns?' Barratt asked. 'Was there forensic evidence? Shell cases?'

'They were positively identified by the manager of the shop as those used in the robbery.'

'Identified?'

'The manager is a qualified expert on handguns Mr Barratt, if anyone can recognise a gun, he can.'

'You said it Sergeant, *if anyone can!*'

'You know these weapons don't you Chris?'

'I've told you, I don't know them.'

'Oh really, is that right? Well what about Karel Lecved, do you know him?'

'Who?'

'Karel Lecved. He's in the same nick as your brother these days or, should I say, was. He was moved yesterday, up north. Does Gavin's influence reach that far?'

'I don't know what you're talking about.'

'Oh don't you? Lecved comes up for trial in a little over two weeks and I would bet my house on the fact that he'll be found guilty and get a nice long stretch. And nice long stretches tend to seem a damn sight longer when you're over sixty. How long do you suppose it will be before he breaks down and talks?'

'My client has already told you that he doesn't know Mr Lecved.'

'Well, just so that there's no confusion, I wanted to

give *your client* another chance to think about it. Do you know Karel Lecved?'

Evans stared at me from across the table with bated breath, imploring me to confess, while I mulled over what he'd just told me. Sure, now that they'd spirited Karel off to the frozen tundra of Durham or Manchester or wherever out of harm's way, there was a chance he might talk, but then, there was also a chance he might not. Fear is a powerful motivator. And unlike danger, fear is much harder to shake. Fear can travel with a person. If one is susceptible to fear, then fear is ever-present.

Besides, nicks are funny places. No one likes a grass, and word travels from nick to nick just as prisoners do. It might take a year or two for Karel's reputation to catch up with him, but catch up with him it would. Did he know that already? Probably. (Whatever the reason, Karel never said a word, not before his trial or afterwards.)

What to do?

Deny everything, that's what. I mean, what's the point in telling the truth, it doesn't impress anyone.

And that applies in all walks of life.

'I've told you once, I'll tell you again, I don't know no Karel Lecved.'

The deflation in Evans' persona was notable.

'Well I don't know, I just don't. Your friend next door (meaning Vince) has been a lot more co-operative than you and he's the one that'll get off lightly while you're doing the serious porridge. That'll impress Gavin won't it?'

Vince, co-operative? What bollocks. The only way I could imagine Vince was being co-operative was by not smashing the room up.

'I'd like your client to take part in an ID parade.'

'I bet you would,' Barratt said.

'Are you declining?'

'What other evidence do you have against my client Sergeant, if any?'

'Are you declining?' Evans asked again.

'You don't have a single scrap of evidence to link my client with this robbery do you?'

'Are you declining?' DC Roach repeated.

'I was just merely stating, Sergeant, that if my client agrees to take part, and if, by some mistake, he is identified, then that is all you'll have. Hardly a cast-iron case now is it? I doubt the CPS will even prosecute, much less a jury find for guilty. I was just wondering whether it was even worth your time.'

'Let us worry about how we spend our time Mr Barratt, you've got enough to worry about. Now, are you declining?'

Barratt laid it on thick and I finally got the message. Basically all that old guff was for my benefit rather than Evans'. Barratt was telling me: 'Chris, if you nobble the witnesses, they've got nothing. Not a thing, got it?' Which we would.

Of course there was always the danger that Roger and his wife might be given police protection, but in all honesty, police protection really isn't all it's cracked up to be. Like I've said before, this isn't America, we don't have the equivalent of a witness relocation programme. A couple of drive-bys in the area car twice a week is about all British police protection stretches to. In this country, the onus lies with the bravery and stiff-upper-lippedness of the prosecution witness in coming forward. And as luck would have it, our witness was Roger and I doubted whether it would take too much to scare the shit out of him sufficiently enough to force him to withdraw his testimony. In fact, one phone call would've probably seen him swimming in a bath of Scotch for a week.

Besides, Barratt was right, with a case as flimsy as this, where the chances of conviction were less than fifty-fifty, the CPS, the police and their purse holders would undoubtedly decide that it really wasn't worth the money or manpower to pursue it.

Hallelujah for budget-capping and resource management.

Not that any of this really mattered in the end. We just declined.

Well, you can do that, you know.

Vince and I spent a few more hours in the cells and were subjected to the absurdity of a direct confrontation identification, after we also declined the offer of a group ID,* before we were informed that no charges were to be brought and that we were free to go.

Evans came and visited me just before I was released to tell me that he was making it his own personal crusade to see me banged up for good.

'I won't rest, you hear, not for a minute, not for a day, until you're back here where you belong.'

'Everyone has to have a hobby, I guess.'

'Very good, very funny, a hobby, yes that's it, a hobby. Well now you're mine.'

[* Group ID: picking a face out of a crowd at a public place, e.g. tube station, shopping centre; Direct Confrontation: bringing the witness into the holding cell to identify the assailant face-to-face. Neither are considered as particularly credible evidence.]

'You shouldn't allow your personal feelings to cloud your judgement Sergeant, it's very unprofessional you know.'

'The guns, the ones you stole, I know it was you.' He lowered his voice and leaned in a little. 'I know what you're up to. You didn't nick those to sell, you nicked them to go active.' He shook his head and almost laughed. 'You won't get a fucking chance I can tell you that right now. I'm going to be watching you day and night, you won't be able to make a move without me knowing it. Your career's over. And when I catch you with those guns, I can promise you this, you'll go down for life.'

'Full of promises aren't you Evans?'

'You better be clear on one thing Benson,' he started menacingly. 'I consider you a very dangerous man. How many guns did you get away with? Twenty? Twenty-five? What were you, like a child in a sweet shop or something? You want to talk about unprofessional you consider your actions. Why d'you take so many? Who are you passing them out to?'

He took a step closer, which I didn't like at all. Personal space and all. 'I find any of those weapons out on the street and the deals I'll be offering to get you in the dock will be so sweet they'll melt teeth.'

'You're a man who enjoys a cliché or two aren't you?'

'Don't fucking try me Benson, don't even think about it. I'll be seeing you around.' And with that he left.

'Yeah well whatever, good luck with it all.'

Seven days later I was in Corfu and, to Evans' frustration, that's where I stayed for the next four years (give or take the odd business trip or half a dozen).

Still, it was nice to see Roger and his old lady again.

9. Party games

Get this:

I was at my neighbour's party (barbecue actually) some time back when this old sort sidled up beside me, plonked herself down in the adjacent seat and went to work trying to get a conversation out of me.

'Hi,' she said.

'Hello,' I replied.

'I'm Catherine,' she told me for reasons best known to herself.

'Hello,' I repeated. 'Chris.'

'Pleased to meet you Chris,' she said in a way that made me think she already knew my name. 'You're new aren't you, number 17 isn't it? I live just down the street from you at 31. Alan and Brenda invite you?'

They had. Well, they'd invited Debbie anyway. I can be the most evasive man in the world when I want to be and I think Alan had grown tired of trying to track me down long enough to rope me into whatever sad suburban schemes he had going that particular week, so he struck directly at my Achilles heel and told Debbie about Peter and Annie's garden party. Underhanded, sneaky bastard that he was, he knew he'd only have to mention it to Debbie and she'd do all his dirty work for him. And she did. She nagged on and on and on and on and on and on and on until eventually, a week later, there we were, standing around in some deputy headmaster's back garden, competing to see how many people could handle the food before it was dished up and served. You might wonder why I didn't just say no and let Debbie go along by herself, but then, you don't know Debbie.

'Alan and Brenda invite you?' I think was the last thing she'd said.

I was about to answer when she moved right along without me.

'They're a lovely couple those two; real martyrs to the cause. He does so much for the community you wonder where he gets the time. Nice buns as well, but don't tell him I said that,' she winked at me.

She needn't have worried. I tried not to screw up my face too much as the image fought to enter my brain. I looked over at Alan as he wheeled my wife from one gruesome neighbour to the next and came to the conclusion that only Billy Bunter and Jumbo the Elephant could possibly see the attraction in Alan's buns, with perhaps an outside interest from the judging panel of East Anglia's annual Most Misshapen Bun competition.

'Oh listen to me,' she said before I had a chance to tell her my thoughts on Alan's buns. 'What am I like! You'll have to forgive me, I always seem to get into trouble when I open my mouth.' She smiled cheekily and gave a little girlish giggle. I rolled my eyes and wondered what it would take for her to fucking go away and leave me alone, but she seemed to miss the gesture.

'You know, these parties can be so boring,' she sighed. 'I wish, just once, something exciting would happen; like everyone strips off their clothes all of a sudden, and just does it with everyone else right there on the lawn. That would be good. What do you think?'

God give me strength was what I was thinking, and as if by magic, it arrived. Up steps this chinless wonder in non-iron pants and an M&S pullover. He doesn't say a word, doesn't look at either Catherine or me, just stands a little overly close to Catherine and looks out across the garden. Catherine clamps up straightaway and all three of us survey the rest of the guests in uncomfortable silence.

After a bit, Catherine touches his arm and introduces me to Mr Knitwear. He turns out to be Catherine's brother and I loved the way he feigned pleasant surprise as if he hadn't noticed us.

'How do you do?' he said squeezing my hand in a chest-beating display of strength.

'Would anyone like a drink?' Catherine asked. We all said how lovely that would be and she wandered off towards the kitchen. The brother replaced his sister beside me.

'You'll have to excuse my sister, I think she's a little worse for the drink.' I managed to get out a 'not at all' before the brother continued. 'That's her husband over there, David. Have you met him yet?' I said I hadn't. 'Oh you should, he's a terrific fella, really nice guy. I went to school with him back when the hunt still ran across this land. Introduce yourself when you get a moment, I'm sure you'd both get along famously. This is a very friendly little estate,' he told me in no uncertain terms.

I looked at the man in the seat next to me and he held my stare until I turned away.

'My sister and David have only been married for about eighteen months and like all new marriages it's taking a little time to get properly bedded down. Too many marriages fall in the first couple of years because one or other of the couple give up too quickly. It's sad, they don't seem to realise that these things take time, they do for some people, it's a fact.' He took a thoughtful bite out of his drumstick and continued the sermon.

'With time comes commitment, with commitment comes contentment.' I hated this cunt with all my heart and ached to grab his chicken leg off him, shove it down the back of his shirt and push him off his chair.

'Me? I took to marriage like a fish to water,' he said, mixing up his analogies with effortless stupidity. 'And I'm sure you and your wife – that's her over there isn't it? – are very happy too. My sister, however, my sister needs a little help, a little encouragement, from people who are there for her. People like me, people like Alan, like Tony – have you met Tony? Do introduce yourself if you get a moment, he's a terrific fella – she doesn't need any distractions. Do me a favour would you – and please don't take this personally – stay away from my sister would you?'

And with that, he pulled himself out of the chair, went through the formalities of telling me how nice it was talking to me and sauntered off like John Wayne.

Debbie came up with a minor look of concern scrawled across her face and asked me what the hell all that was about.

I was fucked if I knew.

'They were all talking about you back there. It was only when Alan stepped in and pointed out quietly that I was your wife that they all got embarrassed and clammed up. They're probably back talking about us as we speak; who was she?'

'No-one, I don't know.' I tried to tell her what had happened but she wasn't listening.

'Look, I'm going to go back and try and save a bit of face with Alan and Peter.' She pointed to some dickhead in a chef's hat doling out undercooked burgers in over-toasted baps. 'Behave yourself for ten minutes, remember where we are. Just be pleasant and don't go causing a scene. These people don't need any excuses to have a gossip.'

And with that she trotted off, back to the inner circle. This was ridiculous, I hadn't done a thing and yet somehow I had managed to cause a stir. Jesus these people needed a life!

Just when I thought I was off the hook, Catherine came storming towards me and launched into a torrent of accusations.

'Just what have you been saying to my brother?' she demanded of me. All heads turned. 'Come on, out with it; I want to know what you've been saying about me. You seem to think it's alright to tell everyone else at the party so why not me?' I tried to answer but she wasn't stopping for breath. I also noticed she hadn't brought me my drink.

'I stop to have a bit of a chat, just to be friendly, and suddenly you're putting it about that I'm chatting you up!' she ranted.

'I didn't say . . .'

'No and neither did I, but that doesn't seem to have stopped you doing your level best to put it about that I'm out for a bit of hanky-panky when my husband's not thirty feet away.'

She was wrong about this as well. Her husband wasn't thirty feet away, he wasn't even twenty, he was about ten and closing.

'Catherine, are you alright?'

'I'm fine, it's this little creep who's got the problem,' she told him, causing about sixty pairs of staring eyes to widen with fascination.

'Listen you, this is my wife,' he said, presumably for the benefit of late-comers or those that hadn't been paying attention. 'If you've got something to say to her you can say it to me.'

'I didn't . . .' I started but too late; the brother was back and he meant business.

'I warned you,' he said, 'to just bloody leave it alone. I don't know what I've got to say to make you understand.'

'I didn't do anything David,' Catherine implored her husband. 'He's totally twisting everything I said.'

'I know, I know darling,' David said.

'I'm sorry,' the brother piped in. 'It's not my sister's fault, it's this little plonker trying it on, now suddenly everyone's got the wrong idea.'

At that moment Debbie appeared, closely followed by the prat in the hat.

'Chris . . .' she started but Peter cuts her off before she could get another word out.

'Listen, I'm sorry about this, but I think it's best if you both left.'

'Peter really, I'm sure it's all just been some big misunderstanding,' she tried. I didn't bother, I'd long given up any hope of making anyone see reason.

'I'm sure it has, but I think that's enough for one day. Come on David, Catherine, let me cook you some sausages.'

The small, angry lynch mob dispersed at the prospect of yet more cooked meat, leaving Debbie to stare down at me in disgust.

'I didn't do anything,' I said, but she merely turned on a heel and marched towards the gate. I got up and quickly followed. All eyes watched me exit in disgrace; only Alan's reflected a glimmer of sympathy.

Can you believe that?
Not!
Well neither did I.

Of course none of this really happened to me, it happened alright, but not to *me* – it was Debbie. See, I thought I'd tell it to you exactly as she told it to me. I even tried putting myself in her shoes, reversing around all the characters in her little fairy tale so that Catherine was David and her brother was her sister and I was Debbie and she was me and then looking at it from there. Sometimes you have to do that if you want to see a situation from someone else's point of view. It's a little confusing and at the end of the day it doesn't make any difference because it's still a load of bollocks. You see, Debbie seems to forget that no matter how much I loathe my neighbours, hate their pettiness and mistrust their motives, I know her. I know my wife. I don't know about David, and I don't know about Catherine, but chatting up a perfect stranger and laying it on a plate at a Sunday afternoon barbecue is exactly the sort of thing she would do.

As it turned out, it all worked out for the best. Debbie's improper behaviour alienated the entire neighbourhood just nicely. Even I was snubbed when out and about, presumably for not keeping a tight enough leash on that little hussy of mine. It was great, almost perfect in fact. We got to keep ourselves to ourselves and no one speculated about anything other than my wife's incredible low moral standards. Debbie had unwittingly created us a perfect cover story. Sometimes, I adore her. And sometimes I want to put a bullet in her head. I think I was between the two camps on this one.

Only Alan made any contact to stay neighbourly (only Alan, not Alan and Brenda) and even then it was only a cursory hello, or a quick doorstep chat to listen to my latest excuse as to why I couldn't make that night's Neighbourhood Watch (always after the hours of darkness though).

Yes, I suppose you could say that I hated suburbia at first, but once the suburbanites stopped fucking with me, it suddenly became bearable.

10. Cover-up

The best job I think I've ever been involved in was probably that first one me, Vince and Sid pulled after Roger's shop. Actually, it probably wasn't the best one, it didn't net us the most cash or involve hitting an impossible target or anything; what I think I meant was, it was the cheekiest job we've ever pulled.

I'd been six months in Corfu by this time and itching to get back in the habit. Vince and Sid got in contact and said that they were ready for another job and that they had an idea where. Like I think I've said before, Gavin had always been the man with the plan and so it had taken a little time for us to get into the habit of standing on our own two feet. Saying that though, we'd also wanted to give it a little while just in case that arsehole Evans had managed to whip up any interest in us. Six months of lying low, we could afford it; especially Sid, all he ever spent his money on was bait and plastic Spock ears anyway.

After half a year though, the money was starting to run low – perilously so for Vince who liked a flutter – so we got it back together to earn a few quid. Actually, I was especially pleased, sitting around on beaches and taking boat trips to hidden coves might be some people's idea of heaven, but I was bored out of my mind and longed to get back to what I enjoyed.

The job, as it turned out, was a peach.

Post Offices are excellent places to rob, particularly if you've got the sort of contacts that we've got. You see, there's so much to steal. Besides cash (Thursday mornings – pension day is best), there's huge books of stamps of all denominations, coupons, licences, tax discs, Giros, certificates of all kind, ID documents, replacement log books, rubber authentication stamps, everything the bent motor mechanic or housing estate forger could ever wish for.

It was a four-man job at least; Sid in the car, me behind the counter bagging the loot, Vince and someone else covering the doors and customers. But who? We decided on Benny.

Benny was one of the original crew – with Gavin, Vince, Sid and Benny – and the guy I'd replaced when he'd come down with the flu, if indeed it was flu. See, shortly after that Benny had hung up his guns and retired from the life after getting on with some bird. It was the real thing by all accounts, she hadn't made him give up or threatened to leave him or anything; come to think of it I don't think she ever knew. But Benny, the old sop, chucked it all in because suddenly, for the first time in his life, he had more to lose than his liberty if he was caught.

Fair play to him I suppose, if he was happy. I guess true love would hurt more if it was taken away from you than, say, the dogs, or the horsetrack, or your tackle box or Debbie or something. I don't know, never been there.

Still, it's one thing to get out of the game, it's another to stay out.

The real world's a tough old place for ex-blaggers. Suddenly you find you have to get a job and because of the huge great gaps in your working history and your education, the only ones you can get involve back-breaking labour or peanuts for pay or both. Then you've got some cunt of a boss whose mission in life is to get back at the world for bullying him at school or not picking him for sports.

Let's face it, it's horrible enough for most normal working plebs, but when you've gotten used to £20,000 for a morning's work and pistol-whipping anyone who even dares frown at you, well, you better prepare for a major ego downgrade.

Benny was no different, he'd stuck at going straight for quite a while by the time we approached him, but the nice little nest egg he'd built up over his years of thieving had all but gone. It didn't take much persuading to get him back on the firm, albeit for just a couple of jobs, and how well it worked out for all of us. Benny had been sitting on an idea for pulling a job for the last couple of years and had been dying for a crack at using it. To be honest, I know what that's like, and it was probably this, just as much as the money, that made up his mind to pitch in. Whatever, it fitted the bill for our Post Office caper just nicely.

See, the problem with robbing banks, Post Offices, building societies, etc, is that, ideally, you want to do the job and protect your anonymity at the same time. Fine, no problem, all you've got to do then is wear a mask. But in wearing a mask you tip everyone the wink as to what you're up to the moment you set foot in the door. Not a problem if all you're doing is running in, scaring everyone to death and then running out. But if your plan requires a little more subtlety to it, then things start to get a lot more tricky.

Take our Post Office for example. It was a large main branch with about fifteen cashier windows taking up two walls of a large square room. In the middle of that room was a long, zig-zagging train of old ladies slowly shuffling towards either £65 or a hundred cans of cat food, depending on which way you look at it. On the far wall, next to the last of the windows, was a door, giving access to behind the counter. Now Vince reckoned that if we hung around by the door and struck as soon as a member of staff came through it (as they always seemed to be doing), then we could get the jump on them and clear out the place in under three minutes.

The only trouble was that the staff were pretty unlikely to open the door while three masked men wielding sawn-offs were hanging about the place. Most places, they won't even let you in wearing a crash helmet. It was a problem.

How do you enter a Post Office (or bank or building society for that matter) fully disguised and carrying weapons, without alarming anyone? Benny had the idea.

Muslim ladies.

You must have seen them. The old Middle Eastern birds who wander around Tooting, Southall and Bradford covered from head to foot in black robes; most leave only a little slit for their eyes, though some even cover this up with a piece of black veil. I don't know why they do it, none of my business, but the fact is that people have got used to seeing them out and about these days, shopping in Sainsbury's and picking up the family allowance, maybe not in Surrey, but in South London certainly, no-one bats an eyelid at them any more.

This was Benny's idea. We could saunter in, hang

around by the door filling out a few forms, biding our time, waiting for the right moment and then strike as soon as someone used the door. We could even carry some heavy weapons under our robes, shotguns and so on.

Just let someone tell us to fuck off back to Africa then!

Brilliant idea. And so that's exactly what we did.

'These things fucking itch,' Vince moaned in the back seat. 'They're like wearing fucking Brillo pads.'

'Oi, man in the car. Speak when you're spoken to,' Sid – the only one of us not done up like Lolita of Arabia – cracked as we turned into the high street.

'No talking when we get in the Post Office,' Benny said a little unnecessarily.

'Right, almost there,' Sid told us. 'Three minutes once you're behind the counter, no more.'

'Okay, one last check, how do I look?' I ask Vince.

'Oh yeah, beautiful, a real pin-up.'

'No you cunt, is my veil straight and everything? You can't see any skin?'

'Yeah, you're fine, come on.'

Sid pulled up just outside the Post Office and we all jumped out.

'Good luck girls,' he said and immediately pulled back out into the traffic. He couldn't stop; the pavement out front was all double-yellowed up and it could've been ten, or even fifteen, minutes before we were able to go. Vince had Sid's pager number pre-programmed into his phone and buzzed him the moment we got to work so that he was waiting when we came out.

We looked at each other for one moment and then, in single file, went on inside.

It was early, not even ten, so the Post Office was only moderately busy. Vince hung around looking through a carousel of postcards by the front door, while me and Benny wandered over to the door to pick our way through a pile of leaflets. We'd been in there only five minutes and the looks we were getting off all the old codgers bordered on scandalous. Most of them just muttered things under their breath but several made themselves more verbal.

'Oh just leave it Arnold,' one of the old biddies was saying.

'Well they're not in the desert now, are they? I don't see why they have to dress like that in Croydon. If they want to live over here then they should have to behave like normal people . . .' etc etc etc!

He's in for a shock in a minute, I thought to myself.

'Oh my good gawd, they're everywhere. Here comes another couple of them.'

Me and Benny spun round to see our numbers swell by two, as a couple of the genuine articles walked into the place. I didn't realise this at first though and I initially thought that they'd come to rob the place too. They wandered past Vince, eyeing him up and down, and joined the back of the queue behind the Goerings.

'Why don't they just go back home if they think this place is so rotten,' he was saying to his wife who was trying her best to ignore him.

The Muslim ladies stared at us for a couple of minutes while me and Benny tried not to catch their eye, which, considering we all had blankets over our heads, was harder than you would have thought. Eventually, one said something to the other one and then left the queue and came wandering over. She stood a couple of feet from us for a little bit, waiting for an acknowledgement and then looked over at her mate when she didn't get one. Benny realised this couldn't go on and the whole Post Office was now looking at us so he stepped over to the women and very quietly whispered to her to fuck off and leave us alone. The lady didn't have time to react for at that moment the door came open and an overweight forty-something stepped out and managed to say the words, 'Doreen, could you . . .' before Benny pushed her over and ran inside.

I instantly recognised the gift horse for what it was and grabbed the Muslim lady and her friend. Vince screamed at the rest of the customers to get down on the floor and so I told the Muslim ladies in a loud and clear voice to: 'Stand here, guard this lot,' then ran in behind the counter after Benny. The others saw what I was doing straightaway and played along with it all the way.

'You two, stand right there,' Vince told them. 'Keep a close eye on this lot, if anyone moves, shoot them.' The Muslim women looked at Vince and then at each other and to all intents and purposes, stood guard for us while me and Benny were able to fill the bags in record-quick time. No-one behind the counter gave us any shit, particularly not the three Asian-looking blokes, who must've thought that they were having a bad dream for the most part.

When we were all done and dusted and legging out of the place, I gave the old duffy a swift boot in the ribs and told him to have a bit more respect in future. As we left, I'm sure he was thinking: 'fucking darkies, coming over here, robbing our Post Offices . . .' etc.

'Come on, come on,' Vince shouted at the Muslim women and duly they came. When we all got outside, me and Benny piled in the car, and Vince sent our accessories running off down the street. We shot off once Vince was in and we were in the pub in time to watch it all on the lunchtime news.

The ladies that had helped us had been picked up within ten minutes of the robbery and grilled for a solid twenty-four hours before being reluctantly released (that's one ID parade I would've loved to have seen). One of the officers on the case was none other than your friend and mine, DS 'I can promise you this' Evans. Life's little ironies hey!

We used this idea successfully another couple of times over the next year – firstly in Southall and then in Bradford – and should've quit while we were ahead, but Vince insisted on giving it one last shake; and so, less than a month later, we walked into the main Post Office in Tooting, South London, armed with pistols, shotguns and over-confidence.

Like Bradford and Southall, Tooting is a very Asian area. Looking back, it probably wasn't the smartest decision in the world to tackle these places. I mean, if anyone was ever going to spot the flaws in our costumes, it was going to be real Asians. This never occurred to us however, and this is exactly what happened.

We were barely through the door when several of the local Mujahedeen start having a pop at us. I don't know what the reason was – whether it was that we were dressed wrong or not bowing our heads properly or the fact that we were white men dressed up as their mums, who knows – what I do know is that several of them left the queue and came stamping over towards us waving their arms and fists and ranting at us something rotten. Me, Vince and Benny backed off a bit, but more and more of them came at us and joined in the shouting.

We looked at each other uneasily and made up our minds to quit the place there and then. There were about a dozen of them by this point, less than a foot from us when one of them tried to grab Vince roughly by the arm. Vince was having none of this; he yanked his arm back out of the bloke's grip and with one swift move and a quick 'fuck off', he brought out his pump-action and blasted matey back ten feet.

Me and Benny needed no second invitation and whipped out our pistols and started firing madly into the ceiling. Everyone in the Post Office dropped to their bellies and covered their heads, including the Cat Stevens fan club.

'Get back,' Benny shouted at them and fired a couple of rounds into the floor inches from one of the ring leaders' heads. 'Get back now.'

The caper was blown. The alarm was going, people outside in the street were running for cover and the lads inside the Post Office that had started it all in the first place were showing a marked lack of respect for the threat we carried and their own safety. Brave, I don't know if they were, but angry, of that there was no doubt. The way we were dressed, I think they saw this as a massive insult to their religion (I suppose they had a point) and it took a barrage of constant firing to keep them at bay.

Vince had paged Sid to pick us up the moment it all kicked off but three minutes later there was still no sign of him. He tried it again and again as we sheltered by the door firing sporadically. 'Where the fuck is he?' Vince screamed over a volley of fire. I peered out of the door and looked up and down the high street; the traffic was still brisk but the pavements were now empty. Every few yards a face peered out from behind a parked car or shop doorway as the cowering crowds strained to see something stressful that they could later use as an excuse for having four months off work. I fired a few shots into the air and a dozen South London counselling centres became booked solid for the next six months. Still there was no sign of Sid.

Back in the Post Office several of the women who had been attending to the lad with the shotgun wound started wailing notably louder and I figured he must've checked out. Some other Asian bloke then shouted loudly at us from the floor, something in Arabic, and started to rise. 'Get down you fucker,' Benny shouted back but matey ignored him. 'I said get down,' Benny repeated as the guy made it to his knees.

'Get down,' Vince ordered and plugged him in the shoulder with a white hot discharge of shot. Gunga Din spun round like a top and fell to the floor clutching his arm and screaming blue murder. Someone else started to crawl to his attention but Vince blasted them in the side, stood up and roared at the rest of the Post Office to keep still. At that moment, a sound outside, way off in the distance, got everyone's attention.

It was the filth.

'Come on, let's go,' Benny implored.

'Where?' I shouted.

'Anywhere, let's just get the fuck out of here.'

'No-one goes,' Vince told him. 'We wait for our ride, he'll be here.'

The sirens got louder and louder as every cop in the area converged on our position. The first car screamed to a halt about fifty yards up the road and started ordering the throng of onlookers to stop creaming themselves with excitement and get clear of the scene. The second car pulled up twenty yards the other side of us and three cops with submachine-guns and dodgy moustaches leapt out.

'Armed response is here,' I told the boys and checked the watch. Four minutes, we were cooked. I was starting to seriously doubt our chances when, behind the ARV, I saw Sid tearing down the high street like an express train. The pigs must've heard him behind them because they turned around at the same moment and good job they did too. Lead moustache had barely a second to fling himself out of the way as Sid smacked past the bastards, taking off the driver's door and front wing as he did so, mounted the kerb and pulled up less than ten feet from where we were crouching. The doors swung open and Sid cordially invited us to a very fast drive through the city. We launched ourselves out on to the street in a blaze of guts and gunfire. Vince who, fuck knows how, still had an armoury's worth of cartridges left, levelled his pump-action at the crippled cop car and finished it off. The two pigs tried to return fire but Sid's ramming tactics had knocked them on to the back heel and handed the advantage to us.

'Come on, come on, we can't wait any longer,' Sid shouted and I immediately recognised that exact same phrase as something Scotty was always saying in the *Star Trek* videos Sid was frequently forcing me to borrow. I pondered later as to whether he'd done it deliberately or whether he was so brainwashed by them by now that he couldn't tell reality from the bridge of the *Starship Enterprise*.

I made it into the car first, followed closely by Vince, but Benny had lagged. I turned around to see what the hell was keeping him and saw Benny dragging his limp body into the car and on to our laps. Blood spewed from his belly and out of his mouth. 'Jesus,' I said. 'He's shot.'

Vince ignored my childish outburst and he was right to do so; pointing out the obvious to everyone wasn't doing anything but wasting valuable seconds. 'We're in, let's go,' he told Sid and before he'd finished his sentence we were off.

This was where Sid earns his money. I haven't really mentioned Sid up till now because, I guess, there's nothing really to him. He keeps himself to himself, he doesn't really mix with us and spends most of his time camped out by various lakes or wandering around the Kensington Olympia in fake plastic ears when the Trekkies are in town. Driving however, driving is a different matter. I've never known a better driver in all my life than Sid, he is in a class of his own. If a job goes smoothly and we get in and out in time, and the Old Bill don't turn up, then no-one really notices the work Sid puts in. It's only when everything goes tits up and we're cornered with no way out does Sid really earn the plaudits. And worthy they are too.

Everyone thinks they can drive, particularly blokes. Everyone thinks that they're shit off a shovel or hell on four wheels, but being a good getaway driver isn't about being able to take a corner at a hundred miles an hour or handbrake turns on the M4; of course it helps if you can do that, but mainly it's about using your brain, knowing when to do a handbrake turn on the M4 and when to casually cruise by a convoy of speeding cops at a steady forty.

It's also about preparation. There are so many little things that people just take for granted that a getaway driver has to do. For a start the cars have to be in perfect working order. From the moment Sid steals them to the morning of the job, he works on them constantly. He checks the brakes, tunes the engine, cleans the carb, checks the tyres, the electrics, everything. Everything is checked and then double-checked to make sure it is in peak working order and then some, because once you're being pursued, it's rather too late to call for the AA. Actually, Sid is a brilliant mechanic. If you're fortunate enough to get your car nicked by Sid and used on a job, as long as it doesn't get riddled with bullet holes or smashed to pieces against a police roadblock, you'll never get it back in better working order. There's also learning the lie of the land. When Sid drives for us, he'll know the surrounding area better than most cabbies. He'll know every side street and alley and verge and turn, and he'll spend days poring over a map until he's got a dozen different routes for a dozen different eventualities.

The last thing you need to be a good driver is a total disregard for life or limb other than that in your charge. It's all bollocks on the telly when you see a Cortina full of blaggers flip over because they swerved to avoid a puppy. If he had to, Sid would happily drive through a crowded playground at a hundred miles an hour if it meant us getting away; he'd take the route with the least amount of children if he had the choice, but he wouldn't do twenty years just for the sake of a few sticky-faced kids. I'm sure I'm in the minority but I find that a comfort.

Everything is up to him once we're outside. It's our job to get the money, it's his job to get us away. It might sound obvious but you wouldn't believe the number of boy racers who don't realise that. Like I've said, most think that driving like Damon Hill is all that's required, well I'll tell you, Damon Hill will win you the World Championship, but Sid will keep you out of nick.

Bullets impacted on the rear of the car as we motored away from the Post Office and past the first police vehicle. The back window fell in around us as Vince and me huddled out of sight behind the parcel shelf. 'Fuck this,' I said brushing the glass off my dress. 'Let's get out of these things, for Christ's sake.' I dropped my gun by my feet, pulled the knife from my ankle strap and cut my way out of my coarse black disguise.

'Me too, cut me,' Vince said and turned his side to me. I sliced up in one long cut and Vince shed his yashmak.

'What about Benny?' I asked.

'Don't worry about him, concentrate on the pigs.' I looked out of the back window and saw the first patrol car right behind us. Up ahead, another had parked half-blocking the road, though suspiciously enough, it left a gap just big enough for us to get through, which is exactly what we didn't. Sid mounted the kerb and drove straight at the cops. At first, I thought he'd done this to put a couple in hospital but when we went past the panda I saw the retractable stinger laid out in the road for us. We rejoined the road the other side and watched as the cops wound in the zig-zag of spikes to let their mates through. Vince hung his shotgun out of the window to give them something to think about, but his shot went wide when Sid flung us down a side street without lifting his foot off the accelerator. Our manoeuvre must've come too late for the cops to do anything about because they overshot the turn by a couple of lengths. Sid turned once more at the next right as the cops were backing up, and then again almost immediately after that. Soon we found ourselves back on the main road and haring west. The traffic was light, which meant there were roadblocks around us and Sid had a good idea where. He pulled off the main road again before we saw any more cops and stopped in this quiet, leafy avenue.

'All change,' Sid announced, jumped out from behind the wheel and went and got into the car in front of us. This was our first change of car. Sid had four cars for this particular job: this one, another parked a mile from the Post Office in the opposite direction, in case we'd had to go that way instead, and one other, parked about four miles away to the south; that was our second changeover and the one we'd drive home, or well, not home, but back to the garage.

We moved as quickly and as quietly as we could, transferring our weapons and kit from one car to the next until all that was left to transfer was Benny. Benny was breathing hard and trying to say something, but with all the blood in his mouth I couldn't make it out. Vince took his pistol from him and checked the barrel.

'You get his shoulders, I'll get his legs when they drop down,' I told him pulling Benny out of the back seat. Vince ushered me to one side, aimed the pistol at the top of his head and plugged him twice. I recoiled back, half expecting him to then turn the gun on me, but he merely got into the waiting car and looked back.

'Are you coming or what?' I didn't have time to think, I just had to move. I climbed in behind Sid and eyed Vince as we pulled off sharply. There was police activity all around, but thanks to Sid's knowledge of the back streets, we made it to the next car trouble free in a little under twelve minutes. As we drove the last leg of our journey, Vince finally turned around and answered my accusing stare.

'What did you want me to do, take him to the hospital? He was dead anyway.'

'Then why bother shooting him?' I asked.

'In case he got better.'

Again, I guess, Vince was right. With a chest wound like that, he was as good as dead, he just weren't dead enough. Medical attention might've saved him but we couldn't offer him that and it really wasn't in our best interests to let anyone else offer him it. The way that Vince had done it though and the way that he'd behaved in the Post Office made me realise, as we left the town and headed into the country, that that could've easily been me instead of Benny lying in the back of that car and it wouldn't have made any difference to Vince.

Vince had always been a bit nutty though, ever since I'd known him, I just took it as one of his strengths and adapted myself to accommodate him. Lately though, I'd been getting more and more concerned with his temperament, I no longer felt comfortable about having an unstable sociopath on the crew. In truth, I should've recognised the signs years ago and distanced myself sooner. It would be harder now. The first time he really worried me wasn't during a job or anything, it was when we were off together one weekend in Norfolk. I hadn't been part of the crew that long and thought I should try and get to know the other lads a bit better, so I let myself get talked into a trip to the sticks with Vince to play paintball – that silly war game where you fire paint pellets at each other and run around the woods like you're ten again. Vince had never done it, but he'd seen a poster and thought it might be a bit of a laugh. I thought it might be too.

I was wrong.

11. The Dirty Two

'Okay, we'll split you up into two groups,' some plum sucker was announcing. 'Allison and Terence will be your team leaders – Allison, you take the red group, Terence, you'll be yellow. If everyone wants to divide up then, roughly fifteen to a group, armbands and bibs are up the front here. Allison, present your troops for inspection once you've got them all sorted. Terence, line up your forces over here for . . .'

'Oh fucking shut up mate,' Vince murmured to himself and rolled his eyes. We were right at the back and keeping well out of the way of the eager brigade. 'When are we going to get started that's what I want to know. All this fucking "let's see you standing in a straight line" bollocks.' We'd been here and ready a little over an hour and that's a long time to expect Vince to hold a gun and not threaten someone with it. He'd already shot a couple of the new arrivals within the first five minutes of us turning up, when one of the marshals had come over and explained to him that shooting was only permitted during a game and besides, the people that he'd just shot hadn't had a chance to change into their combat fatigues yet and were still wearing their own clothes. One of the girls looked particularly put out at having a huge great blue paint splash over her nice M&S roll-neck. So, we waited. We waited for a coachload of computer engineers to turn up. We waited for everyone to get changed. We waited for everyone to have a vote on who was going to be team leaders (Vince voted for himself, not a popular choice) and we waited for General Patton up front to get his speech on team bonding and pincer movements out of the way. I don't think it was what Vince had been expecting.

Allison came over with a couple of red armbands and bibs for me and Vince after we'd decided to sit out the mad scramble to be on Terence's team. Five minutes and a certain amount of sulking later we were organised into two groups; one, a steely, motivated band of experienced weekend warriors, and the second, their girlfriends and half a dozen people with glasses. Guess which group me and Vince were in?

'Okay people, you're ready for action,' Patton started up again. 'But just try to remember this isn't a game. Once you enter the combat zone, this is war. We will be simulating conditions and scenarios that will test you to the very limit of your mettle. Today, you don't work for a living, you fight for it. Today, you are soldiers. Whichever team is the hungriest, at the end of the day, will be victorious. Our motto on this base is "No guts, no glory". Live by that, and fight for each other. God speed ladies and gentlemen.'

'Yeah, and may the fucking force be with you,' Vince chuckled out loud. 'What a cunt!' Several of the people around us eyed Vince with disapproval and moved away the moment our lines dissolved.

'Okay, game one, defend-attack. Very simple stuff, one team defends, the other attacks. Up in the woods, there's a base which guards a flag, the team attacking must capture the flag and make it back safely to this point. Now I know that some of you have been with us before and that you're probably already working on your tactics – Terence, I'm talking about you and your motley crew of vets (all laugh) – so why don't we let Allison and her team have first crack in defence!'

'No problem Robert.'

'Okay, Rachel here will take you reds up to the base and get you tucked in. The yellows will commence their attack ten minutes from now when you hear one blast on the air horn. The game will last about an hour or until the flag is captured. Two blasts on the air horn, game over and everyone back here. Remember, if you're shot, raise your hand and make your way back here for five minutes then rejoin your team. The marshals will be at hand to make sure fair play is observed. Lastly, and most importantly, masks on while you are in the combat zone. These pellets may be paint but you don't want to get one in the face. Head shots are forbidden and won't count as a kill. In fact, anyone seen deliberately aiming for the head will be disqualified for the rest of the game. Does everybody understand?'

'Yes,' said everyone.

'Blah-dy, blah-dy, fucking blah,' said Vince.

What Patton should've said was: 'Does everyone except Vince understand?'

'Yes.'

'Then let battle commence.'

'It's fucking worse than Speaker's Corner this,' Vince said, no longer bothering to whisper.

'Okay you reds,' Rachel started in a thick Aussie accent. 'Everyone follow me.'

'At last,' Vince sighed. As we made the short walk to this little log fort in the middle of the woods, Rachel banged on about how we should all keep our eyes open for ridges and gullies and shit like that because these were what the enemy forces would be exploiting to make their approach, etc, etc. A couple of dweebs also came up to me and Vince on the march and tried to make friends.

'You boys look like you've seen your fair share of action, why don't we hook up together and make up the perimeter patrol?'

'Fuck off,' Vince told them, which they immediately did.

'You know Vince, they are on our side. We are meant to pitch in together and work as a team,' I said.

'Oh don't give me that, I ain't playing soldiers with those two comedians.'

'This was your idea to come here and do this,' I told him. 'I thought you wanted to play soldiers.'

'No, I just want to shoot people and have a laugh. Show 'em, what's what. These silly bastards haven't got a clue. When's the nearest any of this lot have been to any real action? You and me, we'll fucking piss 'em, we don't need any of this other lot. Tactics and team leaders and perimeter patrols, fuck all that, we'll just do the lot of 'em.'

An inspiring speech and one that made me see what an awful mistake I'd made coming along. At that moment though, I didn't know the half of it.

Our group took up positions inside and around the camp, with me and Vince crouching in a little ditch at the top of this wooded embankment. We both had a little nip from his hip flask and smoked a couple of fags while behind us a dozen white-collar workers discussed in hushed voices who could see who. The air horn sounded off in the distance and Vince immediately trained his rifle on the slope below us.

'Fucking hell Vince, it took us five minutes to get here and that was a straight walk. They're going to be at least ten minutes what with ducking and diving all round the shop.'

'I ain't getting shot,' was all he said.

'Don't worry, it won't hurt.'

'I don't care, it ain't that. I just ain't being taken out by no pleb. They don't know what it's all about.'

'It is just a game, no matter what Stormin' Gormless says,' I tried to tell him. 'You're right when you say that this lot don't know what it's all about. Do you think anyone here would really be creeping through the woods, acting like Rambo, if this ammo was live? Of course they wouldn't. See, that's the real difference Vince, it's easy to be brave and warrior-like when you know for a fact, that there's no way you're going to get hurt. It's like when you're kids and playing war; everyone's champing at the bit to charge the machine-gun nest and fling themselves into the long grass in hammy death throes, it don't mean anything though. It's just fucking playing.'

'I ain't getting shot,' Vince insisted.

'Well, whatever.'

'I could've been a soldier you know, for real, in the war,' he nodded.

'What war?'

'The Falklands.'

'You weren't in the army were you?'

'No, but as soon as it was on the telly, I went down to the recruiting centre to sign up. Fucking loads of us did. Trouble is, they reckoned we wouldn't see any action as it would all be over by the time we finished our basic training and everything. I told them I didn't care about training, just stick me on the boat and send me down with the rest of the Task Force, I'd take my own chances, but they weren't having any of it so I told them to stick it up their arseholes then. Loads of us did. Just goes to show what sort of people they've got in charge doesn't it.'

'Yeah,' I said. 'Strange hey! What about the Gulf?'

'Nah, didn't fancy it, couldn't be bothered. Hang about, what's that?'

We looked through the trees and, off in the distance, saw several figures making their way towards our position. Vince indicated that he'd counted four and I concurred. They were some way off so we let them draw closer before opening up. The rifles we had were the best in the camp shop, they had a large canister of compressed gas on the top, a big clip of ammo and they cost loads more than the little cheapy pump-action pistols the rest of our team had. Vince drew supreme confidence from this fact though he should've perhaps noticed that Terence and at least half of his team didn't need to rent guns as they owned their own.

'Alright,' Vince whispered. 'Wait until they get past that grey-looking tree and out in the open and we'll wipe them out.' We hung our rifles over the edge and stayed as low as possible, but the opportunity to fire never presented itself. The closer the yellows got, the quicker they darted behind trees, mounds and suchlike until they were less than forty feet away. We hadn't made a sound and were sure they couldn't have heard us, so we bit our lips and bided our time for a clean shot. Vince was the first of us to think he had it and let rip with three or four rounds in quick succession at the nearest yellow.

'Cover,' one of them shouted and all four disappeared before I had a chance to get any off.

'I fucking got you, you fucking cheat,' Vince shouted at the top of his voice.

'No you didn't,' matey shouted back.

'Yes I fucking did, I got you in the waist.'

'You didn't, I assure you, you missed,' came back the response.

'I fucking never, I got you,' Vince told him. 'Chris, didn't I get him?'

'I didn't see,' I told him.

'Whose side are you on, his or mine?' he insinuated. I looked at him for a moment and tried not to laugh at his phrasing.

'I would've thought, judging from where I'm sitting, yours.' Vince screwed me for a bit then turned his attention back to the bloke behind the bush.

'I fucking got you, stand up and show us that you ain't got no paint on you then.'

'Bollocks!'

Several paint splashes exploded in front of our faces and we ducked down behind the parapet. At that moment we heard voices and shots fired on the opposite side of the camp as the whole of the perimeter came under attack.

'Keep them pinned down,' Vince told me. 'I'll go and work my way behind them and shoot the fuckers in the back.' Just as he finished speaking, blue paint exploded painfully all over our backs as two of the yellows stood over us and fired volley after volley down on us from point-blank range.

'Bunker neutralised, move up!' one of them shouted.

'What? Where the fuck did you come from?' Vince said. The yellows ignored him as the four decoys in front joined them and they all melted into the foliage. 'Oi, I'm fucking talking...'

'You'll have to retire to the assembly point now gentlemen. Come on, quietly as possible,' a marshal wandered over and told us.

'But, we ain't dead,' Vince argued. 'They cheated. That other lot was behind us.'

'You have to go to the assembly point,' the marshal insisted.

'I got that other one,' Vince said. 'If it weren't for them cheating we wouldn't have been shot.'

'I'm very sorry but...'

'Fuck off,' Vince shouted.

'Come on Vince, let's go. It's only a stupid game anyway.' I grabbed Vince by the arm but he wrenched free and defiantly stared out the marshal. 'Vince, this is bollocks. Everyone gets shot in this game, it's the whole point. Just wait till it's their turn, we'll slaughter them.' Vince unfixed his stare and climbed out of the ditch. You could see it in his eyes, he was dying to go after the blokes who had just shot him but he knew the day was still young. There was still time to prove in later games what an exceptional warrior he was.

'Fuck 'em,' he said and we walked back to the assembly point.

Halfway down the track Vince got another splat in the chest and went ballistic.

'Who shot that? Who fucking did that? I'll fucking kill you you motherfuckers.'

'Got you,' someone shouted from the undergrowth.

Vince was about to go tearing in after the voice when Rachel came running up. 'It's alright, these two are already dead. Hold your fire.' She turned to us and smiled sympathetically. 'Sorry guys, but you have to walk with your hand up so that people know you're dead.'

'Who fucking shot me?' Vince continued.

'Come on fellas, let's get you back to the start. Plenty of hours left in the day for payback,' she joked patronisingly. Vince drew strength from the mental image of taking out the camp single-handedly in the next game and followed me back to the assembly point, arm aloft.

'Got you too, hey,' some goofy bird with a perm commented.

'Get lost Bugs Bunny,' Vince told her and again, like the blokes earlier, she did very quickly.

'I'll tell you what our problem is,' Vince started.

'We're taking it too seriously?' I said.

'No, we were stuck in one place. It's easy to sneak up on someone when you know where they are. What we want to do is get back and take out the yellows from behind. They won't be expecting it and we can just pop them off in the back as they sneak up on everyone else. What d'you think?'

'Yeah, well, sounds alright. I'll follow you,' I told him.

'Come on then,' he said and started to move back off towards the woods.

'Don't we have to do five minutes first, Vince?' I asked.

'Yeah, we've done them. That's five minutes more or less innit!' I would've said a lot less. In fact, I would've said we hadn't even done fifty seconds, but Vince wandered off around the corner, out of sight of the marshal on watch and started off towards the treeline. At that moment several yellows rushed out of the woods, on the opposite side of the clearing, and threw down a flag in front of General Patton. Before Vince could comprehend what was going on, Patton blew twice and the game was over.

'What?' Vince mouthed. 'I . . . Cunts!'

'Don't worry Vince, now it's our chance.'

Vince spent the next twenty minutes silently seething as the rest of the reds wandered down to join us at base camp and everyone charged their batteries with a cup of soup. After a while, Vince attempted to pacify himself by buying two great box loads of ammunition from the camp shop even though he already had enough to redecorate all our front rooms with. He eventually had to give me half of it to lug about after realising that he didn't have anywhere near enough pockets to stash it all in. I could understand his mind state though. What was going on in Vince's head was no different to say food shopping when you're hungry. It wouldn't be until he got stuck in that he'd realise he couldn't use it all if he came back here a dozen times. That didn't concern him though, and it didn't concern me either. He'd stopped glaring at Terence and muttering to himself under his breath like a nutcase, so that was good enough for me.

'Okay chaps, grab your weapons and let's move out,' Terence shouted. 'See you in hell dog breath!' he directed at Allison. Before Allison could open her gob, Vince responded for her.

'Yeah yeah, stick it up your arse wanker, we're going to have you!' This prompted the marshal to trot over and ask Vince if he'd like a refund. Vince told him no and, after a brief and frank exchange of opinions, managed to calm down sufficiently enough to be allowed to continue with the day's events. By this time, everyone in our team had already moved off, probably to try and put the relative safety of a battle between themselves and Vince.

'Come on then, let's go,' Vince said pulling his mask over his face. I started trotting off towards the forest but Vince called me back. 'Don't be daft. We go up there with the others, we'll be picked off like ducks. Come on, let's skirt right round the back and approach from the north-west.' I wondered how Vince knew which way north-west was before he showed me his army surplus field compass.

'That'll take ages,' I said. 'It'll all be over by the time we get round there.'

'Will it bollocks. You heard the man, these games last an hour and you don't think any of our team'll get close enough to get the flag do you? Come on.' And with that, we were off and trotting through thick brambles and muddy ditches.

Way off in the distance, we could hear shouting and screaming as the reds engaged the yellow positions, but we were too far off to make out who was splattering who. We had a fair guess though. Terence was well up on this silly nonsense and no doubt had deployed his men in a way to ensure Allison and her idiots were done over in a couple of coats before they even got to see the fort/pile of logs.

It was hard going the route Vince had chosen. The easy criss-crossing paths that covered the combat zone hadn't made it out this far and for most of it, me and Vince moaned about getting tangled up in thorns or stepping in a deep puddle of something wet. Vince even slipped over on something and put his hand in a big pile of nettles – which was good. After a considerable hike, we came across a big stream and wasted a good twenty minutes pushing over several little trees to form a plat-form for us to swing across before discovering, two minutes later, that it flowed in a big U-shape and we were now stranded on the wrong bank. We pissed away another ten minutes getting back, soaking our feet in the process, and decided that we'd come far enough; it was time to attack. The march to the fort was even worse than the route we'd just come. The shallow slope we'd ambled down became a hill, with every inch covered in either something soft and nasty or hard and painful. By the time we reached the crest, Vince and I were well and truly knackered. I prayed, for mine and everyone else's sake, that it wasn't all over, and thankfully, it wasn't. Way off to our left, we heard a dozen voices shouting 'I got you' at each other and just up ahead, there was the fort.

The pair of us carefully moved over the crest and dashed to cover behind a couple of big trees. No-one in or around the fort was looking back. Vince almost grinned with excitement, then chastised himself for his lapse in concentration. He took the safety off his rifle and signalled for me to do the same. We spent another five minutes waiting for our moment and scouring every inch of foliage between us and the fort for any potential ambush before deciding that there wasn't one.

Our tactics were simple. All we was going to do was charge the ten metres to the fort, stick our rifles in between the logs, and kill every defender inside. After that, we could pick off the other defensive positions at our leisure (or at least force them out into the open). Vince gave me a countdown from three on his fingers and, on one, we leapt out from behind our cover and hurled ourselves towards glory (as Terence might've said) for all we were worth. Neither of us managed to even string a dozen steps together though before every defender in the fort turned around and let us have it. 'Got you,' someone shouted, then two seconds later they were all facing front again and getting on with the game. I expected Vince to explode but, to my surprise, he simply dropped his shoulders, stood there silently for a moment, then trudged off towards base camp. I caught up with him after a bit and attempted to say something before realising he wasn't listening. He was beyond angry now, he was serious. He'd retired to his own little land where recrimination and violence over-ruled rationale and reason on every decision and the desperate screams of the soon-to-be-dead was sung as the national anthem. It was another five minutes and a couple of nips of Scotch before he rejoined the sane world, and when he finally did, he'd brought a plan with him.

'Let's stop fucking about,' he suddenly said. 'Let's forget about all this tactical bollocks and fair play and just go and get that fucking flag.'

'How?' I asked. 'I thought that's what we'd been trying to do all along.'

'No, we've been playing it their way all along. Let's start playing it ours.'

'But wait. What . . .'

'Come on,' he ordered and jumped up. 'Let's go to work.'

I followed Vince across the clearing and up the path. 'Vince! Vince!' I repeated as he marched up the hill purposefully, checking his weapon, but he never replied. Our fellow dead yellows we met coming back down from the fray avoided all eye contact with us and thought nothing of wandering into the stingers to give Vince as wide a berth as possible as his aggression con-sumed the whole of the path.

The first contact we made with the reds was their advance ambush. There were two of them hiding in a little ditch twenty yards ahead of us when they opened fire. The first couple of shots missed us but soon enough we were peppered with blue and I was just about to make some comment to Vince about 'so much for that plan', when he accelerated at great speed towards the dugout roaring like a nutter.

'Oi, we got you,' someone started to say as Vince leapt feet first into the trench. Before he was able to finish the sentence, however, Vince brought the butt of his rifle round at lightning speed and smashed him in the face with it. The guy's face mask disintegrated under the force of the strike and he dropped to the ground with a muffled shriek. Seeing this, the second lad tried scrambling out of the ditch but was pulled back by Vince and battered about the head and body with merciless efficiency. The battering went on until both lay in their ditch bloodied and unconscious. I stood over Vince as he ripped off his mask to wipe the sweat from his brow.

'Have you gone fucking nuts, you can't do that?'

'Fuck 'em, had it coming. That's what it would be like if it was real war.'

'If it was real war Vince, we'd both be lying over there riddled with lead.'

'Yeah well, it's not is it!'

'Hang on . . .'

'Stick close, from here on in there'll be a lot more of them so we'll have to charge. Come on, follow me.' And with that he clambered over the bodies and charged off up the hill. It was a couple of seconds before I managed to get my legs working and went after him, in which time he'd laid out another red with the butt of his gun as he ran past him and a marshal.

'You fuckers, come and get it,' he was shouting as he

went, firing from the hip in all directions. Splat after splat of paint responded to his invitation and took him out with precision accuracy, but bullet-proof Vince ploughed on through, walloping anyone stupid enough to stand up and try and tell him that they'd got him. Suddenly we found ourselves in the thick of the action and Vince set about the red's defences like Sylvester Stallone, crunching bones and gouging off noses, until reds and yellows alike threw down their weapons and ran to overpower him. Half a dozen blokes jumped on top of him and wrestled him to the ground. One or two fell away with bite marks on their faces but superior numbers soon pinned him to the ground. It was about this time that I realised I couldn't let this happen. If the police were called, Vince would end up doing some serious time for this little farce and that would attract unwanted attention to him, me, Gavin and our business. Not only that, I knew the kicking I'd get off Vince, once he got out, for not wading in on his side. With that in mind, I grabbed Allison, who was standing only a couple of feet away from me, ripped off her mask and held my gun to her face.

'Let him go,' I shouted and everyone turned to face me. 'I said, let him go or I'll shoot.' Several toy soldiers and a marshal moved towards me until I shouted again. 'I fucking mean it, get back. I'll do her in the side of her face if you don't fucking get back.'

'Wait, wait,' Terence said. 'That could really hurt her.'

'I mean it, let him go!' Allison tried to wriggle out of my grasp but I had her firmly round the neck.

'No wait, listen to me, I'm not joking, that could really hurt her at that range.'

'Then let him go,' I repeated.

'No, you don't seem to understand,' Terence was

saying as he strode towards me. 'I'm being deadly serious. Close up, these guns are powerful enough to even blind a person.'

'Come on, game over,' one of the marshals was saying as several of them strode towards me. 'Give it here.' I could see it in their faces, most of them thought I was still playing around, or that I wasn't aware of what I was doing. There was only one course of action left open to me, I had to prove that I wasn't playing, so I pulled the trigger. Allison screamed as the paint pellet exploded off her nose and showered her eyes. Immediately my negotiators tried to rush to her aid, but I dragged her back a few paces and pushed the gun into her eye socket. Only then did they see how serious I was. Allison fought to pull the barrel out of her face but I was too strong for her and tightened my grip around her neck until she lowered her hands.

'That's your warning, one more step and I'll have enough time to take out both her eyes. Now let my mate up.'

'Okay, just wait, just wait,' Terence was saying.

'I mean it.'

'Jesus, he means it,' someone finally realised. No-one else moved for a second or two, though the guys on top of Vince must've relaxed the weight because he soon broke free and no-one attempted to stop him. Vince picked up his weapon and grabbed a hostage of his own. Again, it was another girl (girls make great hostages; they're weaker, they're more compliant and they invoke more caution and sympathy amongst would-be rescuers. Even in an era of equality and political correctness people are still much less likely to risk the safety of a woman over a man. Always make your hostage a woman – that is, if there aren't any kids about). The first thing

Vince did, behind his human shield, was shoot Terence in the back of the head from about three inches. Terence dropped down clutching the start of a nasty bump and everyone else backed off to a safe distance.

'Come on, let's go,' I said behind Allison's whimpering, but Vince stayed put.

'We haven't got the flag yet,' Vince said and I looked at him to see if he was joking. Vince was never joking. A flurry of murmurs rushed around our surrounding foe, most of it I couldn't make out, though I did quite clearly hear the word 'bananas'.

'Fuck the flag, let's have it away.'

'I came up here for the flag and I ain't leaving until I've got it. You,' he pointed at someone. 'Hand me that flag.'

'Fuck off!' matey exclaimed. Vince fired his weapon into his hostage's ear and twenty people took a choreographed step back.

'Give me my fucking flag,' Vince shouted as his hostage fell over holding her ear. Vince dropped down on top of her and somehow pushed the gun into her mouth. 'Now!' Rachel sprinted across to the flag, pulled it out of the ground and handed it to Vince. A volley of blue exploded into her chest and Vince was away, running down the hill with flag in one hand and rifle in the other. I pushed Allison into the dirt and ran after him. I half expected an angry posse to pursue us but no-one did and, with hindsight, I don't blame them.

We ran past the base camp and Vince hurled the flag into the soft turf in front of Robert who, unaware of all the excitement up the hill, told us well done. Neither of us hung around to collect our medals though (figuratively speaking) and, instead, jumped into the car and skidded our way along the winding country track back to the main road.

Vince laughed about it all the way home and even slapped me on the shoulder one or two times, but I failed to see the humour. We'd gotten out of a potential pickle by the skin of our teeth and, thanks to false names and a lack of communication between police forces, avoided any follow-up. But still, there was no need for it in the first place. I made up my mind to give up mixing business with pleasure and to only see Vince, Sid and whoever else when we had a job on. I thought that as long as it was in the context of a robbery, I could tolerate Vince's excesses.

I badly underestimated Vince.

12. A question of respect

It was a dream.

Sometimes you can tell you're dreaming and sometimes you can't. I don't know at what point I realised it was a dream (probably when a herd of horses ran through my gran's front room) but it was obvious by the end.

I was in my old classroom, back in school, and Mr Ross was attempting to drum physics into us. It wasn't going well and we were all totally fucked off. It was about five minutes into the lesson when I realised that I was in my thirties and didn't need to put up with this shit any more. I was standing up to walk out when Mr Ross turned around and roared at me to get back in my seat. I told him to fuck off, I was going home and everyone in the classroom gasped and asked each other if you could do that. Mr Ross shouted at me again and I turned and ran for the door. I couldn't understand why I'd put up with this sort of shit for so long. And being completely straight here, I couldn't understand why I'd decided to come back to school when I'd made a pretty good living so far robbing banks, but then, that's dreams for you. When I got to the door, Mr Ross was already there, blocking my exit. I tried to go around him but he grabbed my arm. I punched him in the face over and over again but it had absolutely no effect on him, like he wasn't even feeling it. I pulled out my gun and tried to shoot him, but the bullets merely rolled out of the barrel and dropped to the floor. I even tried flicking the gun as I fired to get more force behind the slugs but they just popped out harmlessly. My gran then asked me if me and my friend wanted a cup of tea. I tried to tell her that he was no friend of mine but suddenly we were all too busy trying to stop the horses from stampeding. I finally slowed mine down and even got it to do a Lone Ranger wheely, but when it came down, it knocked over my gran's favourite lamp which somehow led to my old man being electrocuted in the bath upstairs. We all rushed up and gathered around the old fella, who was shivering and sobbing, and tried to comfort him, but the damage was done. The doctor told my mum to hold him still while he gave him an injection to put him down. My dad was crying and saying he was scared and didn't want to be put down but the doctor was saying that he had no choice after I'd electrocuted him (they kept emphasising this point). 'But I don't want to die, I feel okay,' he was blubbing, and then my mum joined in and told him that they had to and that it was for the best after I'd electrocuted him. Then everyone was crying and saying how terrible it was that I'd electrocuted him and I was just beginning to feel guilty about it when I thought, no, fuck off, it wasn't my fault, it was an accident. 'But you knew he was in the bath,' my mum said. Yeah, but I didn't know knocking over a lamp with a horse would kill him, did I! 'You were showing off,' my gran said. I wasn't, gran, I was just trying to get the horses under control (although secretly I knew I was showing off). My dad started screaming as the doctor shoved the needle in his arm and everyone told him to be quiet and take it like a man and I was just about to run away when I woke up.

It was dark and it was quiet. I looked at the clock. It was 4.08 a.m. My heart was thumping heavily in my chest and I was sucking in air like a marathon runner. Other than that though, I was mildly relieved not to have really electrocuted any relatives. I took a sip of wine out of the glass by the bedside, then sunk back into the pillow and turned to face Heather. It was too dark to see her, of course, but I could hear her purring away in her sleep. I could also feel her, the broad expanse of her naked back was invitingly warm and I snuggled up as close as I could without waking her. It was so nice. Not like Debbie, Debbie wasn't invitingly warm, Debbie was like a fucking radiator; a radiator that insisted on wrapping itself around me every time I fell asleep. No, Heather was comfortable, Heather was good to be beside.

Of course the dream was a load of bollocks. None of my teachers would've ever dared talk to me like that, not even Mr Ross. I was Gavin Benson's little brother and I didn't have to go around telling anyone that, everyone already knew it. Gavin had a certain reputation even then. While I was in my final couple of years, Gavin was in HMP Brixton doing three out of a five stretch for armed robbery. Now, what self-respecting physics teacher is going to mess with a boy whose brother is inside for threatening people with shotguns? As for the other kids, let's just say, I was the daddy, and I didn't even apply for the job.

Brixton was where Gavin met Vince. Vince was in for aggravated burglary and set to serve every single day of his six-year sentence and then some, what with his private crusade against the system. Gavin put him straight, helped him see that the only person he was hurting was himself and that the best fingers up he could give the screws was to walk out the door at the earliest opportunity. Gavin got Vince down the gym and got him working his frustration out on the punch bags, the skipping ropes and anyone stupid enough to get in the ring with him. Together, they boxed their way out of nick and never looked back. As for the rest of the dream, I've never been on a horse in my life, and as far as my dad is concerned, he's still alive and well and living on the south coast with Jill. And I can't be sure, but as far as I know, the old soap-dodger's never set foot in a bath in all his life.

Heather prodded me awake a moment later and told me it was six o'clock.

'Come on, Chris, you'd better get up.'

'Hmm! Oh yeah, okay, just give me a moment,' I murmured and instantly fell back to sleep.

'Chris, come on, you've got to go,' she said and ripped the covers off me. The cold morning air quickly got my attention and any effort I made to drag the sheets back met with stiff opposition.

'Get up, the kids'll be up soon.' I felt her feet against me and the edge of the bed closing in fast and just managed to right myself before I went over. God, why was it when ever you woke up in the middle of the night, the couple of hours' kip that followed were always heavier than concrete? I sat up and rubbed the sleep from my face. Heather was pulling on her pyjama bottoms and before I could talk her into a quick one before I left, it was all covered over and off the agenda.

I stood up and walked towards her to give her a kiss and a cuddle, but she pushed me away and told me to get my clothes on.

'Just one morning can't I stay?' I asked her.

'No, we agreed, the children can't see you here in the morning.'

'Well, I'll go and sleep the rest of the night on the sofa then,' I said, stepping into my trousers. 'They won't know.'

'No!' she said again. 'Now we've been through all this before and I'm not about to stand here and argue it all over again and wake the children.'

'Listen, if I stayed, I could take you all to the pictures or something a bit later, they'd love that.'

'Chris, I don't need this right now, okay. Please, just get your stuff together and let's go.' It upset me how cold Heather could be in the mornings, particularly bearing in mind all the things she'd say the night before. It was like she was two different people. Gone was any attempt at civility, any feeling, all she seemed to want was me out of the way. I'd slept on her sofa a dozen times when Gavin was out and she'd always woken me up with a cup of tea and a five-minute countdown to breakfast, I didn't see what was so different now. Sure, we were sleeping together, having sex, but no-one knew that except me and her. The kids didn't know. In fact, I would've been surprised if the kids even knew what sex was.

So she was worried about Gavin finding out about us? But she was my sister-in-law wasn't she, what was suspicious about me sleeping on my sister-in-law's sofa?

We'd been having sex now for about six months and it'd become harder and harder to leave in the mornings. I almost couldn't face Debbie these days and whenever

Heather asked me about her, I'd almost become embarrassed about talking about her. I'd even started lying and telling Heather that Debbie and me weren't having sex any more because I didn't want to make Heather jealous. That only seemed to accelerate the cold war between us though. I don't know, it seemed like the more thought and consideration I showed Heather, the less she showed me.

'Have you got your keys?' Heather asked.

'Downstairs,' I said, so she shooed me in that direction. I grabbed my keys, wallet, and everything else that had been flung about in all directions in a fit of frantic undressing and made my way to the front door.

'Listen, I'll give you a call over the next couple of days, make sure you're okay,' I told her.

'I'm fine, don't worry about it,' she said opening the door.

'Well, I'll give you a call anyway. See you next Friday?'

'No, you can't. I've got to go over and see your mum,' she said opening the door.

'I'll come with you,' I said.

'No, you'd better not. I don't want her getting the wrong idea.'

'What wrong idea, I am your brother-in-law aren't I?'

'Yes, you are,' Heather said, and then punched it home. 'And that's all you are. Please try and remember that.'

'Remember what? I don't know what you're talking about.'

'Look, if Gavin ever found out about this . . .'

'He's not going to, is he? No-one knows about us. Christ, I'm not going to tell anyone, am I?'

'I don't care. It doesn't make any difference. Listen, I've been thinking. Perhaps it's best if we didn't see each other for a bit, put a bit of distance between ourselves.' This was unexpected. I took about half a second to quickly think back and try and pin down what I'd just said to bring this on. Then I set about undoing the damage.

'Wait a minute, wait! What's the matter? What have I done?'

'You haven't done anything. Look, it was a bit of fun while it lasted but now we've got to get back to how we were, for Gavin's sake and mine.'

A bit of fun?

'What is it? What's changed? What have I done? Tell me.'

'You haven't done anything,' Heather said.

'Then why can't we just go on as we are?'

'Look, I love Gavin, don't you understand?'

Then I said: 'But it was you who started all this,' and instantly regretted it.

'I don't need another husband, I've already got one.'

'I'm not trying to be your husband, I thought we were friends,' although secretly I knew it was way beyond that.

'We are friends and that's how we've got to be again.'

'Well we will be. But that doesn't mean that we can't still see each other like this, does it?'

'Yes it does. It's just gone too far. I never meant it to be like this and it can't go on.' This didn't make sense. If it was just meant to be sex, a simple quick fuck between consenting adults, Heather would never have said some of the things she'd said. It was more than sex, it was way beyond sex. It was mutual reassurance in a shitty world. It was a closeness I'd never known before.

It was . . . it was . . . but I couldn't bring myself to face the word, I'd avoided it for so long.

'Just fucking go, please. If you think anything of me you'll go.' But I did think something of her. I thought the world of her, that's why I didn't want to go. Didn't she understand that?

I bowed to her request and left. I tried to give her one last kiss, but she wouldn't even grant me that. The door closed behind me the moment I cleared the threshold. Not even a wave goodbye.

I started my car and drove off as quickly as I could before I could think up ways to dig the hole even deeper for myself.

At that moment, and for the first time in my life, I hated Gavin.

13. Little fish

Someone was banging on my door and yelling my name. 'Chris, quickly, Chris help!' It sounded like Brenda and it sounded like she was in real trouble. I quickly turned up the telly and poured myself another Scotch, but the banging didn't go away. 'Chris, Debbie, please, open the door, it's Alan.' At this moment in time, I didn't care what was 'Alan' – a heart attack, a traffic accident, an attempted suicide that had become horribly prolonged – all I asked was that it stayed over in Alan's house and left me alone while I was watching the telly.

Debbie finally emerged from her slumber and traipsed down the stairs. 'Chris, there's someone at the door,' she said, then let a hysterical Brenda in to annoy me at closer quarters.

'It's Alan,' she was saying. 'Please Chris, you've got to help him, I couldn't stop him.' Debbie stepped in to try and take charge and get some sense out of her.

'Calm down, calm down. Quick, have a drink,' she said, ever on the lookout for a good excuse to knock back half a bottle of rum. 'What's happened?'

'It's Alan, oh Chris, you've got to go after him, please, they'll kill him.'

'Well there's nothing I can do,' I said without knowing even a fraction of the facts.

'Who'll kill him?' Debbie asked. 'What are you talking about?'

'There were burglars, they were breaking into Mr Ashley's house when Alan spotted them out on patrol.' Brenda's eyes flicked at me for a quick half a second as we all knew whose turn it really was to be on Neighbourhood Watch patrol tonight – but then, who could be bothered? 'He alerted Peter, the Watch leader, then went after them himself. Please Chris, you must go after him.'

Fact: Brenda hated me.

Fact: I couldn't stomach her.

Fact: The neighbourhood was full of do-gooders ready to give up an evening's telly to save each other's lives.

So why me?

Fact: I was the youngest and most surly-looking resident on the whole estate. If most of my neighbours were asked who they would least like to pick a fight with, it would be me. However, if most of my neighbours were asked who they would most like to have on their side in a fight, it would probably be me again. This was, at least, something we all had in common; if I was to get half-killed in a fight, I'd want most of my neighbours there with me too.

'Chris, what are we going to do?' Debbie said, suddenly involving me.

'Debbie, what can I do? You know I can barely make it up the stairs with my knee these days.'

'What?' she replied.

'Can I stay here until the police arrive?' Brenda asked bringing home the delicacy of the situation to me.

'No, you can't,' I almost yelled at her, then quickly added: 'Debbie, go and take her back across the road and stay with her. I'll go out and find Alan.'

The fat cunt!

This was just what I didn't need, Inspector Nosy and his troops, stomping through my house, taking notes and checking names. I don't think there was anything outstanding they could've carted me away for, but still, I didn't need anyone knowing who, or where, I was. As Debbie took Brenda back to her house, I grabbed my pistol and headed out into the night.

The street was buzzing with activity; about half a dozen cardigans had been courageous enough to venture out into battle, though none had quite found it in themselves to wander off on their own from the main lynch mob. Curtains up and down the street twitched as the Horlicks heroes passed by to show off their balls and a fine selection of gardening tools. Their numbers swelled momentarily by one as some spotty seventeen-year-old ran out to enlist, only to get dragged away by his mum to his mortal embarrassment. All the men laughed – wankers.

I walked off in the opposite direction from the main party and stuck to the shadows. If there was a burglar out there they weren't going to catch him by wandering around under the street lights – that is, if they actually wanted to. As quietly as I could, I checked behind fences and up alleyways and side roads until I found what I was looking for. It convinced me that Alan was right about the burglars, and, more importantly, they were still here.

The van was parked next to a big hedge, just around the back of mine and Peter's houses. I approached it stealthily and checked inside. There were several tools, a couple of old sheets and a road map; nothing concrete, but I knew. The silly bastards had obviously been spotted and ducked out of sight while the 'string 'em up' brigade milled past in a great trembling mass. I squatted down in the shadows and waited for them to emerge from their hiding place.

After about ten minutes something poked its head around the corner of the hedge and surveyed the ground. It then disappeared back behind the bush and didn't reappear again for another minute. When it did though, again it carefully swept the crescent for any signs of movement. I was just about to let myself be impressed by their professionalism when some great lumbering silhouette said: 'Oh fuck this' and walked straight out under the cover of half a dozen bright orange street lights. He looked back at the hedge and shouted something like: 'Are you coming or what?' The smaller, more cautious animal told him what a stupid cunt he was and that he was going to get them both nicked, but the bigger one simply rebutted him with: 'But I want to catch last orders.' Neither noticed me dart out of the shadows towards them until it was too late. I whacked the big stupid one over the head with the butt of my gun, sending him to sleep in the middle of the road, and thrust the pistol in the other's face.

'Shit! Don't hit me,' he said before he saw that he had bigger problems than that. 'Don't shoot me either!'

'Shut up,' I hissed at him.

'Okay, okay, just don't shoot,' he replied.

'I said shut up,' I repeated.

'Alright, no problem,' he blurted out.

'Shut up!'

'I am, I am, I'm shut up.' I realised then and there

that my original opinion was grossly complimentary and that, in actual fact, they were both fucking idiots.

'What part of shut up don't you understand?'

'What d'you mean?' he asked.

'SHUT UP!!!' I growled.

'Okay,' he replied yet again and I finally accepted that this was as close to shutting up as he could manage. 'Now listen . . .' I started but before I could say another word he said:

'What?'

'Look for fuck's sake just shut your gob, will you?' I told him and really emphasised the fact that he had a gun in his face and that he had to do what I said.

'Alright, alright,' he said. I slammed him up against the side of his van and shoved the gun hard into his throat.

'Say something else, go on. Just one word. Just one syllable. Something,' I dared him. At last, nothing. The penny finally dropped with the moron and he made not a sound – well, not counting the congested rasping he probably referred to as breathing. 'Right, now that I've got your attention, I want you to listen to me very carefully as this is your one and only chance. This estate is off-limits. You are not to come back here again, not you, sleeping beauty down there or any of your other sticky-fingered little mates. You're to spread the word, the next tea leaf I catch in my street gets one in the knee-caps. Do you understand?'

He nodded, though I doubt he truly appreciated my sincerity. I kept the gun to his throat a moment longer for effect before slowly releasing him from my grip. I was about to underline my point with a little finger wagging in his face when both of us turned our attention to the half-dozen or so voices that were coming our way from around the corner.

'Shit, quick, open up the side door,' I told him.

'What?' he said in total confusion.

'Open up the side door and get in the van.'

'But, I thought . . .'

'Don't think. Just do!' I told him and he quickly started searching his every pocket for his keys. The voices were getting louder now and, though I couldn't hear exactly what they were saying, I recognised it to be the 'big'un'. Spotty finally found his keys, opened the door and jumped in. 'Oi, are you forgetting something?' I said, pointing at his half-dead whale of a friend sprawled out on the tarmac. 'Give me a hand with him you fucking moron.' I shook my head with disbelief as we loaded fat boy into the van. Was it really so unobvious to everyone but me that a hiding place wasn't much of a hiding place when one of your mates is two feet away from it, face-down on the deck, outside. With all three of us inside the van, I slid the door shut just seconds before the mob made it round the corner.

'Quiet,' I told him and was genuinely surprised when he didn't say 'okay' or 'sure thing' or 'okee-dokee' or something. The voices passed by outside and, for several moments, the bravado clarified enough to make out individual crap.

'Just give me five minutes, in a room alone with them and I'd show them . . .'

'In my day, people had respect for property . . .'

'It's scum like this that lead to Hitler. And look at the bloody nose we gave him . . .'

Through the darkness I could make out matey as he gave them all the 'wanker' hand sign. The procession passed and we both relaxed a little. 'Aren't you going to hand me over to the Old Bill then?' he asked.

'What, and have you land me in the dock on firearms charges, I don't think so.'

'I was going to say, it's illegal to threaten someone with a gun,' he said. 'If you hand me over I could get you done.'

Christ! Do you ever feel that you're having one of those conversations where ... oh, what's the point, it would've been easier if I'd just shot the fucker and been done with it.

'I know,' I told him. 'I just said that. That's why I'm not handing you in. Look mate, I don't care if you want to go around stealing videos, tellies or frilly knickers for that matter, just do it somewhere else. Have you got it?'

'Who are you?' he asked cautiously.

'Let's just say, I'm a bigger fish than you, and this is my pond.'

At that moment, fat boy on the floor started to stir. He kicked his legs, mumbled a few things, then said: 'Please mum, don't sell my bike,' before drifting off again. I opened the side door, got out and told him to get going before the cops arrived. Halfway down the hill, as he drove past me, he beeped his horn, gave me a wave and left me wondering how stupid the police around this area must be to have burglars of that calibre on the loose.

I tucked the gun away underneath my shirt and knocked on Brenda's door to give them the all-clear. Brenda answered and swept me inside on a tide of newly found admiration and gratitude (bonds formed out of adversity, that sort of thing). Debbie was stretched out on the sofa, half-cut, and Alan was sitting close by. He jumped up at the sight of me and flustered about for a bit before disappearing into the kitchen to do the washing up. 'It's not going to do itself,' he informed us. This was very untypical behaviour from Alan. Normally he'd seize this golden opportunity to bore the tits off me with both hands, but if anything, he looked a little uncomfortable around me. I wondered if he'd seen me with the gun, or if he'd overheard me talking to the burglars. I was about to get seriously worried when I noticed Debbie shifting awkwardly to avoid my gaze. Suddenly I got it and tried all I could not to start laughing in disbelief as I guided her back home.

It was amazing, Debbie's complete lack of standards never failed to amaze me.

14. Diamond geezers

The car went by right on time. Vince patted me on the shoulder but I'd already seen it and was letting a few more cars pass before I pulled out. There was no rush anyway, we didn't need to remain in visual contact, we knew where they were going. I twisted back the accelerator and eased the motorbike out into the traffic eight cars behind Ray. I felt Vince adjusting himself to make sure he could get at his gun quickly and easily. Poor Ray, I did hope he wasn't going to take this personally.

I'd met him only twice before, once at my brother's club and once at Gordon O'Riley's. He was a blagger, with a small-time CV but big-time ambitions. He started out robbing people in the street at gunpoint. One story I heard was that he once held up two little old ladies in the underpass in the Elephant and Castle with a sawn-off shotgun. Talk about taking a sledgehammer to crack a nut, a knife would've done, even a frightening word, but a shotgun? Some people are pure class.

Since those tender beginnings though, Ray (I don't know his surname) went on to hijacking lorries, doing over petrol stations and even the odd sub-Post Office. This job, however, was definitely a giant leap upwards for him – a diamond merchant's in Hatton Garden. The word was, it wasn't his caper, he was just recruited for the job by one of the big boys. Me and Vince both knew it was John Broad's job, because Vince had been given the full running order for the day by Brian Faulkner, one of John's blokes. John, of course, wasn't on the job himself, he was just the brains behind it. Actually, he wasn't even the brains behind it, someone else would've thought up the idea and taken it to John. John would've sorted the talent to do it, regular boys or some up-and-coming wannabes like Ray (blokes basically who'd do it for peanuts in order to prove their worth to John), everyone would get about ten grand pocket money, while John would keep the rest. Nice work if you can get it.

John Broad wasn't really into blagging; his main vices were . . . well, vice, gambling, protection, racketeering, anything to bring in the pennies. But blagging went on, and if it went on on his patch, he'd receive a cut, kind of a gratuity for allowing you to poach on his land. If he didn't receive a cut, then generally, you'd receive several. Occasionally though, someone would come along with a plan or some inside information or something and John would put together his own crew. According to Brian, it was the assistant manager of the diamond merchant's who'd approached John by way of settling his crippling gambling debts. He'd provided a time when the alarm would be out of commission, the background on the best stones and some bent merchants out in Amsterdam who could shift the booty. How could he refuse?

What precisely Brian was getting out of passing all this on to us, Vince wouldn't say, a big fat cut and a little payback for years of running around after John without so much as a pat on the back, I imagine. 'Poor little sweetheart feels unloved,' Vince had said.

John was about to find out that if you pay peanuts, you get monkeys.

Ray's driver pulled up just outside the store and all three of them sat inside the car for about five minutes looking at their watches. The daft bastards had arrived early and instead of circling like pro's would have, they simply sat out front drawing attention to themselves. Vince and me pulled up on the bike a hundred yards behind them and waited for them to make their move. Ray was the first out of the car, followed closely by some other chimp. The driver sat out front and acted as lookout.

'Alright,' said Vince, pulling the revolver from his pocket. 'Pull up behind him nice and easy.' I gave a little rev, covered the distance between us in about ten seconds and pulled up on the driver's blind side. Vince hopped off the bike and began browsing in a leisurely way in next door's shop window. We figured they'd be about two minutes, so we readied ourselves to go the second they stepped out on to the street. I pulled out my revolver, held it low, down by the bike's engine, and made out I was fiddling with the spark plugs.

Somewhere inside, someone shouted: 'And stay down,' then two masked men ran from the store towards the car. In a flash Vince had his gun up and fired into the nearest. He spun like a top and hit the ground with a thump. The second of the two had lightning reflexes and managed to fire his shotgun in Vince's general direction before he took two in the chest and went down. I had no time to look to see if Vince was okay because I was too busy dragging the driver out of the car at gunpoint and clubbing him on the back of the head. People were screaming and running in all directions and from some of the shouts I could tell that someone nearby had been hit in the crossfire.

I looked up over the car and saw Vince standing over the two fallen figures picking up the bags they'd dropped. He tucked them under his arms and I was about to look away when, to my horror, calm as you like he fired a single shot into each of the blokes' heads. I heard a woman's voice cry out: 'Oh my god. Murder!' along with several other people shouting at each other to get down, but I was too hyped to take most of it in. Vince rushed around to my side of the car, told me 'Good work', pointed his gun at the back of the unconscious driver's head and pulled the trigger.

Click!

'Shit, I'm out, plug him and let's get going,' he said.

'Plug him?' I replied, staring at him through the black visor of my helmet.

'Do it now, we've got to go.' Still I didn't move. 'Two murders, three murders, what's the difference, it's all murder now. We can't be traced for this, we're dead if we are.'

I couldn't think and, at that precise moment in time, I didn't have time to. I levelled my gun and fired twice into the guy's head, splattering the pavement with blood and brains. I don't even remember taking the next few steps because the next thing I knew I was on the bike and we were motoring down Hatton Garden and towards St. Pancras where Sid was waiting with the car.

Now that I've had time to think about it I can see Vince's reasons for killing them, even though I don't agree with them. We couldn't get caught for this job, it would've meant a sticky end for both of us. John Broad has absolutely no sense of humour about being fucked over. The last time anyone tried it they ended up being covered in petrol and burned to death in some abandoned warehouse somewhere. I'm sure John was there to oversee the horror and light the puddle personally.

'The silly bastard tried to have it away with the Thursday night pot didn't he,' Brian had told Vince. The Thursday night pot was an illegal card game held once a month at a secret venue. There was always a huge amount of money involved, we're talking hundreds of thousands, and always cash. Nice little number if you can pull it off – lots of money, all untraceable, no police – but a fucking disaster if you can't, as matey boy found out. His accomplices, quite sensibly, disappeared off the face of the earth with their share after the job, but predictably, the ring leader stayed in the Smoke and shot his mouth off to all the wrong people trying to earn a reputation. 'He's certainly got a reputation now,' Brian said. 'As the dumbest motherfucker in town.' You said it, short arse.

So in a way, I could see Vince's point of view in leaving no witnesses, and with Ray and whoever else in the crew, they were *expert* witnesses. Just by our builds, voices, style or weapons, they could've probably made an educated guess as to our identities. And in John's court, a rumour or a guess was all the convincing he'd need to go out and buy a gallon of four star. We weren't even going to try and turn the stones into cash, not here or in Amsterdam, we couldn't risk it. These stones were purely for sitting on. They were getaway money. A hundred grand in diamonds is a lot easier to pick up and run with than a hundred grand in cash and me, Vince and Sid all needed a nest egg if ever the worst came to the worst. To be honest, I was thinking about changing some of my cash up into diamonds anyway, so this opportunity was too good to pass up.

But still, I felt uncomfortable about Vince's increasing readiness to use deadly force. Gavin once told me that there were three types of killer: the killer who killed only when he had to; the killer who enjoyed killing; and the killer who killed and thought nothing of it. If I was to fall into any of these categories then I'd say it was probably the first. Vince, however, he fell into the third category, and in my mind, this was the most dangerous of the three. See, someone who enjoyed killing, for him (or her) killing was still a big thing, but for someone who thought nothing of it at all, it required no more consideration than swatting a fly. And when killing became easier than taking a few extra precautions or having a modicum of faith, then anyone was a target. Including me.

In fact, especially me.

Sid and me dropped Vince off in the East End where he sought out Brian to give him his cut but opted for strangling him with a plastic bag instead.

'All done,' he told me over the phone. 'There's no way Broad'll ever be able to trace that job back to us now. We're safe as houses. Listen, I've got another job lined up, why don't we meet up later this week and go over it?'

We met Wednesday night, talked it through and agreed a plan. I didn't know it then, but it was to be our last job together.

15. Easy as falling off the back of a lorry

'How much?'

'Brian reckons in excess of fifteen grand.' I couldn't help noticing Vince referring to Brian in the present tense which, considering he'd strangled him not three days back, he clearly wasn't.

'Fifteen grand! It's not that much.'

Vince swung around from the wheel and looked at me. 'Not much if it was a bank maybe, but it ain't a fucking bank is it, it's just a lorry. A lorry with nothing but a fried-bread-breakfast chomper minding it. Says a lot about you when you don't think fifteen grand for an easy morning's work ain't worth the effort. Better than a kick in the teeth,' which I sensed was the realistic alternative.

'And he didn't say what it was?'

'He didn't know. All he knew was fifteen grand's worth of merchandise was coming in from Calais on the eight-thirty train and it was easy pickings.' Vince went about spelling it out to me like I was a low-grade cloakroom thief; how it wouldn't be protected by anyone other than the driver for fear of drawing attention to itself, and how, whatever it was, it was just fifteen grand because it was only part of a shipment. I knew all this already; I knew John Broad's operation as well as he did. John shifted stuff all over Europe and he always shifted it in part (it was better to lose two out of ten lorries of fifteen grand each than your entire shipment), but that didn't stop Vince banging on about it for the next twenty minutes. I didn't really care though, as long as he was patronising me he wasn't threatening me, or even brooding silently over reasons why he should be threatening me.

'And Brian didn't even have a clue what it was?' I said after the sermon.

'No, I told you he fucking didn't. What, you don't believe me or something?' he barked.

'No, I'm just asking.'

'Well don't. I fucking told you one time, if that's not enough for you then I must be a cunt.'

Vince made a lot of sense sometimes.

'So it could be drugs.'

'It could be antique-fucking-wooden legs for all I know, but at the end of the day, whatever it is, there's fifteen grand's worth of it and that's enough for me.'

'So, how reliable's the information?'

'Rock-solid I should imagine. Brian seemed pretty sure of his facts.'

'But how d'you know?'

'He came through on the diamond merchant's front didn't he, so I'd say his information is beyond question.'

'But why'd he tell you? He didn't get nothing from that job, so what was in it for him?'

'Well how about an extra minute without a plastic bag on his head. I'd say all things considered he got a pretty good deal, wouldn't you?' Vince should've been a salesman. He had a natural talent for making 'the shaft' sound like the bargain of a lifetime, which I guess in poor Brian's case, it was. 'I'll tell you what, shall we just steal the fucking thing first and play twenty questions later?' he growled.

'Hey, I ain't got a problem, just want to be sure of what the score is that's all.'

We sat in silence for a little longer. Vince clearly had the arsehole with me because he lit up a fag without offering me one – what a child! Of course, when you think about it, what had I done? I'd asked a couple of questions about something I was preparing to do that could land me in nick for the remainder of my good looks. Was that so unforgiveable? I glanced over to Vince and saw that unblinking grimace of silent smouldering I knew so well. He hadn't reached the 'muttering to himself under his breath' stage yet but that weren't far off. And normally from there to 'come on then you bastard' was just a short hop and a skip away. Not today though. Game on.

'No Sid?' I said.

'No, no Sid. It's a two-man job, no point in giving away an extra share for fuck all, is there?' he said. 'And not just an extra share, an extra share plus.' By the plus I took it he meant Sid's expenses. Sid always got a little bit extra to cover expenses, though that was only fair. As far as I was concerned anyway. See, while me, Gavin, Vince and whoever else used the same guns, togs and equipment, job in, job out, Sid needed to weigh out each time. Well, the cars he nicked didn't come suped-up, resprayed and bullet-proofed on three sides did they, that was Sid. I'd noticed Vince enviously eyeing Sid's little expense pile each time we'd come to divide up a few times before but this was the first time he'd mentioned anything out in the open. 'You want to know something?' he said as if he was letting me in on a secret. 'Never trust a fisherman. My dad told me that.'

Why? I wanted to say, what was he, a fucking tench or something?

'Sid's sound,' I told Vince. 'Safe as houses.'

'You reckon?' he replied.

Off the top of my head I couldn't think of a single thing Sid hadn't done. Well, I mean, he'd always kept himself to himself but, in our business, I would've said that that was a plus point not a minus. Sid liked to keep his distance, probably for this very reason; psychos like Vince were always more likely to turn on the people closest to them. In the end, I just asked the question.

'What has Sid done then?'

He turned to me with a look of disgust. 'He's never shot anyone.'

'And that's a bad thing?'

'Look, if we ever got turned over, who's the most likely to talk? Me and you, we've both killed people, so we're not going to say anything. We're in it as much as each other.' I hated the thought that the one or two people I'd put down would be viewed, in the eyes of the law, on an equal footing as the scores (well, maybe not scores) of innocents that Vince had gleefully dispatched. 'But Sid, Sid's never done anyone, he's the weak link.'

'Well, of course he's never shot anyone, I mean, he drives the car.'

'Doesn't matter, he's always had a gun on him by his side when we've pulled a job.'

'Well, what do you want him to do, lean out of the driver's window as we're pulling away and earn himself a few Brownie points?'

'I ain't saying he should've done someone, I'm just saying he never has. So while we both go down for murder, he gets let off with speeding or something.' I almost laughed. What stopped me was the realisation that in Vince's mind, he probably actually believed that.

'Vince, you know as well as I do, that if we're on a job and I kill someone, we all get done for murder by proxy, regardless of who was in the car, who had the gun or who was shouting, pleading and begging me not to do it.'

'Yeah, that's what they fucking say but who believes that?'

'Vince, it's true,' I told him. 'You remember John Tanner. He went down for murder and he wasn't even in the same building when it happened.' This was true. John Tanner was waiting outside, acting as lookout while his cousin bludgeoned some poor old night watchman to death with an iron bar, all for a few quid out of the company safe. In fact, by all accounts, when the Old Bill pulled him in and charged him with murder, he actually laughed because he was convinced they'd made some sort of big cock-up and tied him in with the wrong job (his cousin failing to mention to him that he'd killed someone inside). For a job like that, burglary, John could've expected to receive about three years. As it was, John had now been in the Scrubs for some twelve years.

'I'm telling you, he could cut a deal. It could happen.'

'Well, what do you want him to do about it? Sid's the model professional, he's never let us down once.'

'I'm just saying, I'd be happier, and trust him more, if he'd killed someone.' Before I could say anything else, Vince gave me a glimpse of his full madness. 'It could be arranged. We could get someone, take them out to the woods, give Sid a gun and get him to kill them.'

'What!'

'Hey, we've both fucking done it, I just need Sid to fucking do it too. Next week, we'll just get someone.'

'Who? Get who?'

'I don't care, just anyone. We'll grab someone off the street and just do him.'

'Vince, this is crazy. You can't just kill someone at random. That's not being a blagger, that's being a serial killer.'

'One person, just one fucking person, that's all I want him to do. We'll dig a hole for him, stick him in and no-one'll be any the wiser.'

'Vince, you can't just kill an innocent person.'

'Why not, there are millions of them aren't there?' I had to stop arguing there and then before Vince began imagining me with six inches of dirt covering my face. This was a real problem though. If Vince was nuts enough to dream up an insurance policy like this, he was certainly nuts enough to think about silencing Sid once and for all before Sid ever got the chance to spill the beans. And if Sid went down, I wouldn't be far behind. I also wondered if he'd actually done it already; picked up some poor postman early one morning and driven him out to a hole in the woods.

More than likely.

Vince didn't say anything more on the subject though I knew he was thinking about it, probably trying to fathom out what on earth my objection could be. It was something Vince was too far gone to understand. The next twenty minutes crawled by and my usual pre-job nerves were all but forgotten as I mulled over Vince's plan. In a strange way, there was a logic behind his idea and I could see how he'd arrived at it. But it was a logic I wanted no part of. I have killed people, but for every one of those I put in the ground, I'd died a little bit too. A cliché I know, but then most truths are.

We spotted our target leaving the terminus at around nine. It was a big white van, like a furniture van, with KEYSTONE HAULIERS written down the side. We'd been parked a little way up the road and pulled out and joined it for the drive to London after it went past. It was a piece of piss to keep tabs on, so we were able to drop back a few places and lose ourselves in amongst the rest of the mid-morning traffic.

We followed it for about forty-five minutes until it pulled into this lorry park just outside Ashford. Taking it nice and easy, we pulled up behind the van just as the driver was climbing from his cabin and rolled our masks down.

That last step out of the van must've seemed like it went on for ever for old porky pie as Vince gave him a swipe of his cosh and rolled him under the lorry in the next space.

The next thing I knew there were voices and two sets of footsteps heading our way fast. I looked up to see a couple of likely lads ten yards off and charging like the cavalry. Just for once I beat Vince to the draw and stopped them in their tracks half a van length away.

'Down on the floor, down on the floor,' I shouted and they complied instantly, even going so far as to put their hands on their heads.

'Don't shoot, it's alright, take the fucking thing I don't care,' the older one was saying. Their threads were too nice and their hands too clean for truckers, they had to be Broad's men, come to meet their shipment. 'It's not mine, makes no odds to me, I don't want no trouble,' he kept flapping. Vince patted me on the shoulder to show that he approved then moved behind them.

'Get your hands off your head grandad,' he told wrinkles, raising his cosh.

'Do it in one, alright,' he told him back.

'No problem,' Vince grunted, bringing the cosh down on his head in one long arcing swing and laying the old boy out cold. His number two, this younger lad, saw what was on the menu and panicked.

'No don't hit me,' he implored Vince, trying to get up from his knees. Vince grabbed his shoulder and pushed him back down.

'Get down,' he barked. 'Now get your hands away from your head.'

'No please, don't hit me, I won't say nothing,' he was begging.

'Get your fucking hands away from your head,' Vince ordered pulling at his arms.

'No, please, don't hit me.'

'Get your fucking hands off,' I shouted, pushing the gun in his face. Vince yanked away at his arms but only succeeded in tipping matey's balance and pushing him down on to his face.

'Don't hit me,' he was yelling as the two of us tried prising his fingers away from his scalp. 'I don't want to be hit.'

'Take it like a man,' I told him.

'No,' he replied. 'Get off me.' Vince pulled him back up to his knees and smashed the cosh down onto the top of his head, cracking his knuckles painfully. Instinctively, the lad ripped his hands away giving Vince a free target, though it still took two or three whacks before he was out cold, as he insisted on wriggling about like a captured scrumper. Incredibly, we'd managed all this without alerting another solitary single soul in the whole park. Lorry drivers hey! If it isn't a fried breakfast or the sports section they just couldn't give a fuck.

We rolled them out of the way underneath another couple of vehicles and peeled our masks off.

'You take our van and follow me out of here. I've got a nice quiet spot about six miles from here for dumping this shit-heap,' Vince told me and a minute later we were back on the road.

I followed Vince away from town and along several miles of winding country lanes until we got to a dirt track which looked like it led up through the middle of a forest. Vince jumped out, opened the gate and we both drove through and up the hill. Several hundred yards up the track we came to a little clearing and Vince stopped in front. He jumped out and waited for me as I spun the van around and backed it up.

'Come on, we'll start with the cargo. Go through it and anything you find that looks valuable, give me a shout,' he said. We cropped the padlocks off and swung open the doors. We jumped in together and started tearing open the crates stacked top to bottom inside. The first few were full of crockery; pots, tea cups and plates, all wrapped up in bubble-wrap, though what we found towards the back, we couldn't believe. It was me who came across the first one, and when I did, I shat myself.

'Fuck Vince, get over here. Look.' Vince darted over to where I was standing and looked down at what I'd just found.

'Eng-land? We Eng-land,' he was saying.

'What the fuck?' Vince mumbled and tore some more of the packaging away from the grubby, brown face. 'What the fuck are you doing in there you thieving little

Arab?' Vince shouted at him as he dragged him out of his hiding place by the neck.

'Shit, I've got another one here,' I said, ripping into the next crate. Vince spun around to look as matey behind him continued to show off his multilingual skills.

'Eng-land? We?'

'Get it out of there,' Vince told me, hurling his catch towards the back of the van so hard that the poor, confused fucker rolled out of the door and landed in his new home with a right almighty thump. 'Get out there and keep an eye on that one, make sure it don't go wandering off. I'll see how many more of the little stowaways we've got.' Vince tore through the back of the van like a mad thing. As each new face was uncovered, he pulled them out and gave them a kick up the arse in my direction until we had a total of eight jabbering chatterboxes, all trying to ask us in Romanian where the free houses were.

'Shut up the lot of you,' Vince shouted at them, slapping the nearest one down to the ground.

'Blah blah blah, bang bang bang,' they continued unabated.

'Shut up!' he yelled again and when this didn't work, he pulled his gun from his pocket and fired a couple of rounds in the air and around by their feet. They backed off a bit and huddled together, but the one thing they didn't do was shut up.

'Dip-lom-mat-eek Emun-o-tee,' one was saying over and over again, while another just kept saying 'Pleeeeese!'

'Eng-land. We,' their spokesman was telling us until Vince lumped him on the nose.

'Who do they think we are, fucking immigration or the Old Bill or something?'

'Probably,' I nodded. 'This is probably how the Old Bill in their country treats them isn't it?'

'Alright, you stand here and guard them, I'll go and look for the gear,' Vince said jumping back into the van.

'Vince, this is the gear,' I told him pointing at Her Majesty's newest subjects. 'These people are the merchandise.' Vince eyed me suspiciously.

'What the fuck are you talking about. Who'd want to buy one of those fucking things?'

Me and the lads looked at each other and then back at Vince as he set about ripping the floorboards up. It took him twenty minutes of desperate searching before he reluctantly accepted the truth. 'I don't believe it,' he said slumping down on the tail gate. 'I just . . . I just don't believe it.' By this time, the cargo had quietened down and were staring at us with apprehension. 'What's he smuggling this fucking lot for?' This was, of course, a rhetorical question. The fact is that people are an incredibly lucrative thing to smuggle; £2,000 a head, a life's savings to most of these poor wretches, and once that's paid it doesn't matter a jot if the cargo's picked up or lost at sea after that because people aren't actually worth anything. Of course, if you did get them into the country, they all needed jobs and accommodation and therefore could be milked for even more cash if you had a string of sweat shops and fleapit bedsits to offer them. It's hard to believe, but it was tantamount to people buying their way into slavery.

And no matter how many got intercepted en route, or died in transit or got rumbled after a couple of months and deported, there was a never-ending supply back East willing to risk everything just to get the chance to call Eng-land 'home'.

Of course, when they did get over here, they still

supported Cameroon or Albania or wherever they came from whenever we met them in the World Cup so go figure.

'Chris, I said what's he smuggling this fucking lot for?' Vince repeated, making me realise that it wasn't a rhetorical question after all.

'Money, what d'you think. Easy money. Come on, let's get out of here.'

'Alright, but hold on, this track's used quite a bit. Let me drive the van up around the corner and dump it up there where no-one'll find it. I'll meet you down by the gate,' Vince said waving me off.

I've run over this sentence in my head a hundred times since to try and ascertain whether it hid any clue as to what Vince had in mind. I've tortured myself with guilt for dropping my guard and failing to spot the unbelievable danger this situation presented. I didn't think. I was sick of the job, sick of the woods and sick of Vince. All I wanted was to go home and forget all about the day, but instead it turned into one I'd take to the grave with me. And if there's a hell, beyond.

I sat in the car at the bottom of the hill for about twenty minutes before Vince jumped in, slammed the door and told me to go. After several minutes and a cigarette each, I looked over at Vince and saw him wiping spots of blood off his face with a handkerchief in the passenger side vanity mirror.

'What the fuck's that?' I asked him.

'It's just blood, get's fucking everywhere don't it?' he answered nonchalantly.

'Why've you got blood all over you?' Even before I asked the question I knew the answer. I prayed that he'd say something like he'd just fallen over or cut himself but I knew he wouldn't.

'Well, I had an idea that maybe those Pakis had something in their bellies, you know, like smack or diamonds or something, so I opened one of them up to check it out. You were right though, there wasn't nothing in there.'

This is the moment I relive over and over again. The sudden, crashing realisation that I'd left eight perfectly harmless innocents to a psychotic maniac to dispose of in the quiet woods. The shock drained the blood from my face and left me barely able to breathe. I couldn't believe I hadn't seen the danger. Vince was never going to just chase them away and leave them to fend for themselves; they were potential witnesses. It didn't matter how unreliable they were, or even if they realised what they'd just witnessed. They were a threat. And when life was as worthless as it was to Vince, there wasn't even a choice to consider.

'Where are the others?' I asked.

'Don't worry, no-one'll find them.'

'Where are they?'

'They're still in the back of the van I suppose.'

'And where's the van?'

'It's about forty feet under water by now. There's an old flooded gravel pit up the top of the hill, I just drove it off the edge after I'd checked out matey boy's guts.' He turned around to reassure me. 'Don't worry, it's got sheer sides and a bottom so murky it'll be years before anyone finds the fucking thing – if it ever is found. We're in the clear. Waste of a day though.'

A waste of a day?

I'd already decided, that morning, that I would never work with Vince again. But suddenly, I realised beyond all doubt I had to kill the evil fucker.

16. Killing Vince

Three days after the lorry-jacking I phoned Vince and told him me and Sid were waiting for him in the blue van at the end of his street.

'What?' he mumbled, half groggy with sleep.

'We've got one,' I said.

'What are you talking about?'

'Oh for fuck's sake Vince rise and shine, this was your idea, remember? I thought you said you wanted to see our mutual friend plug someone?'

'You've got someone?' he said, snapping awake immediately. 'Where d'you get them? Who are they?' The excitement in his voice was really horrible.

'Look come down will you, this isn't really a conversation I want to continue on the phone. We're in the blue van on the corner. Be quick.' I hung up and waited for him to appear. It was early morning, not even light yet. The streets were empty save for milk, post and bogey men. We fell into the latter category.

It was ironic really. After much soul-searching and heated discussion me and Sid had finally agreed, by mutual consent, to kill Vince. The only problem was, how? Vince solved that one himself, he'd come up with the plan for his own murder just three days earlier in the van outside the shuttle terminus. Well how else were we going to lure him into the woods and get him to stand over a shallow grave with his back to us? Nice one Vince.

'Look at that?' Sid said as Vince closed his front door behind him and did everything but skip down the street towards us. 'He's creaming in his fucking pants.'

Vince opened up the passenger door and jumped in. 'Where is he?' he said as Sid started the engine and quietly pulled away.

'Back here,' I told him and lifted the blanket just long enough to give Vince a glimpse of Peter's terrified expression.

'Fucking superb! Where d'you get him from?' he asked and, for a moment, I thought he was going to lick his lips.

'Oval,' Sid told him. 'He was half-pissed and waiting for a night bus. It was easy.'

'He looks sober enough now though, don't he?' Vince gloated.

Peter tried to say something, or scream something more like, from beneath his electrical tape gag, but nothing audible came out. What Sid had told Vince was, of course, true. We'd nabbed Peter from a stop in Oval a few hours earlier, we didn't know him or anything, he was just in the wrong place at ... well you know how the rest of it goes. We weren't planning on actually killing him (hopefully) it's just the thing was, we needed someone to bait the hook with (that was a Sid analogy as you can probably tell). Vince wouldn't have come with us if we didn't have someone. And we couldn't very well use a friend or one of our own in case something went wrong and they really did end up getting rubbed out. Besides, no self-respecting criminal would ever allow themselves to be trussed up like a turkey and marched out into the woods by men with guns as part of a ruse, in case it turned out that they were the object of the ruse. People never kill each other honestly any more. No, we had no choice. So Peter – Peter Baker I think I remember him blubbing – became our unwilling accomplice in the murder of Vincent Stanley Fairchild.

'Look at him, he's fucking really scared,' Vince helpfully pointed out.

'Well let's be fair Vince, so would you be if you were in his shoes,' I told him.

'No I wouldn't,' he snapped back like a big kid.

We'll see, I thought to myself and then realised I was going to really enjoy this. And that was wrong. Vince clambered over the seats and into the back with me and Peter. 'Let's have a look at him,' he said tearing back the blanket.

'Vince, leave him,' I said quickly recovering him.

'What's the matter with you?' Vince demanded pushing me back. What the matter was, was that so far, me and Sid had managed to avoid showing Peter our faces. If he was to walk away from this with his life then he couldn't know what we looked like. He couldn't even know what Vince looked like because that again would set DS Evans' ball rolling nicely in the right direction regardless of whether they found Vince or not. We'd thought about putting tape over his eyes but Sid figured that would tip Vince the wink – everyone knows you only have to hide your identity if you're planning on letting someone live. This was a dangerous moment, not so much for us, but for poor Peter. Vince, for all his bleak outlook, could end up taking him with him.

'Wait till we get out in the woods, we ain't home and dry yet,' I told Vince.

'Fuck off,' he told me back and ripped the blanket back. Peter's eyes were wild and full of a terror I can't even imagine. Vince gripped him by the throat with one of his shovel-like hands and lifted him off the floor to within inches of his own grinning face. 'We're going to kill you,' he whispered to Peter then began squeezing his windpipe.

I leapt forward and had to wrestle with Vince before he let go. 'You're going to fucking kill him Vince! That's not the idea. Sid's got to do that,' I said then cursed myself for mentioning Sid's name in front of Peter.

'Hey get your fucking hands off me,' he growled and pushed me back violently.

'You were going to kill him.'

'I wasn't, I was just playing. I was going to let up after a bit.'

'Shock Vince, shock. You're shitting him up so much he's going to give up the ghost before we even get out to the sticks.'

'Vince, I can't do this twice,' Sid said from up front. 'You've got to leave it to me.'

Over the next five minutes we all managed to calm down and get Vince to move back into the front passenger seat away from Peter who must've been going out of his mind listening to a clutch of murderers arguing over who was going to kill him.

We reached our destination, a large, sprawling, bracken-covered wood just outside Guildford, a little after seven. Me and Sid had been here the day before and dug – and concealed – a deep, but narrow pit three quarters of the way up this steep, slippery hill. It was a good spot for a body; isolated and inaccessible, what with its tangled thick flora, I doubted anyone but botanists and murderers ever came up here. We parked the van in amongst the trees off this little lover's lane that wound its way through the trees for a few dozen yards. Sid jumped out and had a quick scout about before coming back and giving us the all-clear.

'Right, let's get this over with,' he said dragging Peter out of the side door and pulling a flour sack over his head. Peter tried to scream but the tape, the sack and the deafening early morning birdsong did for that. Me and Vince grabbed shovels from the back of the van and we all set off into the trees. Peter was determined to leave this life without the slightest shred of dignity and did all he could to delay proceedings; tripping over things, refusing to get up, grabbing hold of trees and bushes and not letting go. After several minutes of laboured struggle, Vince stepped forward, gave his shovel to Sid and pushed him aside.

'I'll take it from here, Florence Nightingale,' he said yanking Peter up by the elbows.

'Enough of this fucking about.' Suddenly, to my dismay, Vince pulled the sack from Peter's head and stuffed it in his jacket. 'You don't need this any more,' he told him.

'Don't Vince,' I blurted out a little too quickly. 'Leave it on.'

'What's the matter, Chris,' Vince replied, 'can't look in the eyes of someone you're about to plug?' then swung Peter around so that he was looking right at me. My instinct was to avert my gaze but it was already too late, he'd seen me, he'd seen Sid and he'd seen Vince. Ours were faces that would be etched on Peter's mind for the rest of his life. We'd haunt him in his dreams, we'd peer out at him from every passing car, we'd never leave him. 'Look into his eyes,' Vince ordered me pointing Peter's head right at me and Sid. 'Fucking couple of pussies you two are. Now come on, let's get moving.' I turned around to Sid who shot me the exact same look. Vince insisted on fucking up everything for us, even his own murder. What a cunt!

We followed the pair of them up the hill for another couple of minutes. The going was hard, steep, overgrown and slippery, but Vince's grip was such that Peter didn't get the chance to fall over again. 'Come on you bastard, come on,' Vince shouted as he drove him on.

You know, it always makes me laugh when people in this country talk about the second world war and the gas chambers and the camp guards and all the atrocities they committed. 'It couldn't have happened here,' they always say. 'We're not like that in this country.' What a load of bollocks! I've been around a bit and I'm telling you this, some people (and I'm not just talking about Vince here) are fucking animals regardless of what flag they salute in the morning. I'll tell you this, if Hitler stuck a card up in my local newsagent's window advertising for camp guards you wouldn't be able to get in to buy a paper. Queueing round the block they'd be.

Sid directed Vince to where we'd dug the hole and after a little search we found and uncovered it. Peter, by this time, was incoherent with fear. His face was red with tears and his jeans were soaked with piss. His sobbing had got so bad that his nose had become completely blocked, forcing Vince to remove his gag. At this stage it didn't matter, we were too far into the woods to be heard by anyone and Peter was hyperventilating too fiercely to muster up anything that could be mistaken for a shout. Vince threw him to his knees in front of the pit and ushered Sid forward.

'Alright, do it,' he told him.

'Please,' Peter cried. 'Please don't. Sandra help me!'

'Do it Sid, shoot him,' Vince ordered pulling his own gun out. Sid looked around to see that I had my gun out too.

'Okay,' he said. 'Let's do it.' Sid brought up his gun and aimed it at Peter's head. Peter closed his eyes and said nothing more. Vince was so engrossed in what he was about to witness that he didn't see my gun levelled at his back. This was it, I thought to myself. Goodnight, you evil fucking scumbag.

'Vince,' I called out from behind him. Vince shot a very reluctant glance my way, fearful of missing the action. Our eyes locked for the briefest of moments before he suddenly noticed the gun.

There's your look motherfucker. Now die.

The penny dropped much too late to save Vince's life and even before he'd managed a half-turn I'd fired the first shot into his midriff. Such was the force of the impact (and his footing) that he fell head first into the hole just as Sid opened fire on him as well. Here was another little irony of Vince's murder. Me and Sid had agreed that we both had to do the killing – three bullets from him, three bullets from me – so that if Vince was ever found the police would know that he was killed by two people, not one, thus ruling out the possibility of me or Sid ever being able to sell each other out.

Vince's original plan unless I'm very much mistaken.

The only trouble was, I got completely carried away and emptied an entire clip into Vince and was in the process of reloading when Sid stopped me. 'I think he's dead now Chris,' he said, snapping me back to my senses. I looked down at the dropped crate of tomato ketchup that used to be Vince and found myself shaking with rage.

'That fucker can never be too dead,' I said and fired two more shots into the hole. 'Shit! Where's Peter?' We looked around and saw Peter twenty yards up the hill and scrambling for dear sweet life.

'No! No! No! No! No! No! No! No! No! No!' he was yelling over and over again by the time we caught up with him. Sid got hold of one elbow, I got hold of the other and dragged him back to the hole. He was so exhausted from the all-encompassing terror that he didn't even put up a struggle. We dumped him down a few inches from the edge and Sid looked at me.

'You do it, I can't,' he said turning away.

'We do it together, as agreed,' I told him back. Sid stared down at Peter who had turned lily-white and had all but accepted his place in the grave. I hated to do it but what choice were we left with; he'd seen our faces, he knew our names, he'd seen us commit murder and could lead police right to the body. It had never been our intention to kill him, that was Vince's doing. And there was nothing we could do about it now.

'Sorry Peter,' I said pushing the gun to his temple. Sid clicked the safety off his weapon and took a deep breath. I was just about to pull the trigger when the strangest thing happened.

Vince saved Peter's life.

I admit, it sounds a bit bizarre to say the least but it's the only explanation I can offer. I was all set to blow his brains out when Vince's words about looking the man you're about to kill in the eyes came echoing back to me. Without thinking I fixed my gaze straight at his and studied his cobalt blues; the desperation, the helplessness, the complete despair, all brightly decorated with brilliant sparkling tears. I couldn't do it. I had to do it, but I couldn't. No more. No way.

I dropped to my knees beside Peter, put away my gun and told Sid to do the same.

'Okay, listen to me and listen good. You're dead. You are standing by a shallow grave in the middle of the woods with two murderers and, at this precise moment in time, you are dead. We have no reason to let you go and every reason to kill you. You're already underground and there's nothing you can do about it.' I grabbed his face as he tried to turn away and stared him hard in the eyes. 'But what if I was to make you an offer? What if I was to tell you there was a way out of this? What would you give for that second chance? Your car? Your job? Your house? What about your word? Would you give us your word that you'd never speak of this day again, to anyone, in return for your life?'

'Yes, yes, I promise, I would,' Peter blurted out re-animated with hope. 'Please, I would.'

'Don't go promising too quickly because I fucking mean it. I'm not talking about keeping your gob shut for five minutes until we're out of the way, then going running to the police . . .'

'I wouldn't. I swear,' he interrupted.

'If we let you go – and I say "if" – you don't tell anyone. Ever. We'd have to trust you. If you can guarantee us that trust, we can guarantee you your life. Is it a deal?'

'It's a deal. It's a deal. I promise I won't ever say anything, please I promise,' Peter was spluttering. It took half a minute and a great outpouring for him to settle down and shut up and when he did I explained a few further things to him.

'Look, we're sorry we got you into this but we needed you. The man we killed was a psychotic murderer.'

'A serial killer,' Sid chipped in.

'Yeah, well, as good as anyhow. And the only way we could lure him out here was if he thought he was going to get to kill someone – you. Okay, you understand? You saw what he was like. It was a trap. We just made the world a nicer place. So, keep schtum, and I can promise you this, you'll never see either of us again as long as you live.'

'Grass us up to the Old Bill though, and we've got a lot of friends. Particularly in the police,' Sid lied. We didn't have any friends in the police, in fact they fucking hated us. 'One word and you'll be back up here before you can say Jack fucking Robinson.'

'I promise,' Peter said for the thousandth time.

'Alright then,' I said and cut his hands free. 'Don't go running off now.' I pulled a handkerchief from my pocket, wiped my gun clean of all prints and tossed it in beside Vince. Sid did the same as I picked up and counted all my loose shell casings and tossed them into the hole as well. Sid dug up a large plastic sandwich box he'd buried beside the hole yesterday and peeled off the lid. Inside, a thousand hungry maggots wriggled and squirmed.

'Never trust a fisherman,' he said and scattered them over the entire length of Vince's body.

It took the three of us just a few minutes to backfill the hole and disguise it with foliage before we all headed back for the van. We dropped Peter off in South London somewhere and gave him a couple of hundred quid to go out and get drunk out of his mind on and even as he was getting out he was still saying, 'I promise. I promise.'

All the things we'd discussed over the last few days, me and Sid, the one thing I'd omitted was the lorry-jacking. I couldn't tell him about that. I couldn't tell anyone. It was too terrible. Even to admit to being an unwitting partner in it, it was way too much. That's one job I'll take to the grave with me. It's also the one job I'll think about every day until I'm there.

Sometimes it's a shame you can only kill someone once.

17. Collars

I'd been scouring the papers for weeks now to see if Peter had broken his word and gone to the police and was mildly surprised to see that he hadn't. Well, so far at least. While I was scouring though, I came across one story that really caught my attention. This young lad, only twenty-three he was, had been convicted on eighteen counts of armed robbery and sent down for a total of fourteen years (only one less than Gavin). His mum, dad and former school friends knew him as Clive Mason, though to the rest of us, he would forever be remembered as the Baby-Faced Robber, a name given to him by the morning rags and one I'm sure he probably hated. There was also a picture of him, his police mug shot, to titillate and shock polite society over their morning cornflakes. It was this that caught my eye, for straightaway, I recognised him but couldn't think from where. It annoyed me all day trying to place his face and I racked my brains trying to figure it out. It was late in the afternoon, when I was thinking about Gavin and the similarity in their sentence that I finally realised where I knew him from.

It was Clive. You remember, Clive 'take me with you' Mason, that little idiot cashier from the bank all those years ago. It was that last job we did before Gavin was nicked.

Well, you could've knocked me down with a feather. Clive, eighteen robberies, over £160,000 stolen in total – top man! Gavin had been right about him all along, he turned out to be a great little thief. And gutsy too. The first five robberies he carried out he did with an air pistol. Can you imagine that? Walking into NatWest with nothing more than a single-shot peashooter that you could just about break skin with (if you got someone in the face), and walking out with ten grand? The balls on this lad must've been big, hairy and made of the right stuff. He did the next two with a crossbow, which is even dafter, and then all the subsequent robberies with what was described in the papers only as a semi-automatic handgun. It was probably a Beretta though. No-one knows where he, and his gang, got the weapons from because he never grassed, not a single name. Nothing. He took his punishment like a man and didn't ask for any favours. He didn't blub in the dock when they were leading him down either, unlike so many of these supposed hard men rappers you get on the telly – Iced Tea and all the rest of them – who bang on in their songs about being funky mean cop killers, then cry like fucking babies when they get four months for drink-driving or exposing themselves in public. No, not our Clive. He just looked up to the public gallery, gave the thumbs up to his family and then walked down the steps with his head held high. How disappointed all the old ghouls from the press must've been when he didn't spill a tear! For some reason, people love hearing about that don't they? I don't know why. I guess it's that some people find it satisfying, or edifying . . . (do I mean edifying? Actually I don't think I know what that means. What's edifying? Oh never mind.) My point is, that people like to see a baddy get his (or her) come-uppance to remind themselves that there's still order in the galaxy and the cowboys in the white hats will always win the day. I'm surprised they don't televise it; *Beadle's Baddest Bawlers*. It'd be a sure-fire winner.

I'd definitely watch it.

Not that they got any such satisfaction from young Clive. The police described him as 'careful and calcu-lating', and 'ultra-professional' like that was a bad thing. I never get this. Why is it, if you're a criminal and good at what you do, that is seen as something negative? Criminals, particularly robbers I have to add, are prob-ably the only people in society who are penalised if they exhibit high standards of competence. Would it have been better if Clive had been a bumbling fool and blown a pensioner's bobble hat and his own foot off during a string of prat-fall hold-ups? I don't think so. Give him a bit of nous and a will and determination to see a job done right though and he ends up with an extra five years on his sentence. Some backward crazy world this is.

To get away with eighteen robberies is some feat though, particularly for someone with absolutely no formal education in the ways of blagging. I don't know if I could've managed it. He would've got away with more as well, had he not been grassed up by his former girlfriend after she was caught with dealer quantities of cocaine on her. The police fucked up actually, they moved in too soon. They picked up Clive, found his gun, crossbow and ski mask and thought all they had to do was give him a shake and the names of all the gang members would come falling out of his mouth. It didn't happen. The cops mistook his boyish features for weakness just as me and Vince had all those years ago. How that must've pissed them off. There you go, there's another four years on top of your sentence thank you very much. If he'd been picked up by the SS trying to make it to the Swiss border on a stolen motorbike and not said a word, he'd have been a hero and would've been played by Steve McQueen in *The Great Escape*. However, stick him in a police cell and charge him with robbery and suddenly he's no longer brave, he's just cold and evil. Am I the only one who thinks this smacks of double standards? Probably.

Something else about Clive's case fucked me off greatly. Several of the charges laid against him (and he was subsequently convicted of) were conspiracy to commit robbery. Now, I'm not sure how this works but somehow the police dug up this star witness to testify that he'd met Clive on several occasions and had discussed the robbery of the Abbey National in the Elephant and Castle with him. Now, the fact that they never carried out this raid is neither here nor there (taking a guess and reading between the lines I would've said that matey got cold feet and didn't show, compromising the whole plan – another good call on Clive's part). This guy's evidence played a crucial part in convincing the jury that if Clive was capable of planning the robbery of one building society, then he was capable of carrying out the actual robbery of eighteen other establishments.

Now, I have a big problem with this conspiracy nonsense.

Whatever happened to the freedom of speech? The freedom of assembly? So what if Tom, Dick or Harry talk about robbing a bank? People talk about robbing banks, shops, art galleries and so on all the time, doesn't mean they'll ever do it. For most people, it's just fantasy. Should we arrest them? And not just robbery. I bet half the workers in Britain have fantasised about murdering their bosses after a bad day at the office. I'd put money on it they'd even discussed it with their mates in the pub after two hours of unpaid overtime and five much-needed beers. Isn't that conspiracy? The fact that they'd never do it in a million years doesn't matter. If we're applying the same criteria that earned poor Clive an extra line on the charge sheet, then they're breaking the law as well.

The smug answer here, of course, is that you'd never be able to catch them or prove it unless you bugged them or one of them went to the Old Bill. But even then, if that happened, the police would have a hard time in court convincing a judge and jury to take your slurs about 'smashing that cunt's fucking head in' too seriously.

Okay, so let's forget about the plebs and talk about someone you could convict for conspiracy to commit murder and there's proof – the government. As far as I'm aware, under the Geneva Convention, the use of nuclear weapons is banned. In fact, so is genocide, which for you thickos out there, is like murder but there's more of it. Britain owns nuclear weapons. In fact we pulled out all the stops and kissed America's arse until we got them, even though after Hiroshima and Nagasaki, it had been given the big thumbs down by the international courts. We've even got stockpiles of chemical and biological weapons as well and they're illegal too. Now, I accept the likelihood of us ever using them is slim, and that it's the use of these things that is illegal, but surely, again using the same criteria as that used against Clive, just having them makes the British government (and the Yanks, Frogs, Ruskies, Chinese, Indians and every other cunt who's now got the bomb) guilty of conspiracy to use outlawed weapons and conspiracy to commit genocide. You know me, I'm not some fat, ugly lesbian living in a tent on Greenham Common, I just think that there seem to be some fundamental inequalities in the law of this land, particularly with regards to bank robbers. And I think we pay for it heavily enough already. But then, that's just my opinion, though I'm more than happy to back it up with examples of heavy handedness till Tuesday if you want.

Take Clive's fourteen-year sentence, for example. This might seem a fair and just punishment for such a dangerous criminal, but let me just point out a few things here. Blue collar crime (robbery, burglary, muggings, shoplifting, etc) accounts for less than ten per cent of all the money stolen in this country each year. In fact, I think it's lower than that, I saw the figures once but can't quite remember them in detail. The simple fact is that it's white collar crime (fraud, embezzlement, insider trading, etc) that makes up the vast majority of the figures, and we're talking billions and billions here. However, if you do your robbing with a pen or a computer or a share option, your sentence, should you get caught, is likely to be ten times less than that of a blue collar criminal, regardless of how much you stole. Let's take Ernest Saunders for example. Ernest Saunders was the Big Cheese at Guinness and therefore, I would imagine, a rich man already. A few years ago though he, along with several others, was convicted of . . . I'm not quite sure of the actual wording of the charge, but it was a typical 'Suit' crime. He was selling or merging or floating the company or something and him and all his mates exaggerated the share prices so they'd get more money. And when I say more money, I'm talking more than I could fit in the back of the transit and still get it up a hill. Anyway, the point is poor old Ernest, he got five years. Five years, that's all. And typically of all these old Etonians, he got to serve his sentence in fucking Pontins' holiday camp. However, this just wasn't enough for Ernest, he got his lawyers to petition for his early release on compassionate grounds, citing that he had Alzheimer's Disease and didn't feel very well, 'can I go home please?' and they fucking let him! I'm sorry, but that deserves two exclamation marks at the very least!! This is in a day and age when the courts are locking up single mothers for not paying their TV licences.

Incidentally, you'll be glad to hear that Ernest's condition miraculously improved once he was released and he was able to lead a full and active social life on the dinner and golf circuits. Funny how they didn't tell him to get back in-fucking-side and finish his sentence then, isn't it?

Can you imagine some old lag, halfway through a thirty-year stretch, asking for the same consideration? He'd be laughed out of the Masons' get-together chamber . . . sorry, I mean courtroom!

Shame – that's what the old toffs always cry when one of them is caught with his fingers in the sweet jar. 'The shame and humiliation of the whole affair were punishment enough.' Bollocks, send him down. When Profumo, the Minister for War back in the early sixties, was found out to be sharing a mistress with a Russian spy, his political downfall and the shame he'd brought upon his family were deemed a suitable penalty for endangering the lives of countless of his countrymen. Yet, that same year, when the Great Train Robbers were convicted of stealing a couple of million quid's worth of cash – money that was intended for the incinerators anyway – they all got thirty years apiece. What about the shame their families felt? Why wasn't that taken into consideration? Don't the working classes feel shame or are we all too busy wrestling with each other in the mud over the price of a bottle of gin?

Years later, when films based on both incidents came out at roughly the same time, Barry Norman himself pooh-poohed both movies; *Scandal* (based on the Profumo affair) for unnecessarily dredging up the past for the poor, shame-faced adulterer, and *Buster* (based on the Great Train Robbery) for portraying such violent, notorious criminals in a sympathetic light. In fact, in the film *Buster*, Buster Edwards himself refers to the Profumo Affair saying something like: 'Nick a bit of cash and we get thirty years, give away all our country's secrets and he don't get invited to no posh parties any more', or maybe that was just Phil Collins. It doesn't really matter who said it, the important thing was that it was said, and by someone other than me. I don't think my opinions are so out of touch with the rest of the world. Well, not the rest of the criminal world anyway. I find it difficult to take Barry's film reviews seriously these days.

I saw this documentary on Lord Lucan the other day; he's another one who's meant to have experienced great shame, for accidentally murdering his nanny (he thought it was his wife you see, very understandable). All his old toff pals stood in front of the camera and talked at great length about his sense of duty and honour, and the fact that, as one of the aristocracy, his fall from grace was all the more tragic. Asked whether any of them thought he was still alive, they all gave roughly the same answer. 'No,' they said. 'He was a gentleman. I'm convinced he did the decent thing,' meaning kill himself, most suggested by chucking himself into the sea off the back of a cross-Channel ferry. It's funny how the decent thing, when you're one of the upper classes, is always to disappear without a trace, it's never to give yourself up to the police or not to murder your nanny in the first place, is it? I have no doubt Lord Lucan is still alive and well and sporting a very nice tan indeed, while the nanny's family are still mourning the death of a loved one and the justice they once believed in. Incidentally, if Lord Lucan had just been plain old Alf Lucan off a London council estate he'd be ticking off nearly a score of years of being behind bars at this very moment. But then, I suppose, Alf would find it a bit harder handshaking his way past the police and out of the country, wouldn't he? Maybe that's a bit cynical of me, but it's what I believe.

I guess the point I'm trying to make is – and this is where my young mate Clive fell foul – that when the law feels your collar, it starts by feeling to see what colour it is.

18. A quiet night in

You have to be so careful who you work with in this business. We might've been wrong about Clive but for every decent pro, there are a dozen wankers. And I seem to have worked with more than my fair share. A few months had passed since the lorry-jacking and I was itching to get back to work, but I had a bit of a problem there; my crew had been decimated. Gavin was still a good few years shy of daylight, Vince had taken an enforced early retirement and Sid, well his incapacitation was the most tragic. He'd been arrested shortly after we'd murdered Vince and was currently seeing out a six-month sentence for theft. What was it he stole? A fucking ray gun, what else! Apparently he was at this *Star Trek* conference up in some hotel in Leicester and some bloke had one of the original stun guns – what are they called? Phasers or something – from the first series and Sid decided he had to have it. This one apparently was really special for some God-knows reason (Captain Kirk had kept it up his arse or something, I don't know), but it was the Holy Grail for Trekkies everywhere. Anyway, Sid offered the owner £1,000 for it, but the guy said no. So then he upped his offer to £2,000, but still the guy said no. When the guy said no to £5,000 Sid decided to steal the fucking thing and be done with it. So he followed matey out to his van, waited for him to disappear back inside to validate his parking pass after he couldn't get out of the car park (Trekkies always do this apparently), then just broke in and had it away with the gun. Sid would've got away with it as well, had he also not had to go back to the hotel to get his parking pass validated.

I got a letter from him just after he went down reassuring me that there wasn't anything to worry about as far as any other matters were concerned, all in a roundabout way of course. He signed off by letting me know that he wasn't going to waste his time inside, he was going to spend it constructively doing a correspondence course, Klingon for beginners, which, I was sure, would come in very handy when he got out.

On the down side though, all this meant that I had to either wait probably four months to do another job or take on someone else. I plumped for Tom Fincham.

Tom Fincham was a young lad on the up and up who'd made a bit of a name for himself pulling off some pretty crazy shit. One of his most famous jobs was when he nicked this big JCB forklift off a building site in the middle of the night, drove it half a mile down the road to the high street and straight through Abbey National's glass front. He then picked up the two cash machines, loaded them on to the back of his mate's lorry and drove away £60,000 better off. It was in all the papers and, what with the fucking racket he made, there was no shortage of witnesses. But they were masked, daring and lucky. It was thanks to Tom, and a couple of similar jobs up North, that banks started fitting their cash machines with paint bombs that go off if they're moved. I'd got to know Tom in passing through Gordon

O'Riley and understood that he was looking to get in with an established crew, so I decided to give him a try.

The nature of bank robbery is changing all the time, it's been getting harder and harder to just walk in off the street and demand money at gunpoint what with modern-day security. Criminals, inevitably, are constantly having to rethink and adapt their methods if they want to stay in the game. Probably the most popular way to rob a bank these days isn't to go through the doors with a gun, but to kidnap a bank employee's family, usually the manager's, and keep them hostage until he empties the safe for you. This method has a number of advantages over the traditional 'give me all your fucking money' formula. Most obviously, it's less risky. Bank employees' homes are considerably less protected than the banks themselves. Secondly, it only takes two of you to do it. And thirdly, only the manager and his family are aware of the robbery while it's being carried out. Everyone else is oblivious, so there's less risk of alarms and cops being called.

On the minus side though, it takes a lot of preparation, a lot of planning. You've got to follow the manager and his family around for a week or so and get to know their routine so that you can pick the best day to strike without anyone else knowing. I mean, if the wife normally goes to her mother's every Wednesday, or the family always go swimming with their friends on Thursday, then you'd better know about it, especially if you're settling in for the night at their house. You're likely to be spending fourteen hours in their company, that's a long exposure time, and if anyone suspects that there's something wrong, then the game is up for you my old son.

Homework, that's what it's all about. But I'd done

mine, so I couldn't see a problem. I was wrong, of course. The human factor, that's something you just can't second guess.

'Nina, it's just me,' Gus Harrison called out, dropping his bag in the hall and hanging up his coat. 'Simon was an arsehole today. A first-rate tosspot.' He walked into the room and was about to tell us about Simon nicking his favourite elastic band or something when I shoved a gun in his face and told him to freeze.

'Don't move, not a fucking muscle, not a hair, or you and your wife are both dead.' He looked over my shoulder and saw, to his horror, Nina and his grown-up daughter, Yasmin (don't the middle classes give their kids stupid names?) bound and gagged on the sofa with Tom standing over them. 'Do exactly as I say and do it slowly,' I whispered. The whisper was for two reasons, to disguise my voice, and to sound more sinister; people are less likely to mess with sinister folk. 'Stick your hands out behind your back and turn around.' Gus complied and I stepped forward and pulled his jacket off with one swift tug. I laid it on the chair behind me and told him to turn around again. 'Now your trousers. Undo your belt, very slowly,' I emphasised with a hiss, 'and just let your trousers fall to the floor.'

'Are you some sort of pervert or something?' he asked.

'You'd better believe it,' I replied. 'But at this precise moment in time I'm more interested in the panic button you've got concealed about your person somewhere. Now drop your trousers slowly.' His expression betrayed him and told me I was on the right track. Gordon O'Riley had told me about these things. It could be as little as a key ring or tie pin or something similar and managers were meant to keep them about themselves day and night in case of this very thing. Fuck knows how Gordon knew about them but there you go. A classic example of 'man down the pub' information. Tom stood guard while I undressed him myself until I found what I was looking for. It was a clever little device and hidden in his tie, which was activated when the tie was slipped the whole way, alerting the local police station that all was not well at the Harrison residence. I loosened it just enough to slip it off his head and let him get dressed again – once I was satisfied that the tie was the only device. We were going to do the same with the wife and the daughter but found their panic alarms in their handbags straightaway. I got the impression Tom was a little disappointed by that.

'Okay, sit down in that chair and don't give us any trouble. We're going to be here for a little while.' Gus did as we told him and sat down. Tom began strapping him down with thick electrical tape while I took the chair opposite.

'We'll co-operate with you any way we can. Just, please, don't hurt my family.'

'Shut up,' Tom said, slapping him round the head.

'I just mean . . .' he started again, but Tom soon silenced him with some tape around the mouth. I hate chatty hostages.

Bank managers are told to try and talk in these instances. They go on courses to learn what to do in the event of a robbery or a kidnapping. It's big business these days. A lot of ex-coppers, and even some ex-blaggers, set up security firms and hold seminars on 'Staying alive: the don't be a hero guide to being robbed'. These companies charge banks and building societies a small fortune pointing out the obvious to a bunch of middle-aged chinless wonders who, in all probability, just look at the course as little more than an all expenses paid piss-up in the country. Maybe it's something I should think about when I finally retire from the life. But then, perhaps not. No, I think I'd rather teach people how to rob these wankers.

Once Tom was finished, I got up from my chair and went to get a glass of water. Tom removed the gag from the wife as I cracked the lid off the bottle of sleeping tablets. 'Take a couple of these,' I told her. 'They'll help you relax and get through this quicker.'

She turned her head violently and started to scream. Tom clamped his hand over her mouth in an instant, subduing the noise. Beneath his hand she was shouting for help and blind with terror. Yasmin, next to her, then started thrashing about and murmuring about something and eventually even Gus joined in the muffled pandemonium. Something inside me told me that she thought we were giving her poison, so I attempted to reassure her.

'They're just sleeping pills, for fuck's sake. They'll knock you out for a few hours, give us all a bit of a rest.' She still wasn't buying it until Tom held the butt of his gun over her daughter's head and told her:

'The hard way or the easy way, it's up to you?' This seemed to strike a chord with Nina and, reluctantly, she opened her mouth and accepted the pill.

'Gus . . .!' she whined. Gus tried replying but thankfully his gag held; I don't think I could've taken any sentimental garbage at that particular moment in time. Mind you, he might not have come out with anything like that. He might've just said:

'Fuck off, leave me alone. I've got my own problems to worry about.' Now that would've been good.

I gave Nina some water and she took a couple of sips and sent the tablets south. 'Good girl,' I said. 'Now I'll leave your gag off, alright. Let you get a bit of air.' I then turned to the daughter, who was puffy and raw with tears. 'Okay Yasmin. Are you going to give me any trouble?' Yasmin nodded and more salty tears spilt from her eyes. 'What? Why?' I asked and took off the gag. Yasmin was so upset she could hardly get the words out.

'I can't swallow tablets,' she whimpered. 'I can only chew them up with toast.' I looked at her for a moment and saw that she'd been panicking about this as soon as she saw the bottle of pills. She didn't want to mess us about, but she was terrified that her inability meant she was going to have to. Tom finally found his voice.

'What are you talking about, fucking toast? Take the fucking tablet!' Which, I think, was exactly what she had been shitting herself about.

'It's alright, leave it. Go and make some toast,' I told him.

'What?'

'You heard the young lady, she can't take tablets. Go and put some toast on. How do you like it?' I asked Yasmin.

'Just dry please,' she said. Tom threw his hands up and trudged off to the kitchen like a spoilt little child being made to do the washing-up. If it was up to him he would've just shoved them down her throat and held her nose until she passed out. That approach didn't sit comfortably with me. Just because we were robbing them, didn't mean we had to be arseholes about it. This isn't any pretence at chivalry, don't get me wrong, it's just good sense. If you do get caught for this sort of crime and you've treated your hostages like dogs, you can add an extra five years to your sentence. That's a high price to pay just to dodge the toaster.

Tom came back with the toast and asked her if it was brown enough. Yasmin nodded warily. 'Okay, how do you do this, fold it up like a sandwich?'

'No, I just break off a little bit, roll the tablet up in it and chew it.'

I did as she instructed and fed her the tablets.

'Can I have a sip of water now please?' she asked once she'd eaten them. I gave her a quick drink and patted her on the head, rather patronisingly. Yasmin whispered a thank you my way and closed her eyes. I looked around at Gus, who was staring at the tablets and shook my head.

'Oh no, none for you. You have to call in at nine and I don't want you to spark out.' Gus looked at me with an expression of shock and confusion. 'We are professionals you know Gus. Give us some credit.' The call I referred to was a security call at nine o'clock every night. Some managers do it, some don't. It was a new thing. Gus had to place a quick phone call to his security division at a certain time every night and give the all-clear password. If he forgot, they would then try and contact him at home or on the mobile. If they still couldn't raise him after that then a procedure would start which would ultimately lead to the Old Bill ringing his bell.

We'd been tapping his phone all week so we knew exactly when and where to call and what was to be said. You know, perhaps I should think about running a course after all.

As the girls slept, we lads settled in for the night and watched a bit of telly. Gus wanted to watch *A Touch of Frost* on ITV but me and Tom had the remote control and the guns so he got to see a UEFA Cup second round match between Arsenal and some part-time Swedish team.

After Gus made his call at nine, we gave him a couple of pills and bid him goodnight. He wolfed them down eagerly and closed his eyes to try and speed up the effect, explaining in the morning that he couldn't stand bloody football. It was a particularly dull game as well. When Gus finally dropped off, we covered his, Nina and Yasmin's eyes with tape and pulled the woollen masks from our sweaty faces. Bliss!

At half-ten, Tom turned in upstairs while I stayed with the Harrisons and made sure that none of them went sleep-walking down to the local cop shop. It's hard to stay awake in a darkened room full of sleeping people, even if you are hyped-up. I ended up drifting off several times in the big comfortable chair next to Gus (once for a whole hour) and finally got so sick of snapping awake over and over again that I went into the kitchen where the light was bright, made myself some coffee and read one of Nina's Mills & Boon paperbacks. At four in the morning Tom came down to take over, though I put off sleep for another half hour because I wanted to finish the book. When I did finally plant my head on the pillow and close my eyes, I didn't open them again until my watch woke me up at eight. I made the bed, pulled my mask back on and quickly ran over the plan in my mind. I couldn't see any problems.

It wasn't until I came down the stairs and walked into the living room that I had the first inkling that something was wrong. Yasmin was gone. My heart leaped out of my chest. 'Shit!' I rushed into the kitchen to get Tom and get us out of here and got my second shock of the morning. Tom had her on the floor, bound and gagged, with her top up and his hand inside her bra. Yasmin turned her tear-streaked face towards me as I looked down on them and closed her eyes in despair. I guess she thought I'd come in to have my turn.

It took me a second or two to take this all in before I lunged forward and dragged Tom off. 'What are you fucking doing?' I hissed venomously at him.

'No wait . . .' he started to say but I knew what he was doing, it was a rhetorical question you see. 'Wait,' he shouted again, but I didn't wait. I threw him bodily across the kitchen and into the cooker. Before he had a chance to catch his bearings I had him up and flying again, this time into the swing bin. Yasmin screamed behind her gag as I set about Tom again, punching and kicking him until my fists were sore. She scrambled across the kitchen floor and curled up into a little ball and stayed that way until I was through. The hardest part was reining back my anger and stopping short of beating him senseless. I needed Tom to finish the job. I hadn't gone through this whole rigmarole just to sleep over at Gus and Nina's; there was money to collect, and collection time was almost at hand.

I pulled Tom's pistol out of his belt and pressed it up against his balaclava and growled at him so menacingly he must've thought his number was up. 'You fucking animal,' I said. 'Not on one of my jobs. I've a mind to blow your fucking brains out you horrible little nonce.'

'I can explain . . .' he spluttered.

'No you can't. Not this.' I looked over at Yasmin who was wide-eyed with fear. She looked like she was expecting a bullet straight after Tom. 'You, come here,' I told her. Yasmin shook her head then buried it in her hands. 'Come here!' I told her again, but still she didn't come. 'I'm not going to hurt you, I swear.' Finally I seemed to get through to her. She picked herself up and pigeon-stepped the distance between us. I pulled off her gag but left her hands strapped together.

'Please don't touch me,' she said, screwing up her face in complete misery.

'I'm not going to. In fact, I want you to do something for me.'

'What?' she blubbed.

'You see that little saucepan on the draining board over there? Bring it over here.' She turned around, made her way to the side and came back with the pan. 'Okay, now you see this piece of garbage down here? I want you to hit him on the head with it.'

'Hey, wait a minute,' Tom said but I simply pushed the gun harder into his temple.

'You don't speak,' I told him. 'You just get hit. I guess if you really want to you can get shot as well, it's up to you.'

At first Yasmin didn't say anything, she just looked at me and then looked at Tom in complete bewilderment. When she finally did speak, I couldn't help but laugh.

'Is this a trick question?' she said.

'Nope, this is payback. Now give him your best whack.' I stood back, still keeping the gun trained on Tom's face.

'Not too hard, please,' Tom implored.

'Are you joking?' was all Yasmin could reply before bringing down the pan and clobbering him with all her might.

'Ahh, fucking hell!' Tom yelled, taking most of the impact on his knuckles as he desperately tried to shield his brain from serious damage. Yasmin was about to swing again when I pointed the gun at her and told her to stop.

'Sorry, but you only get one.'

'But he had his hands in the way, I couldn't get through to his head.'

'I'm sorry, but those are the rules. Unfortunately, I need him alive to get your dad's money. But don't worry, he won't bother you again. That's a promise.' I looked down at Tom, who had his hands underneath his armpits and was grimacing behind his mask. 'Now get up and let's get this over with. Try and act like a fucking professional for the next couple of hours. I thought you wanted to be a crook, not a fucking rapist.'

'I'm sorry, I'm sorry,' he said getting to his feet. 'It won't happen again.'

'You're right it won't happen again. Now you know what's got to be done. So just do it and let's get the money.' I pointed the gun at him to emphasise my next warning. 'And if you try anything like this again when I'm not around, I'll fucking plant you up in Epping Forest.'

'On my word . . .' he started to say but was abruptly cut short with a saucepan in the face. 'Ah fucking get off will you?' he said rubbing his jaw.

'Sorry,' Yasmin said, addressing me. 'One for the road. Too good to waste.'

'Alright,' I nodded. 'Probably best if you put the pan down now, okay.' She dropped it on the side and led the way back through to the living room. Gus and Nina were wide awake now asking what was going on. 'Well, it's gags back on time for you both,' I told them and taped up their faces. 'Here's one for you too,' I told Yasmin stretching a length of electrical tape over her mouth, then retying her legs together. 'Right, go and clear a path to the car,' I told Tom. Tom went back into the kitchen, opened the side door that led into the garage and tidied away all the bits of furniture I'd been beating him up with a few minutes earlier.

'Alright, let's go Nina.'

Nina struggled as me and Tom picked her up and carried her to the car. In fact, she struggled so much I ended up almost dropping the stupid cow on her head. Some people really are their own worst enemies, aren't they? We loaded her into the back of her family saloon and went back and got Yasmin. Once they were both inside and hidden under a blanket, I told them to shut up and stay that way. 'You're going for a little ride out to the country. As soon as Gus has given us our money you'll be allowed to go free. Until then, you'd both better be as good as gold.'

Needless to say, neither of them were. They thrashed about and tried to get up and all sorts until I threatened to club them unconscious with a spanner. 'Fucking pack it in,' I snapped. I think Yasmin was particularly reluctant to be driven into the unknown by a man she'd just whacked with a saucepan, so I let everyone know where they stood. 'You two will not be touched or mistreated by him, me or anyone else as long as we get our money. As for you,' I said to Tom, 'I'm deadly serious what I said in the kitchen. No funny business.'

'I won't.'

'Alright, get the fuck out of here and wait for my call.'

'Sure,' he said, then didn't move.

'Go now.'

'Well, I'll need my gun won't I,' he said.

'What for? They're only fucking women.'

'But what if I, you know, have to ...' he started, leaving the rest hanging in the wind.

'We'll cross that bridge when we come to it, now go.' Tom climbed into the car and started the engine while I opened the garage door. He was about to drive off when I pointed to the mask he was still wearing. He gave me the thumbs up to show that he'd remembered and rolled it up into a bobble hat and hid what he could of the rest of his bruised and battered features behind a pair of sunglasses.

The moment he was gone, I closed the garage doors and went on back to Gus. 'Where have you taken them?' he asked when I ripped the tape off his face.

'They're quite safe,' I reassured him. 'Well, as long as you get us our money.'

'But how do I know that? You could've taken them anywhere.' That being the whole fucking point of the exercise. It was this very uncertainty that would ensure Gus's co-operation. If Tom had just stayed in the house with his wife and kids there was always a chance Gus would play the hero and phone the cops while we were sitting around like ducks. Take away a location to direct them to though and suddenly we have total control. We're not stupid, you know.

I explained all that needed to be explained to Gus and told him to get dressed for work. 'But let's pick a different tie for today shall we?'

I find it amazing that I live in a day and age when I have to explain to my victims exactly how I'm going to rob them, that stealing is becoming so complicated it requires instruction and understanding on the part of the innocent before I can make it off with their cash. Robbery must've been a piece of piss in the old days. All you had to do was walk up to someone and stick a gun in their face. There were no alarms, no CCTV, no *Crimewatch UK*, no laser beams, forensics, helicopters or infrared, there was just you, a gun and a crotchety old guy in glasses and a granddad shirt. And as long as you got out of the bank and had a good start over the cops, you were sure to get away. If you don't believe me just try and name five famous robbers. You'll probably come up with Bonnie and Clyde, Dillinger, Butch and Sundance, Dick Turpin and Ronnie Biggs, all of whom (except Ronnie Biggs) enjoyed fame while they were still out and robbing. And if you can be famous, a robber and on the loose, then really, just how difficult can it be? There are no famous bank robbers any more, only the ones that get caught. Once people start to look for you these days, then for you those days become numbered. And that number's usually pretty small.

When it got to ten to nine I told him to go outside and bring his car off the drive and into the garage. I told him if he did any different, he'd never see Nina and Yasmin again. 'Don't make the mistake of thinking I'm not capable of it,' I said. 'Just because I've treated you half decently, it doesn't mean I'm not deadly serious.' Gus stared at me blankly for a few seconds as if he were trying to recall exactly what half decent treatment I was talking about, before going out and backing the car into the garage.

'Don't get out, don't look round,' I told him as I climbed into the back seat. 'Your rear view mirror, angle it away from back here.'

'But I won't be able to see,' he complained.

'Use your side mirrors.'

'You can't drive adequately with just side mirrors!'

'Oh for fuck's sake, this isn't your driving test. You only work ten minutes away. Now just go.'

Gus stuck his idiot-proof car into DRIVE and headed for the bank. It was hard for me to tell exactly where we were from my position in the back as I was ducked down low beneath the windows, but I could tell we were making good progress despite the fact that it had quickly become apparent that Gus was a painfully bad driver. Every couple of hundred yards he'd stamp on the brakes or swerve violently and say 'shit' to himself. He was forever apologising to everyone around him as well. 'Sorry,' he'd offer with a hand, then say, 'No, no, I said sorry.' I couldn't see what he was apologising for each time but it was starting to annoy me. One particular arsehole overtook Gus on a bend and called him a 'motherfucker' as he cut in. Again, Gus simply put a hand up and said 'sorry' as the bloke continued to give us the finger in his mirror.

'What are you apologising for, he cut you up?' I asked him.

'No, I should've let him in earlier. My fault.'

'You had right of way. You should've got after the bloke and called him a wanker.'

'Civility costs nothing,' was all he could offer up by way of an explanation.

When we got to the bank Gus parked in his usual spot and opened up shop. He knew what was expected of him and what was not, so all I could do now was keep my fingers crossed. If he decided to call the Old Bill, then I'd stand very little chance of escape. However, if he did that, he'd have to gamble on the fact that me and my accomplice were bluffing about the murder of his family and that I'd use their safe return to buy myself a lighter sentence; that's of course assuming I had any leeway with the other robber. We could've arranged it beforehand that if he didn't hear from me by such and such a time, he'd take the necessary steps on his own. It was a gamble. And the stakes couldn't get much higher, but looking at it from a point of view of priorities, your family were irreplaceable, regardless of how full of shit the gunmen were. If it was you, would you wager their safety against that of the firm's money (which was insured against this sort of thing anyway)?

The half-hour wait for Gus to reappear with the money was the longest half hour of my life (and of Gus's too probably), but when he did I felt like £1,000,000. Unfortunately, he'd only brought £125,000 with him so that had to do.

'Get in,' I told him.

'What? Can't you just take the money and let my wife go now?'

'I'm not going to leave you here with all these phones, am I? Now get in and drive.' This came as a bit of a blow to Gus who, I think, thought his part in all of this was over with the handing over of our cash.

'Please, just let us go,' he was pleading as we headed out of town and towards the country.

'I will, don't worry. Soon.'

We were driving up this little back-country lane when Gus smashed home the brakes, swerved into the verge and hit his horn. I was about to ask him what the fuck he was playing at when I heard the sound of another horn beeping back at him. I looked up from the back to see these two morons leaning out of their van and shouting at us. 'You shouldn't be on the fucking road you fucking poof,' one was saying, and 'Who are you fucking beeping?' the other was shouting. I couldn't see exactly what had happened but it looked like they'd just pulled out in front of Gus from a side turning and we all had ended up on a grass bank as a result. The driver got out and started gesticulating at us while Gus tried to defuse the situation with some 'sorry's.

'I've had enough of this,' I said and climbed out of the car.

'Who the fuck . . .' the driver started to say when I opened fire on his van. Bang! Bang! Bang! Bang! Windscreen, tyres, radiator, lights, I shot them to fuck as van man and his sidekick dived for cover. 'Jesus Christ!' he was shouting as I quick-stepped up to where he lay. I shoved the hot barrel against his neck and told him never to fuck with other drivers again, then climbed back into Gus's motor and suggested that he stepped on it.

'You can't do that!' Gus said flabbergasted.

'Well, you can't rob banks either, but that's never stopped me before.'

It was only another five minutes before we got to the old barn and I told him to pull in. I got out of the car, stuffed the money into the backpack I'd left for myself then wheeled out my getaway bike. 'Hands,' I said leaning through the driver's window and cuffed him to the wheel.

'Where are you going? Where's my family? You said you'd let them go when you had the money. Well you've got the money so where are they?' I held up a finger to silence him and pulled out my mobile (little tip for you: pay as you talk phones; no bills, no contract, no fuss, no way of tracing them back to you).

'Everything's rosy, let them go,' I said then stuck the phone back in my pocket. 'They're about ten miles from here being left in the middle of nowhere same as you. Another few hours and you'll all be back together and on the telly. Oh, almost forgot.' I leaned back in, pulled the car keys out of the ignition and threw them over a hedge. 'Bye Gus.'

'Wait, how will I get found?'

'Are you joking, I've just shot a van to bits half a mile from here. Every police car in town's going to be heading this way soon.' I gave him a wave and, out of his view, switched my mask for a crash helmet and roared off to divide the money up with Tom.

The robbery, especially the shooting bit of it, made all the papers and stayed there for a few days. Gus, Nina and Yasmin all talked of their ordeal and posed for the cameras until everyone got bored of possibly the dullest family ever to be robbed and went off to find the next big scoop. It wasn't until a week after the robbery that the balloon went up.

Wednesday morning, ten o'clock, my mobile rang.

'Chris, it's Tom. Listen, you've got to believe me it's not true.'

'What? What are you talking about? What's not true?'

'I swear to god, she's making it up, I never touched her.'

'Touched who? Tom, what's gone on?'

'Haven't you seen the papers or watched the news this morning?'

'No, I've just got up.'

'It's that little girl, she's saying I raped her.'

'What?'

'When I was alone with her and her mum. She's saying I fucked her in the car and I didn't Chris I swear, not after what happened, I didn't touch her, I promise.'

I couldn't believe what I was hearing. What the hell? I rushed to the front door, pulled the paper out of the letterbox and sure enough, there she was, front page and outrage all rolled into one. ROBBERY VICTIM RAPED was the headline and I quickly scanned the copy.

'Chris,' Tom was still saying. 'It's not true.' He was clearly shitting himself at the prospect of a brace of bullets in the back of the head.

'Shut up, just shut up, I'm reading.' When I'd finished the article I had to quickly make up my mind what to do. I'd meant what I'd said back at Gus's and would've gladly hunted down Tom and plugged him if it weren't for one thing. Yasmin was a week too late.

If she'd said she'd been raped the morning of the robbery then I would've known it was true, but why wait a week? There was only one reason I could think of. Physical evidence, there'd be precious little of it left after a week so no way to disprove that she hadn't been assaulted. I mean, it made for a completely paper-thin case but that didn't matter, Yasmin wasn't making her statement for the police's benefit, she was making it for mine. I'd promised in front of her that I'd murder Tom if he touched her, now she was testing that promise. I'm sure Yasmin thought he deserved it for what he did to her in the kitchen and for what he helped put her family through, but that was the only thing I was sure of. I couldn't be sure that he'd raped her. In fact, I just couldn't bring myself to believe it at all, not after the warning I'd given him. And Yasmin's failure to come forward earlier only stiffened my belief.

However, that wasn't the end of our problems. We now had every other legitimate crook in the south of England ready to turn us in if they heard even a whisper. Crooks don't like sex cases, they fucking hate them, especially amongst their own, and Yasmin's accusation was enough to get a few fingers pointing our way (the only time it's deemed alright for a villain to grass). This had to be nipped in the bud.

'You don't know me,' I told Tom. 'From this point onwards you don't know me. Forget me, forget my name, we've never met. This ever gets out and we're dead. You have no idea what you've done.'

'I didn't do it, I swear,' he insisted.

'Maybe not the rape, but your messing around with her beforehand was enough. That's where this has come from. I've a good mind to turn you in myself, if it wasn't for the fact that I'd get dragged down too. You're nothing. A fucking shit stick, and if you ever mention my name again, even to a priest, I'll take you out.'

'Chris, I . . .' but that was all I had to say and all I wanted to hear. I hung up the phone, went and had a pre-breakfast Scotch to calm my nerves, and tried to figure out why there were so many wankers in the world.

19. Priceless paranoia

There's a saying that's always stuck in my mind. 'Just because you're paranoid, doesn't mean they're not out to get you.' Fucking right. I'd always been paranoid, as far back as I could remember and probably even before that. Gavin always used to take the piss out of me and tell everyone that when I was born I poked my head out first to make sure the coast was clear. They'd all laugh at me and crack jokes at my expense but then I wasn't the one who ended up eating all the porridge was I?

It was just my way and recent events had hardly helped me to relax. The double hit on John Broad's merchandise, Sid going down, the rape allegation and all the shit I was getting off Heather; I was becoming a nervous wreck. The Heather situation was a particularly hard one to swallow. I'd tried phoning, but just lately I hadn't even managed to get past the answerphone. I knew she was there, listening to me on the machine, but there was nothing I could say to make her pick up. When did I go from being a lifeline in a sea of loneliness to someone to avoid? It made me feel very bitter, not least of all because it had been a secret affair so there was no-one I could talk to about it. Usually, when something like this went wrong you could at least be guaranteed a hundred and one different reasons as to why you're a fucking arsehole from everyone who's ever met you. But not this time. This time it was just me, a lot of unanswered questions and recorded messages.

There were days when it felt like the whole world was against me. And sometimes it felt like the stars were backing them up as well. If Heather, the one person in the world I'd trusted, could turn against me so easily, then . . . God I didn't know. I stopped thinking, it got too complicated. This seems like a strange thing to say, but I did, I stopped thinking almost completely. I used to ponder and mull over things in my mind all the time, but just lately I hadn't liked the conclusions I was coming to so I just stopped. I became kind of numb. I noticed everything, and I took everything in, I just didn't clutter up my mind any more with explanations. I concerned myself purely with the what, how, who, when and where, and left the why to another time.

It was this mindset that was to save my life. Well, this and fish and chips.

I'd always liked fish and chips as a kid. As a family we always had them on dad's payday or as a special treat and so whenever I'd be feeling down as an adult, I'd go and attempt to cheer myself up with fish and chips. Just lately, what with all my worries and Debbie being regularly AWOL for days on end, I'd been eating them so much that I'd stopped having to ask for what I wanted, the girl behind the counter would see me getting out of my car and have cod and chips wrapped up and waiting for me when I stepped through the door. This might seem nice and quaint in a small-town sort of way, but when you fancy giving haddock a go for a change it can start to annoy you. I ended up having to park my car round in the car park behind the parade of shops to try and pre-empt my increasingly bland cod and chips, and it was then that trouble tried to crash my dinner. Luckily, thanks to paranoia, he'd already RSVP'd me weeks before.

It was half-past seven and a mild Wednesday evening when I finally got to stroll out of the fish shop with haddock and chips under my arm. I'd parked around the back for the first time but, through force of habit, I half expected to see my car in its usual space out front. The sudden shock of finding my car missing set alarm bells ringing inside my head and it was a good full second before I realised my mistake. However, this second was enough to get my body pumped with adrenaline and my senses on maximum alert and, besides the car being missing, my instincts told me something wasn't right.

There were maybe four or five people milling about outside, your run of the mill evening crowd, looking in shop windows, walking to the pub, that sort of thing. One of them though, he wasn't run of the mill at all. I couldn't put my finger on precisely what it was about him, whether it was his posture or his eyes or his over-emphasised nonchalance, but he wasn't right. Not by a long way. It's a difficult thing to explain, particularly to plebs, but when you've been in the game a long time, sometimes you can just recognise a wolf in sheep's clothing. Of course, I'd felt this way about people before and been completely off the mark but, at the end of the day, it's better to let yourself be spooked than let yourself be suckered.

The wolf looked at me when he saw that I was staring. He smiled politely, took a couple of steps my way and, with his left hand, pulled out a warrant card. 'Excuse me sir, police. Can I have a quick word?'

You can have better than that, I thought to myself, you can have my fish and chips if you want. And before he was any closer I hurled my dinner straight into his face and made off in the other direction. There was no way on earth I was giving the Old Bill even a second of my time after recent events. I'd been involved with nothing but really bad shit the last few months, stuff that could bury me for life, and if the cops had finally caught up with me then only bad things would follow. As it turned out, all this became academic once the first shots whizzed past me and cracked into the bakery window.

After weeks of staring blankly at the wall, my brain's work-to-rule protest finally paid dividends. If I'd been a creature of thought at that particular moment I might've hesitated to try and figure out why a plain-clothes police officer was firing on a fleeing suspect and wonder if my brief could use this to my advantage to get my charges dropped if I gave myself up? As it was, acting purely on instinct, my brain simply informed me that a gun was being shot at me and that that was a dangerous thing. It didn't attempt to tackle the why, or who, or wonder if that was allowed, it just told me to get the fuck down and return fire. Dinner could wait. Therefore, this is what I did.

I dived in between the parked cars as a quick succession of rounds smacked the tarmac and kerb behind me and crawled for all I was worth until I found I'd clawed myself enough time to whip my automatic out and blast a couple of warning shots in the direction of the wolf.

The wolf's reply was swift and a lot more serious than

my challenge as all of a sudden the cars around me started disintegrating under a spray of submachine-gun fire. I know it seems daft and it just goes to show how little I was thinking, but until this moment I still assumed that it was the cops behind me. It took me another half a second after that to realise that the submachine-gun was fitted with a silencer and yet another half a second after that to realise that I wasted a whole fucking second sitting around listening to the sound of gunfire when I should've been crawling for my fucking life. I fired a volley of six shots through the car windscreens in the general direction of the closing wolf, but concentrated on keeping my head down so much that none of my efforts could even lay claim to being aimed.

I always hated being shot at.

It had only happened to me a few times in my life and it was never like it was on the telly. When you're Bruce Willis or Rambo or someone, the only shots that ever matter to you are the ones that actually hit you (always in the shoulder for some reason. I think Hollywood producers think it doesn't hurt if you're shot in the shoulder). In reality however, you hear, and sometimes even feel, the shots whizzing all around you and this disorientates the fuck out of you. It's actually an old special forces trick to fire bullets all around a target's head to cause him confusion and loss of equilibrium. This is true, I saw it in a documentary once. Personally though I never understood why, if they could aim around his head, they didn't just unload a clip in the bastard's face and let him never work it out? Not that any of this helped me out at this particular moment in time.

I fired four more shots, then slammed home another clip and wasted two more bullets killing the chip shop window before deciding that the only plan of action was to make a run for it. More machine-gun fire now ripped up the car next to me and the combination of lead on steel, frantic car alarms and my own thumping heart all but left me deaf.

'Jesus Christ!' I shouted as a figure stepped out from behind the long line of cars and sprayed a dozen bullets over my head. My return fire bought me long enough to leap to my feet and make a dash for the alleyway that led round the back of the shops. I didn't even look back when the brickwork around the alleyway entrance started exploding. I just hung my gun underneath my left armpit and let off five shots in the opposite direction to the one I was running.

Pain.

White-hot, searing pain slashed my lower back and almost caused me to stumble head over arse on the pavement to leave me a sitting duck, but somehow I managed the extra two strides that carried me to the semi-cover of the alleyway. My brain shouted at me to get up and run faster, but my back hurt like crazy. This however, was a good sign (relatively speaking). If you've been shot in the back and it doesn't hurt, that's when you've got problems. As it was, the bullet had merely skinned my Special K inch and a pinch to leave me bloody and sore. I rolled on to my side and fired one of my four remaining bullets out into the street to let the wolf know I still had a bite, then pulled myself up and ran for all I was worth down the short, dark alley. When I made it to the end and ducked around the corner without a shot being fired after me, I was more than a little surprised. I even started to think that maybe I'd tagged my pursuer with one of my noisemaker shots. My optimism didn't last long and as soon as I heard the clatter of something rolling down the alleyway I knew he was still after my blood. I looked down at my feet and for a good second just stood there gormlessly.

Well, it isn't everyday you get to see a real grenade now, is it?

'Fucking hell!!!!!!' I screamed diving head first into the tarmac as far away from the pineapple as I could possibly sling myself.

BANG, crash, tinkle, more car alarms, ringing in my ears. I had no idea those things were so loud. And yes, more pain. This time though, not from the grenade, but from the tarmac. When I lifted my head and blinked a few times, I saw that I'd left behind my two front teeth and a nice puddle of blood. Not that there was any time to worry about that at this moment as the next grenade landed a few feet from the first. It's funny isn't it, but sometimes a complete lack of professionalism can some-times save you. I did the stupidest thing when I saw the second grenade. I got up and ran. Any self-respecting army instructor will tell you if a grenade goes off and you escape injury, stay where you are if you see another one because chances are, you're in a safe position. Getting up and legging it is only going to offer the explosion a better target and very few people can outrun shrapnel. This is why I was stupid. However, what they don't teach you in the army is that some sneaky fuckers try and trick you with a dummy grenade so that when they run around the corner, you're lying face down in the middle of the road waiting for an explosion that's never going to come.

I couldn't tell you how disappointed the wolf was when he saw that I was far too stupid to be caught by clever tricks as I was far too busy trying to squeeze myself behind the toy shop's rubbish skip. What happened next though, literally handed me back my life. See, what I didn't know was that there was already someone hiding behind the skip. When the shooting started everyone legged it for cover in different directions and this poor sod probably thought he had the art of concealment all sewn up when he ducked down the alley and found himself a nice quiet corner in which to sit out the storm. I bet he couldn't believe it when the fighting got gradually nearer and nearer until eventually it was trying to get into his hiding place with him.

The wolf must've heard the commotion I was making because he opened up and emptied a full clip on to our position, reducing the big steel skip to Swiss cheese in no time at all. I didn't bother to return fire. I had three bullets left and if I had any hope of saving my life I had to wait for a clean shot. And that's exactly what the man behind the bin gave me. When the wolf's clip ran dry, the idiot decided to make a break for it, and what little luck he may have had with him, he left behind for me. The wolf reacted in the blink of an eye. He slammed home another clip and swung round and strafed the fleeing target with everything he had. In the fading light of the car park and the confusion of battle, I guess he must've thought it was me. It didn't matter, the important thing was that I had my clear shot and I took it. My first round smashed into his upper left arm and spun him round to face me. My second round I squeezed off too hastily and it did little more than buzz his ear, leaving me no option but to make the last one count.

I centred my aim on the wolf's chest but at the last moment shifted it slightly and plugged his right shoulder with a peach of a shot that dumped him helpless on the floor. I rushed over before he had a chance to do anything, but there was fuck all he could do. Both arms were now effectively useless and shock had set in to steal what little fight he had left.

I picked up the machine-gun and scanned the area for witnesses. There was no-one about, but that would soon change. I quickly went through his pockets and found a small arsenal: guns, knives, ammunition, I almost felt flattered he thought he needed to bring all this along to take me on. He also had a mobile phone, a set of keys and a wallet containing nothing but a passport photo of some woman, but no papers or documents or anything. I pocketed the two ammunition clips for the machine-gun and the wallet, then looked down at my assassin.

'Please,' the wolf coughed, 'my wallet.' I retrieved the wallet from my pocket and pulled out the picture of the woman.

'You want this?' I asked him and he managed a nod. I stuffed the picture in his top pocket and trained the gun on his face. 'Who sent you? Was it John Broad?' For some reason this made the wolf smile and he shook his head.

'Dead,' he said.

'Yes, you are, but how you go is up to you, quick and easy or slow and painful. So we'll try again, who sent you?' The name I was dreading to hear was that of my brother's, which was more than possible if Gavin had found out about me and Heather. It wasn't, however, the name the wolf managed to spit out.

'Your wife,' he whispered.

'My wife! Debbie!' I exclaimed in disbelief, though it got even more incredible than that.

'And a fat man,' added the wolf.

'A fat man?' I said and thought about all the fat men I knew before the image of Alan riding my wife over the dining room table presented itself before me. 'I don't believe it,' was all I could utter. I looked back down at the wolf, who was staring off into oblivion, and shook him back to earth. 'Are you sure it was my wife?'

'Your wife,' was all he could reply then he looked away again. 'Adelaide,' he whispered.

'My wife's not called Adelaide,' I told him, knowing there had been a mistake. He looked up at me and shook his head in a way that suggested he couldn't believe I'd managed to get the better of him.

'No,' he spluttered, and if he'd had the strength to call me a fucking moron I think he probably would have. 'Mine is.'

'Oh,' I replied, then switched his lights out forever.

I had to move and I had to move quick. I could hear the first of the sirens off in the distance and knew I had probably forty-five seconds before we were all here, together. I looked at my car and knew it was pointless taking it. By the time I found the keys, got it started and under way, the police would already be here, so I forgot about going out the front and looked to the back instead. The car park backed onto the back gardens of a large residential estate and nothing more substantial than a six-foot fence blocked my path, which I cleared with ease. The windows of every house were crammed tight with a thousand beady eyes and only disappeared when I fired an arc of lead over the tops of the chimneys. I ran through to the front of the street and was immediately reminded of the jubilee. The whole fucking estate and his wife were out and milling around and asking each other what all the noise was. Christ, didn't anyone stay indoors when they heard gunfire any more? They all stared at me blankly when I ran out into the street.

'Ooh look, he's got a gun,' several of them pointed out to each other. 'I told you it was shooting.' *News at*

Ten probably never had it so easy. Neither had the police come to that.

My cover was well and truly blown. Debbie might not have killed me, I remember thinking as I ran past the massed ranks of excited onlookers, covered in blood and carrying a submachine-gun. But one thing's for sure, she's finished me in this town for good.

20. Alan, you gullible bastard!

God knows how I got away from the area without getting picked up. Everyone in the street I ran through must've all been so busy doing their hair for the TV cameras that they forgot to call the police. When I got to the main T-junction at the end of the estate I managed to flag down a car and ordered the occupant out. I told him to sling his hook, which he did when he saw the gun, then climbed in to discover the git had taken his keys with him. 'Come back here you bastard!' I shouted after him but he had a good head start on me. I took my frustration out on his windscreen and gave it a quick spray with the gun then redirected the barrel on the road when the next car happened along.

'Oh no you don't,' I said when the guy started to get out. 'Stay in the motor. You're fucking driving.'

'But I'm married,' he said, pleading to my better side.

'I'm very happy for you. Now shut up and get back in.'

I kept down out of sight in the back and got him to head for the other side of town. It was quieter a few miles away and after locking the handsome groom in his own boot, I hijacked another vehicle, this time without the benefit of the entire Neighbourhood Watch doing precisely that. White van man who gave me my next lift proved to be perfect and got me to London within an hour of the last shot fired. I rewarded him with a big lump on the head and half a night tied up in his own motor.

We'd listened to the news on the radio on the way down. Most of the details were sketchy but the reporter had been able to confirm that three people were known to have been killed, which left me wondering if the bullet responsible for that third victim had been one of mine or one of the wolf's that had gone astray. The ride had also given me time to think about what he'd told me but I still couldn't believe it. Debbie? Debbie had hired someone to have me killed? That fucking bitch. Regrettably it started to make more and more sense though. Debbie hated her existence with me out in the sticks, she missed the high life, the champagne and the nightclubs. She would've probably just left me had there not been one little problem – she didn't have two bank accounts to rub together. She was skint. Everything she had, I'd given her, even her tits. Sure she was free to leave any time she wanted but where was there to go? Now that her looks had started to fade and she'd lost a good chunk of the youth that marked dizziness in a girl's plus column, she wasn't going to find anyone as well off as me to look after her and she knew it. I would've thought she might've tried to blackmail a big kiss-off out of me first but then I guess she figured she could get it all if I was out of the way. And this is where Alan came in. She didn't have the wherewithal to buy a contract with what little she had put aside so I guess she had Alan front the money, the scheming little cow. All she had to do was bounce him around the walls of our bedroom a few times and he'd do anything that fell from her lying lips. I was actually quite relieved at this, believe it or not, that she wasn't banging him out of lust. Any woman I'd driven away into the arms of a pork chop like that I think deserved to see me six foot under.

There was, however, one thing she hadn't allowed for. In involving Alan in her little web of murder and deceit she'd exposed her soft underbelly, in more ways than one. See, Alan wasn't a career criminal, he was a pleb, and therefore an easy mark to panic into making a mistake. As I sat in the back of that van I wondered what I should do about them. Killing them wasn't really an option any more. My name was about to go up on more noticeboards than Bill Posters so I doubted I'd be able to get near the pair of them even if I wanted to. But I didn't anyway. They might've tried to have me killed, but death for them would've been too easy. Particularly for Alan. There were much better ways to turn his screw. So, after I left van man out for the count, I went and headed for the nearest Dixons.

'It's done,' I mumbled into my new mobile.

'It's done!' Alan hyperventilated on hearing this. 'He's dead?'

'Seen the news?' I asked.

'Yes, but they didn't give any names, so I didn't know if you'd got Chris.' You fat bastard. How dare you think you can kill me, I wanted to say but bit my lip. Up until this moment, I still hadn't been a hundred per cent certain the wolf had spoken the truth and listening to it being confirmed for me by one of the perpetrators was a bitter pill to swallow.

'He's dead,' I told him.

'Oh God, okay, alright. I'm okay. Just give me a

moment.' It was a few more seconds before the obvious finally occurred to Alan. 'Wait a minute, why are you phoning me? I thought you were never meant to call us at home? What do you want?'

'There's a problem,' I growled down the phone line.

'What?' he demanded.

'You're a fucking idiot,' I muttered to myself, clamping my hand over the receiver and shaking my head.

'What? I didn't hear you. You'll have to speak up.'

'I need more money,' I said into the phone.

'More money! What for?'

'Complications. I need more money.'

'What do you mean? How much do you want?' Alan was walking straight into my trap. If my idea was to succeed I needed the full details of the entire contract. How much was paid. Where he got the money from. Who he paid it to. Stuff like that. The difficulty was though, Alan was no mug. He'd spot an ambush as soon as one was laid. He was a very clever man.

Only kidding. This was easier than winding up kids.

'I need the same again,' I told him.

'Another £7,000!'

'£7,000?' I couldn't help blurting out. Frankly I was insulted. Was that really how much my life was worth? Jesus Christ, talk about the bargain basement. 'Yes, £7,000.'

'Please, I can't raise that sort of money again just like that. I'm worried my boss will check the books and find out as it is, but another £7,000, that'll definitely be missed. I can't.'

'Just do it,' I snapped at him. 'You've got two days. Then I want the money delivered to the same place as before. You got it?'

'Please try to understand . . .' Alan was attempting to say but I cut him off.

'YOU GOT IT?'

'Yes, I've got it. Sorry.'

'Don't fuck with me or you will be sorry.'

'Please, I just meant . . .'

'I know what you just meant and I won't be fucked with. Now, tell me, what are you going to do in two days' time?'

'Get you the money,' he repeated parrot-fashion.

'And where are you going to take it?'

'The same place as before.'

'Which was?'

'The Lyric in Soho.'

'And give it to who?'

'And give it to . . .' suddenly I heard the blood drain from Alan's face. 'Wait, who is this?'

I allowed myself a chuckle then reverted back to my own voice. 'Enjoy prison you motherfucker.'

'Oh my . . .!' was all I heard before the line went dead. I switched off the tape recorder, unstuck the little sucker-cup microphone and then spent one or two pleasant moments reflecting on how thick some people were, before getting on with things.

Winston Churchill used to come out with some good one-liners in his day and one of my favourites was particularly pertinent to my situation. When he was asked in 1941 how he could even think of striking up an alliance with Russia (people seem to forget that Russia started the war on Germany's side before coming over to the good guys) he replied: 'Sir, if Hitler declared war on Hell, I'd give the devil a favourable reference.' Funny man, hey!

I couldn't help remembering this as I sat in Sid's empty flat and phoned DS Evans on the mobile the next day.

'Where are you?' was the first pointless question he asked me.

'All over the fucking telly and newspapers, that's where. I'm famous.'

'You've got no hope, you do know that don't you? You haven't got a prayer. In fact, I can almost guarantee you we'll have you banged up before the end of the day.'

'You want to put your money where your mouth is? £20 says you don't.'

'I wouldn't touch your money in a million years,' he replied with disgust.

'You mean earn it,' I goaded him back.

'Give yourself up Benson, it'll be easier in the long run.'

'Can't do that Sergeant, might as well go for broke. Anyway, that's not why I'm calling,' I said getting to the point. 'I've sent you a package, you should've got it by now.' There was a brief pause and I heard Evans shout around the office if a package had come for him. Someone pointed out that it was on his desk, underneath his McDonald's breakfast tray and then someone else laughed.

'I've got it,' he said and then there was another pause while he tore it open. 'It's a little tape,' he told me.

'I know, I fucking sent it to you. It goes in a little tape recorder, have you got one there?'

'I'll find one. What's on it?'

'I was set up. That business from the other day, it was a hit and I was the target. The tape's evidence.'

'Who ordered the hit?' Evans asked.

'My wife and porky fat neighbour, they were having an affair,' I told him. 'Oi, don't fucking laugh, I'm giving you two perfectly good convictions on a plate. All you've got to do is nick them and look good.'

'Sorry about that Benson, go on.'

'The neighbour you'll hear on the tape, Alan Robinson, and the other one's me pretending to be the hitman. You'll probably call it entrapment but it'll give you enough to go on. I shouldn't think you'll have too many problems getting more out of him.'

'Why are you giving me this, Chris? Why aren't you going after them yourself?'

'Come on, that ain't my style and you know it. Whatever else I am, I'm not a killer,' I told him though, if the whole truth were ever to be uncovered, I think folks would say I'd killed a lot of people for someone who wasn't a killer.

'I beg to differ,' Evans said. 'You did a pretty good impression of it with Sunny Jim.'

'That was self-defence. Clear-cut. I had no choice. In fact, I'd probably even get let off if it ever went to court.' In a pig's eye I would. I'd executed a man at point-blank range as he lay defenceless on the ground and contributed to the deaths of two passers-by as I blasted away with my illegal handgun. And that's not even taking into consideration all the other shit that would float to the surface from other jobs after I was tucked away behind bars. I'd like to meet the barrister who could've got me a suspended sentence out of that little lot.

'Besides,' I told Evans, 'killing them would be letting them off lightly. I want them to wake up and weep over what they tried to do to me every morning for the next ten years. I want them to remember me their whole lives. I want my payback in daily instalments.'

This was true, and my driving motivation. Prison would destroy Debbie and Alan in a way that death could never hope to. It would rob them of the things they held most precious, yet keep them around to appreciate it. It would be like death for them, but a living death and that's the worst kind. Prison would be particularly rough on Debbie, robbing her of her remaining youth and good looks and the fun life they had brought her. It would be unbearable for her, particularly if the sentence was a long one as it was bound to be (they might not have killed me but several other innocent people died because of their actions). As for Alan, Alan would lose the lot. His wife and kids would go the minute it came to light he'd been unfaithful. His house, job and standing would disappear along with his liberty. And best of all, that pompous, self-assured, smug righteousness that Alan loved to project to all others would shrivel up and vanish the first time he had his creamy round arse set upon in the showers.

It's true what they say, I guess, every cloud has a silver lining.

'I've sworn out a statement and left it with my brief. Just get them for me,' I said to Evans.

'Don't worry, we'll look into this. Now what about you?'

'What about me?'

'Give yourself up Chris, every armed police officer in the country is ready to take you down. Don't lose your life trying to be a hero.'

'Life,' I said. 'It's overrated.'

21. Me against the world

You ever have those days where you feel like the whole world is out to get you? Well let me tell you this, you don't know what you're talking about. I've been there, I know what it's really like.

Your workmates leaving your sandwiches on a sunny windowsill for a joke or waking up on your birthday to find only bills on your front doormat constitute neither the persecution or population levels required to rightfully claim that the majority of the citizens of the planet earth are on your case. Alright, things might not have been that bad for me, but after my little run in with the wolf I certainly had to give most people in Britain a wide berth, which was exactly what I planned to do. South America suddenly looked like my kind of continent and, thanks to some forward planning, I already had enough dodgy documents and a nice little diamond nest egg to get me there and set me up. For a few years at least. I might've gone out of my mind on the beaches of Greece while I was down there with Debbie, but given the choice I'd take that over twenty in the Scrubs any day of the week.

The only problem was, I didn't have my escape kit with me, it was back at the house in a secret safe set in the concrete floor in the cupboard underneath the stairs (I also kept all the mops and brooms and cleaning stuff in this cupboard to keep Debbie away from it). This made things very difficult. My house was bound to have been staked out, in case I developed some sort of brain damage and tried to pop back for my golf clubs, so I was stuck. I needed my stuff to escape, but I couldn't get it without getting caught. And the longer I stayed in the country dithering over what to do, the more likely it was that Evans would come knocking on my door, or should I say, come *back* knocking on my door. I'd been holed up at Sid's place the last week, tiptoeing around in the dark by night, twiddling my thumbs up in the loft by day. The Old Bill had been around twice already, looking through the rubbish, checking the reading on the electric meter, the usual sort of stuff to see if anyone was home. I wondered if they had a warrant to do this and if Sid knew they were snooping around his place. I also wondered if Sid had stashed his escape fund somewhere in his house and spent some time doing a bit of snooping of my own, but I never found it.

No, the only chance I had of getting out of this mess was if someone went to my house and collected my kit for me. And the sooner the better. I didn't know how much longer I could go on crapping in carrier bags and dropping them in the bins of twenty-four-hour garages at three in the morning whilst shopping for cold Cornish pasties and crisps.

But who?

It wasn't much of a choice. There was only one person I trusted enough not to run off with the diamonds or turn me into the police. The trouble was though she wasn't answering my phone calls and mine wasn't the sort of message you could leave on a machine. I was left with no option, I had to go and speak to her in person. I knew it was risky, but it was the lesser of two evils.

Other than a few silent phone calls there'd been no contact between us and, so I hoped, there'd not be much reason for Evans to assume there would be. Round-the-clock surveillance is fortunately a very expensive business and there were more important people to watch than the sister-in-law. She would've been turned over a few times, had the house ripped apart, maybe even been followed to the shops and back for a few days, but it was doubtful the men with the pips could've made available enough funds to keep the cameras pointed at Heather for more than a week. I gave it another three days just to be sure though before I paid her a careful visit.

Heather left the house with Bobby and Barry at 8.30 a.m. and walked them to school. Uncharitable of me to say this but I couldn't help thinking that at seven and eight (or were they now eight and nine?) the boys were a little old to still be hanging on the apron strings like this. I'd walked to school under my own steam when I was just six, which proved I was clearly harder than my young nephews.

She dropped them off at the school gates at 8.50 a.m. and hurried on to her job at the bakery in the shopping centre. Heather was in a world of her own and didn't notice me board the bus behind her and take the back seat. My new short crop, beard and glasses helped blend me into the background and gave me a comfortable degree of anonymity.

The short bus ride ended by the Post Office and soon we were darting along through the swell of early morning consumers. It wasn't massively crowded but there were certainly enough people about to disguise a quick approach, so I stepped up my pace and caught her up just before she reached the bakery.

'Don't look round and keep walking,' I told her quietly when I got up alongside her. Naturally she stopped and turned to face me.

'Chris?' she said.

'For fuck's sake Heather, point why don't you? Come on let's move!'

'What do you want?' she asked when she finally got her legs going.

'I'm in trouble.'

'Well, what do you want me to do about it?' she said a little too quickly for my liking.

'I want you to fucking help me, what do you think I want?'

'I can't help you, I've got to go to work,' she replied. I thought she was joking for a moment until I turned round and saw her looking at her watch.

'Fuck work.'

'That's easy for you to say but I need this job.'

'What are you talking about? I'm looking at life in prison and you can't help me because you might lose your £3 an hour job selling buns? Heather, for crying out loud.'

'I can't get involved, I've got the boys to think about.'

'Look, I'm not asking you to kill someone for me, all I want you to do is go to my house and pick something up for me.'

'I can't,' she said shaking her head. 'Please, just leave me alone and stay away from me.'

'Do this one thing for me and I promise you'll never see me again.'

'I'm sorry, I've got to go, I haven't got time for this,'

she said and started to wander back towards the bakery. I ran after her and grabbed her sharply by the elbow.

'What's this all about?'

'What's what all about?' she asked.

'Heather, what are you playing at? Do you want me to go down for this?'

'Please Chris, just try to understand. I don't ever want to see you again. I don't want anything to do with you any more. I just want to get on with my own life and be left alone.'

'No, you try and understand, if you don't help me I'm as good as dead. I'm desperate. I wouldn't have asked if I wasn't.'

'I'm sorry, you'll just have to ask someone else, I can't help you.'

'Jesus . . .!'

'If I'm even seen talking to you, I could go to prison and have my children taken away from me, lose my husband, everything, and that's not going to happen.'

A row in the middle of a shopping centre is a difficult thing to keep to yourselves, no matter how quiet you think you're being, and inevitably people started to stare and nudge their mates. I knew it wouldn't be too long before someone recognised me.

'Please Heather, you're my only hope.'

'Sorry Chris, I can't.'

'Why? Just give me one good reason.'

'I've got to be selfish from now on. I can't get involved in anyone else's problems, I've got enough of my own. Now let go of my arm.'

'Heather, I'm dead if you don't.'

'That's not my problem.'

'You fucking little bitch!' I spat out in disgust. 'All

the things I've done for you since Gavin went away and you can't do this one pissy little favour for me.'

'Hey, I don't owe you anything. I never asked you for your help and I just wish to God you'd left me by myself.' She tried snatching her arm away from me but I held tight.

'Just tell me why? What did I do to make you hate me so much?'

'If you don't let go of me I'll scream.'

'Heather, please. After all we've been through, please.'

'Just forget about it, it never happened. There is no "we" any more, there's only me. Me, Bobby and Barry. Now go.' I looked deep into her eyes and saw the tears ready to spill out but still didn't understand. Had Gavin found out? Had the police put the frighteners on her? Did she really want to see me locked away for life? What was it? I was stuck for words. I was never very good with them in the first place but I didn't know how to put the same question a dozen different ways.

Finally deep frustration got the better of me and I pulled out my gun and stuck it in her face. 'You fucking cunt!' I shouted with rage, totally oblivious to the screaming crowd that was now running in all directions.

'Don't Chris, don't,' she said, surprisingly calmly. I didn't know what I was doing or what I was hoping for. I guess all my anger and bitterness from my dealings with Heather finally caught up with me in this one moment and what I really wanted was for her to fall to the floor and beg for my forgiveness. It was bloody annoying when she didn't.

'I fucking loved you,' I heard myself say, 'and this is what I get.'

'I can't help you,' Heather replied as she stared down the barrel of my gun.

'Just tell me why.'

'You'd better go.'

I was beyond thinking at this stage. I felt as close to death without being physically injured as it's possible to feel. Despite all other considerations and everything else that had gone on between us, I'd been certain Heather would help me when I needed her most. She had to, she was all I had. The kids thing, that was just an excuse, there were other factors at work here, I just couldn't figure out what they could be. I never really got time to. Before I could say another thing I heard the patter of massive feet and looked round to see half a dozen police running my way.

I turned back to Heather for one last look, tried to think of something poignant and gut-wrenching to leave her with, but when I couldn't come up with anything quick enough, I just settled for pushing her to the ground by the face.

'Stop police!' the shout went out. I wondered if they knew who I was or if they were just chasing me because I had a gun. Either way, I found it slightly inconvenient and so turned and fired several shots over their heads causing them to drop to the floor and fill their pants. After that it wasn't too difficult car-jacking to safety and I arrived back at Sid's sometime after dark.

I don't know why Heather turned her back on me like that. I could take a guess, I have a dozen different theories, but it would all just be speculation and of no real help to me whatsoever. The truth is, unlike on telly, we don't get an explanation at the end of the show and so rarely ever discover why some people react completely differently to the way we expect them to. This was one of the reasons why real life wasn't as good as the telly. I tortured myself trying to come up with the answers all the next day until I finally realised that, in the scheme of things, it wasn't important. What was, was the fact that I was back to square one. I still didn't have my escape kit and, rather dishearteningly, I'd used up all the people in the world I trusted.

This was the worst, the moment when I felt completely alone.

I sat down and examined my life and it finally came home to me what Heather had said all those months ago – I didn't have any friends. There was no-one I could turn to. I'd always had Gavin and Heather, and I guess at a push Debbie, but suddenly I had no-one. My mum and dad were still about, but would've turned me in as soon as looked at me and believed it was the right thing to do. I knew quite a lot of people, it was true, but they all fell into one of two categories: upright honest citizens (i.e. my neighbours) or thieves, neither of which you really want to call on to pick up a small fortune in diamonds for you when you're on the run from the law.

In the end I figured I had no choice, I had to take a chance, so I called Gordon O'Riley to see if he'd be willing to pick up my stuff and arrange a safe route out of the country in exchange for a healthy cut. Gordon agreed and sent one of his burglars along to empty my safe for me, but the police were there and waiting and picked him up the second he stepped out of the door (a bit stupid in my opinion. I would've followed him but I suppose after almost two weeks they needed a body to show for their efforts). All credit to the burglar who didn't talk but, as far as I could see, the game was up. I'd lost my ticket out and it was only a matter of time before they got to me.

I phoned Gordon one last time to see if he could at least get me a passport in exchange for a machine-gun but Gordon made me an altogether better offer. A job – a very big job.

Game on.

22. Broad ideas

'Alright then, that's agreed, Tom, you and Chris go in through the back way, me and Jim'll take the front. Now, some of the lads will have shooters so you'll have to be on your toes and get them on the deck a bit lively. Don't stand for any shit, but at the same time, don't go pulling the fucking trigger unless you can help it. I really don't want any killing. Clear?'

Everyone said 'yes' 'yep' 'okay' 'no problem' and suchlike, only Tom said 'clear' back.

'How many are we expecting?' Jim asked Gordon, though Gordon left this for Eddie to answer.

'There could be about twenty . . .'

'Twenty! Fucking hell!' Tom blurted out not giving Eddie a chance to finish. 'You've got to be joking or what?'

'Oi, put a fucking sock in it for a minute will you, I'm talking here.' Eddie Sinton, or Handsome Eddie as he was known around town because of his phenomenally bad looks, was one of John Broad's men. He'd spent most of the last ten years delivering packages, dropping off money, passing on messages, that sort of thing, but now he'd seen his chance. Broad was gone. Dead. And so was half of his gang. No-one quite knew how but there'd been a big shoot-out down at the docks just two weeks back and Broad and his boys had come away with the wrong result, which must've been what the wolf had mentioned. No-one knew what had gone down or who was responsible so a kind of shock set in where everyone suddenly found themselves waiting for someone else to make the next move so everyone could figure out whose side everyone was on. Eddie decided to make that move.

Sam Broad, John's son, had quickly stepped into the fray to try and pick up his old man's reins, but Sam was hopelessly inexperienced and it was only a matter of time before he was muscled out of the way by proper people. This meant we had to strike quickly. If we didn't someone else would. There was £8 million in cash waiting for whoever got their arse into gear first.

The £8 million was drug money. Well, it was all set to be drug money but John had had the courtesy to die before the deal had gone through and Sam was too shit scared to make a move in case he ended up like his dad, so it was just sat there, in the safe, in John's nightclub. Eddie had seen it. He'd even helped set up the deal with some South Americans, but now it was up for grabs.

The King is dead! So let's all nick his cash.

Eddie had taken the plan to O'Riley and O'Riley had come up with the crew, though to be honest, from what I could see they were all wankers. O'Riley and his mates were small-time villains with small-time experience. They might've been willing to have a crack at it but it was highly unlikely they'd have the know-it-all to pull it off. Enter me and my ridiculously high share of the loot demand. I'd convinced Gordon to leave it to me to plan and co-ordinate the whole affair in exchange for twice as much as everyone else was getting.

'You can't put a price tag on experience,' I'd told him and promptly put a price tag of £1 million on my experience. Gordon mulled it over for a bit before agreeing much too quickly for my liking, my £1 million experience telling me to watch my fucking back after the job.

There were seven of us in all: me, Gordon, Eddie, Tom Fincham – my little sex case friend, which I wasn't happy about – Jim Jackson, and two drivers, Ben something and Gary something, that Gordon knew from his rally days. Gordon had already conscripted them all by the time I arrived, so I was stuck with them and couldn't drop anyone for fear of word getting out.

Jim was a stick-up artist who knew no world beyond petrol stations and corner shops. 'Little tip,' he'd told me before I'd even finished shaking his hand. 'If ever you're going to do over a Paki shop and you don't want to look too conspicuous, stand by the dirty mags and make it look like you want to buy one. Everyone always looks a bit dodgy hanging around by the wank mags so matey'll just think you're waiting for the shop to empty so you can quickly pay for your porn, though really you're hanging for everyone to fuck off so you can rob him.'

'I'm just about to nick £8 million, I think most Paki shops'll be safe from me after tomorrow,' I replied.

The drivers, Gordon assured me, were straight out of the top drawer and for once I was inclined to agree with him. That's where I kept my pants. 'You'll have no problem with these boys,' he'd promised. 'These two can outpace and out-manoeuvre anything on four wheels,' which was exactly where my problem was. Over-confidence was a dangerous thing. I had to remind them that there wasn't a prize for the first one to get back to the hideout after the job. They both agreed and acted all hurt at the suggestion but still looked like they were champing at the bit to race each other to fiery deaths.

'Like I was saying before I was so rudely interrupted,' Eddie continued, 'there'll probably be about twenty of them, though most will be bar staff or cleaners getting the club ready for the evening. Only maybe three or four of them, tops, will have guns or try to give you any grief. Now you can handle three or four of them, can't you? They're not expecting you so you shouldn't have any problems.'

'I was just saying, you know, twenty is a lot of people,' Tom said giving us all a 'just saying' shrug.

'It's £8 million, you expect them to leave it on the fucking doorstep for us stuffed in milk bottles?' Gordon said. 'We've got to earn it. That's why we've got a plan.'

'I was just saying . . .' Tom continued to just say.

'Button it!' Gordon ordered. 'Right, what's next?'

'CCTV,' I told them all. 'Eddie, you've got to knock it out so we can approach from the back without being seen. You know how?' Eddie said he didn't, which made me grateful for a little professional honesty. There was nothing worse than someone fucking up a job just because he was too much of a big man to admit that he wasn't the last word in all things criminal. 'It's easy,' I told him, 'all you've got to do is stop the tape in the recorders, rewind it back a bit and press play.'

'How far back?'

'Well, I don't know, use your loaf. I mean, we're doing it just after lunch so don't rewind it back to the middle of the fucking night or nothing, just an hour or two.'

'But what if it's raining in the morning, then sunny after lunch,' Jim asked.

'Then your garden will come up lovely, just fucking shut up will ya,' Gordon said. 'Like the man says, just use your loaf.'

'Just remember to grab the tapes and shoot up the machine whoever does the security booth. I don't want any of my boys wondering why your van wasn't captured on video,' Eddie said.

'Don't worry, we will,' I told him. 'Just do your bit and we'll do ours. Right, cars . . .'

'Oh wait, almost forgot. I've got these,' Gordon said and, reaching into his pocket, he pulled out two model cars and plonked them down on to the nightclub layout plan. We all looked at them for a moment before Gary gave the question we were all thinking a voice.

'Gordon, did you go out and get the toys to match the cars or the cars to match the toys?'

'Hey, let's just . . .' Gordon started to say but was stopped in his tracks when we all burst out laughing.

'No, it's just that you've actually got a model of a Jag and a model of a Toyota van, the exact same motors we've got lined up for the job, and I just wanted to know if you went out to the toy shop and actually spent time looking through the rack for those specific toys.'

'A little accuracy, what's there to piss yourselves about. It's the little details that count,' Gordon said, clearly a little embarrassed by it all.

'Did you? Gordon, did you?' Ben asked, joining in. By this stage, even Eddie, a notorious sour-faced misery, was laughing at Gordon.

'You wanker!' Eddie said, taking it just that bit too far.

'Can we just get on,' Gordon snapped. 'This ain't a

fucking playground. We've got work to consider. Right, Gary, you're driving the van with Chris and Tom in it,' he said and rolled over to the back exit.

'Broom, broooom, broom!' Ben chuckled as he did so, making us all crack up again.

'Oh, you bunch of cunts,' Gordon moaned and walked off for a fag. It wasn't until later that he confided in me that he'd bought a 99p pack of little plastic soldiers from the shop as well. 'I'm fucking glad I didn't get those out,' he said. 'Don't you do things like that when you're planning jobs then?' he asked.

'What, make an idiot of myself! No, I try not to if I can help it.'

After a short break we went over the plan again until we knew it all backwards. Two of us in the front, two of us in the back, Eddie would have the doors unlocked and waiting for us. Everyone would get rounded up and herded on to the dance floor (including Eddie), Gordon and Jim would look after them while me and Tom went for the safe.

'Remember, it's not the company safe in the office. That's just got all the nightclub takings in it. It's in a second safe hidden in his en-suite behind the shower,' Eddie reminded us. 'That's where all his dodgy stuff is. Hardly anyone knows about it but I've seen it.'

'Then everyone'll know it was you that tipped us the wink,' Gordon said.

'No, only John knew I knew and if he was still about I wouldn't dream of this, but he ain't so it's alright.'

'And Sam definitely knows the combination?'

'Yeah, of course he does, no worries.'

'Good, because we don't want to have to cut his fingers off for nothing.'

'The boy's too fond of picking his nose to hold out

for more than two or three of them,' Eddie assured us and stuck a finger up his nose by way of a practical demonstration.

'Right, keypad codes for all the interior doors are the same combination; four six two three. Repeat it to yourself a few times and don't forget it. What else?'

'Accent,' Gordon said.

'Yes, accents. We'd rather none of Broad's men picked us out as Londoners so if you have to speak, put on a Paddy accent, Northern Ireland alright. You know, sort of "Git dyine yi fock'n bast'd".'

'I didn't understand a word of that,' Jim said. 'What did you just say?'

'Get down you fucking bastard,' I said. 'Listen. "Git dyine yi fock'n bast'd".' Jim and Gary just shrugged their shoulders and shook their heads.

'That didn't sound Paddy to me,' Gary said.

'I ain't going for a part in *Father Ted*, am I? It don't matter if it ain't spot on just so as it disguises my real accent.'

'Do it again,' Tom said.

'Git dyine yi fock'n bast'd.'

'What part of Ireland you meant to be from, Bombay or something? You sound like a Paki.'

'Well you give it a fucking go then Sir John Gielgud, see how much cop you are.'

Cue six assorted Indian accents.

'Can't we pretend we're Tamil Tigers instead,' Gordon quipped.

'Git dyine yi fock'n bast'd,' I said again to show them that I was doing a Paddy accent.

'Yeah and I'll have pilau rice and two poppadoms with mine thanks,' Tom said. 'Come on, shall we call it a night, I'm busting for a pint.'

'Yeah, alright. Big day tomorrow so don't piss it up too much. Couple of beers and an early night,' I told them. 'And watch those mouths. Don't go talking to any strangers,' I added as an afterthought.

'Yes mum,' Gary said as he headed for the door. Him, Tom, Jim and Ben all filed out and went off in search of a good time. I could never understand this; how, twenty-four hours before a job, some blokes could put it all on the back burner and go out as though tomorrow was just another day. What did they need outside stimulation for? Wasn't pulling a robbery stimulating enough? I didn't get it. I'd never got it. For me the job was everything. I'd spend the night poring over the plans, picturing in my mind every eventuality, every angle. I'd clean my weapon, check that it fired cleanly, feel its weight in my hands and rehearse exactly what I would say to the person looking down the other end of it. I'd get so psyched up preparing myself for the work the next day that I'd find it impossible to get even a wink of sleep.

God, I loved it.

How could you not? For me, there was no other good time. The job itself was as good as it got; the planning, the preparation, the conspiracy, the execution, everything else in life paled into insignificance beside this. Why would anyone *not* want to rob stuff? They wouldn't. I've said it before and I'll say it again. If I could guarantee a person that he could walk into a bank, shove a gun in someone's face and walk out with £50,000, and not get caught and not hurt anyone, there ain't a bloke in the whole of Britain who wouldn't do it. The only thing stopping everyone from doing just that was bottle. Something I had no shortage of. Actually, no, that's not true. I got as nervous as the next bloke to be honest, but again, that was just part of the whole package. Wouldn't be nearly as much fun if you didn't shit it a little bit about what sort of risk you were running. And, you wouldn't be human. Fear was nature's way of telling you to keep your fucking head down.

Was I really going to give it all up to go live on a beach?

I couldn't. No way. I'd miss the life too much. Sitting around on my backside, counting my money. That wouldn't be living, I'd go out of my mind in six months, just as I had done in Greece and just as I would if I was banged up with Gavin. I couldn't give it up. All I needed was a break, maybe even a new face, just till the shit died down. Just till it was safe to resurface.

Debbie and Alan were already behind bars, Evans had been as good as his word (and he owed me £20, the 'not-nicking-me-by-the-end-of-the-day' wanker), Eddie had already commented on as much after reading the story in the paper.

'Was your wife really shagging that fat geezer?' he'd asked.

'Yes.'

'Really,' he'd smiled. 'That fat bloke?'

'Yes really.'

'Jesus. A fat man shagging your wife!'

'And your point here is?'

'No, no, nothing. I'm not saying anything,' he was making a point of saying. 'It's just . . .'

'Yes?'

'Well, it's just that, he was a bit fat, wasn't he? And he was shagging your wife.' I almost laughed, he was trying to get a rise out of me but it wasn't going to happen. I had no such Achilles' heel about Debbie, no matter how fat Alan was. They could laugh and take the Mick all they wanted, I didn't care. In fact, I was quite happy for them to do so. I'd rather be remembered for that than remembered for pissing my pants in the middle of a job so that was just fine. They could even recarve my epitaph.

Rip Chris Benson
1962–20??
His wife shagged a fat man

'Wasn't he? Big and fat?'

It meant not a thing to me.

No, the real hurt lay with Heather. I was still miserable about how things had turned out between us. Miserable and confused. Of all the people I'd ever known, Heather had been the only one ever to have given me a glimpse into what it was that normal people got out of life. Perhaps if I'd had a wife like Heather instead of Debbie I'd have been a bit more inclined to make sure I didn't do anything to jeopardise me going home to her at the end of every day. I don't know though. It hurt when I thought about it too much. I felt bad about pulling the gun on her and hoped that one day she could forgive me for it. I missed her a great deal and wondered if she missed me. I hoped that she did. I couldn't bear the thought of her not even thinking about me at all. Just every now and then. In a good way.

I wanted . . .

If it was possible, I just wanted . . .

I don't know what I wanted. It all started to hurt again so I stopped thinking about her and concentrated on the job.

I couldn't wait. It would be a good one tomorrow.

The biggest job I'd ever been involved in. £8 million. The best we'd ever previously taken in one single haul in all our years of robbing, Gavin included, had been just shy of a million. I'd always dreamed about the big one. A job so big that your name would go down in legend. A Great Train or a Brinks Matt or something. It was a shame that it was bent money and not a legitimate target, it probably wouldn't even be reported. It would've been nice if all the plebs could've read about it on the bus or the train on the way home; read about how I'd spent the day while they'd been toiling away in their crappy little jobs. Read and dreamed. Oh they'd shake their heads and tell each other how terrible it all was, but they'd read every line, every quote, every word.

And, just for a few seconds, while they swayed around on packed cattle trains or passed their puckered lips between the boss's rosy arse cheeks, they'd wonder just how it felt to pull on a mask, pick up a gun and walk away with more money than their fathers had earned in a lifetime of drudgery. They'd wonder, but they'd never know.

Did they really think I could've been like them? Christ!

Fuck 'em. They might've had their Heathers . . .

But I'd have £8 million.

Epilogue:
The Evening Standard
front page, early evening edition

BLOODBATH

3 police officers amongst 12 dead in West End gun battle

Leicester Square was turned into a war zone this afternoon when armed police and masked men exchanged
gunfire after an apparent robbery went tragically wrong.
Three police officers were killed and another six
wounded, two seriously, during a ten-minute shoot-out
with men armed with shotguns and machine-guns.
Initial reports claim that four of the gang were also
killed in the exchange, while two more were captured
and placed under arrest. Police have yet to release their
identities.

[*turn to page 2*]